"With a one-of-a-kind heroine and a plot that's just as addicting as checking Instagram, *Two Parts Sugar, One Part Murder* is a fresh take on the cozy genre. I couldn't help but root for influencer Maddy Montgomery, whether she was trying to solve a murder or just not burn the cake. The Baker Street mysteries has already become one of my favorite series! #MorePlease" —Kellye Garrett, Agatha Award–winning author of *Hollywood Homicide* and *Like a Sister*

"Valerie Burns sweetens the pot for cozy mystery fans with this debut in her new series. City transplant Madison Montgomery finds her small-town tribe and new strengths in a delicious story of baking, backstabbing, and murder." —Maddie Day, author of the Country Store mysteries

"A blend of quirky characters, intriguing mystery, and mouth-watering baked goods makes *Two Parts Sugar, One Part Murder* a great start to Valerie Burns' delicious new series." —Ellen Byron, author of *Bayou Book Thief*

"This novel has everything—a spoonful of murder, a sprinkle of romance, and a cup of intrigue." —Raquel V. Reyes, author of the Caribbean Kitchen mystery series

"Stir in a crew of Sherlock-loving Irregulars and a classic small-town mystery for a tasty treat that will keep you reading long past bedtime." —Leslie Budewitz, three-time Agatha Award-winning author of the Spice Shop and Food Lovers' Village mysteries

"A wonderful start to an entertaining new series with a lively plot, sweet setting, and a brilliant protagonist who inherits more than she bargained for with Baby, a champion stud English mastiff. Burns's writing sparkles with wit and charm in this classic culinary cozy mystery. I couldn't put it down!" —Nancy Coco, *USA Today* bestselling author of the Candy-Coated mysteries

"Valerie Burns whips up a deliciously devious cozy mystery! *Two Parts Sugar, One Part Murder* is a perfectly paced page-turner with a fresh protagonist, a cast you'd like to call friends, and an irresistible English mastiff named Baby who steals every scene he's in. Nods to Sherlock Holmes' Baker Street Irregulars spice the tale and the suspects have motives as deep and dark as Aunt Octavia's chocolate soul cake. You're in for a treat! #OneTastyCozy." —Meri Allen, author of *Mint Chocolate Murder*

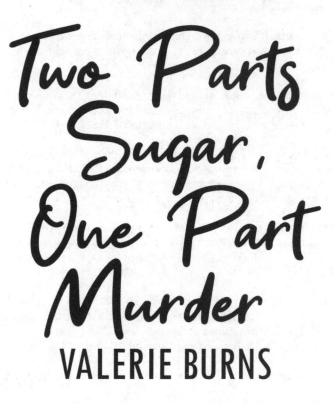

A Baker Street Mystery

# Two Parts Sugar, One Part Murder

## VALERIE BURNS

Kensington Publishing Corp.
www.kensingtonbooks.com

KENSINGTON BOOKS are published by

Kensington Publishing Corp.
119 West 40th Street
New York, NY 10018

ISBN: 978-1-4967-3825-7 (ebook)

ISBN: 978-1-4967-3822-6

First Kensington Trade Paperback Printing: September 2022

10 9 8 7 6 5 4 3

Printed in the United States of America

# Acknowledgments

This book wouldn't have happened if it wasn't for my agent, Jessica Faust, and my editor, John Scognamiglio. Thanks to everyone at Kensington Cozies, especially Michelle, Larissa, and Carly. You all are amazing and I appreciate your hard work and commitment.

It takes a village, and I'm thankful for all the people who are a part of mine, including all of the bloggers, reviewers, and readers. Thanks to Kelly Fowler and Alana Retseck for helping to make my life easier so I can focus on what I love, writing.

I have been blessed with friends and family who are willing to share their knowledge and expertise to help me get the details right. Thanks to Deb Childs, Alex Savage, Alexia Gordon, Michael Dell, Carson Rucker, and Abby Vandiver.

Family and good friends are essential ingredients in any recipe for success. I am grateful to my dad, Ben Burns, and my family (Jackie, Christopher, Carson, Crosby, Cameron, Jillian, Drew, and Marcella) for their love, prayers, and encouragement. Special shoutout to my sister, Jackie, and my niece, Jillian, for brainstorming, but most of all for listening. As always, I am thankful for my good friends Shelitha and Sophia for reminding me of what's most important.

Finally, special thanks to Kellye Garrett for planting the seed for the series, and for all of the unicorns for always being there.

# CHAPTER 1

Like a lemming, I followed the other condemned passengers through the door of our gate, down a flight of stairs, through a long corridor, and outside. A blast of arctic air hit me full in the face, and I stalled. *You have got to be kidding. Surely, we aren't going to be traveling during a snowstorm.* However, the lemmings in front continued out onto the tarmac toward a small plane that looked like something out of a 1950s Doris Day movie. Those behind pushed and jostled around me, leaving me shivering in the doorway. I wrapped my pashmina more closely around my neck, braced myself against the wind, and made my way forward as fast as I could in my new Louboutin heels.

A set of rickety metal stairs had been pushed next to the aircraft, and I grabbed ahold of the handrail and hoisted myself up the steps. About halfway up, my heel slipped off the tread, and I nearly fell backward. The only thing that saved me from bashing my head on the ground was the person behind me, who blocked my fall.

"Whoa, are you okay?"

*Am I okay? If I were okay, I wouldn't be dangling ten feet*

*in the air, hanging on to a steel pole for dear life in subzero tem-*
*peratures in the middle of a blizzard.* I prepared to deliver a
sharp retort but was halted when I saw the black shirt and
white collar of a priest. I wasn't a religious person, but I felt
confident cussing out a priest would send me straight to hell.
Do not pass go. Do *not* collect two hundred dollars. Even if
God wasn't finished torturing me yet, I wasn't prepared to test
my luck before getting on an airplane in the middle of a snow-
nado. Instead, I swallowed the profanity. "Thank you, Father."

He helped me get my feet back on the stairs and gave me a
gentle nudge in the back to get me moving. "Brrr . . . it'll be
nice and warm *inside* the plane."

I would have resented the nudge if it hadn't been so cold. Instead, I carefully climbed the remainder of the way up and took
a few steps inside to my first-class seat. I glanced around, looking for the spacious leather seats I'd grown to love and expect.
When I didn't see them, I stopped so quickly that the priest
bumped into me.

"Stewardess, there must be some problem here." I stared at
the front of the plane, blocking the one and only aisle.

A stewardess who looked a bit long in the tooth for flying, but
well preserved, stepped from the shadows. "Can I help you?"

"Where's first class?" I stared to my left, but that was clearly
the plane's cockpit.

"This is a regional plane. We don't have a first-class section.
May I see your ticket?" She held out her hand.

I rummaged through my purse for several moments before I
remembered I'd stuck it in my pocket. I pulled it out and
handed it over.

"You're right here in front." She pointed to a seat in the
first row.

I wanted to protest, but she'd obviously been trained by the
military to brook no opposition. Considering my dad was an
admiral in the Navy, I recognized authority when I saw it. She

took one step and maneuvered her body in a way that forced me to step toward the seat. Then she took my bag on the pretense of finding a place for it in an overhead bin. Before I knew what was happening, I was strapped in.

"But what kind of plane doesn't have a first-class section?" I asked as she turned to leave.

"There are only twenty-eight seats total."

"But—"

"The flight time is thirty minutes. I'm sure you'll be able to endure it for that short time frame." She turned and walked away.

The priest sat in the seat next to mine. He fastened his seat belt, put his head back, reclined, and closed his eyes.

"Father, I need to confess."

His eyes popped open. "Well, I don't think this is the appropriate time or place."

"But I need a priest."

He gave me a hard stare. "Are you Catholic?"

"No. Do you only listen to confessions from Catholics?"

"Well, normally . . . yes. Other religions tend not to adhere to the same practices. Perhaps you'd be more comfortable talking to a minister from your own faith." He smiled. "What faith are you?"

"I'm not very religious, but I feel like I need to change. I feel like I need a priest."

He sighed and pulled his seat forward.

"Father, I need—"

He held up a hand to halt me.

The stewardess picked up a microphone and started her spiel about the airplane's safety features, cabin pressure, and the instructions for using my seat as a flotation device in the unlikely event that we plummeted into Lake Michigan during our thirty-minute flight from Chicago to the airport in northwestern Indiana.

The priest wouldn't allow me to speak until she finished and we made it into the air. Once the plane leveled out, he turned to me. "Now, what's your name?"

"Madison Montgomery."

"Pleased to meet you. I'm Father Calloway. How can I help you?"

"I need guidance." I have a tendency to overshare when I'm nervous, and I must have been nervous, because I shared how I was raised by my dad on military bases and how I was supposed to be going on my honeymoon but my fiancé had dumped me right before the wedding. I pulled up my cell phone and swiped a few images. "I had everything planned out. It was going to be livestreamed and now look." I held up the phone so he could see. "That's Brandy Denton." I waited, but he just stared at me. "Brandy Denton? You know, she was friends with a friend of the Kardashians and *almost* got her own reality show, but the deal fell through at the last minute."

"Oh, I'm sorry."

"I was, too, until I saw these pictures of her with Elliott, *my* former fiancé. She's always been jealous of me, and now here she is making a move on the doctor that I was going to marry." I heaved a sigh. "And he called *me* shallow. He said I was only marrying him because he was a doctor and didn't really love him. Can you believe that? We were together for eight years."

"Were you?"

"Was I what?"

"Only marrying him because he was a doctor?"

"Of course not. Maybe, but . . . is that wrong? I mean we were perfect for each other, and we've been together ever since freshman year in college. All I ever wanted my entire life was to marry someone . . . like him."

"A doctor?"

"Nooo . . . well, maybe, but it's not just because he was a doctor. I mean, it's the lifestyle. I did my research."

He looked skeptical.

"Have you ever seen the movie *How to Marry a Millionaire*?"

He shook his head.

"Well, Lauren Bacall makes a really good point in that movie. She said, 'Most women use more brains picking a horse in the third at Belmont than they do picking a husband.' And I think she's right. I think most people just wait for a *feeling* and that's it. Hundreds of years ago, marriages were arranged. Parents looked for men who would be able to provide for their daughters."

His lips twitched and he raised an eyebrow. "Most women nowadays prefer to pick their own husbands . . . at least I think they do." He tugged at his collar.

"Well, they probably don't have trouble making decisions. They know what they want. What if you don't know what you want? What if you're terrible at making decisions? Marriage is important. It's supposed to be until *death do you part*. My father always said I needed to stop being impulsive and make wise decisions. I need to think before I leap into things. So I did. I researched careers and decided that the best fit for someone with my skill set would be a doctor's wife." I saw the surprise in his eyes and hurried on. "It wasn't just a one-sided deal, either. I would have been an asset to him. I can host parties and I know how to dress and carry myself, so he would have been proud to be married to me. I was going to be the perfect wife and . . . and the perfect mother." The tears welled up, and the priest handed me a handkerchief. "Anyway, I was humiliated. He left me standing at the altar with a church full of people, and the entire wedding, or non-wedding, was livestreamed all over social media. I just wanted to find a rock and crawl underneath it and hide. My dad said it would all blow over, but he blamed me for the *debacle*, as he called it. I could tell he did. All he kept doing was complaining about the money that he'd spent and how it was nonrefundable." I looked at the priest for sympathy.

"I can certainly understand how disappointing that had to be."

"Exactly, so when I got the letter that my great-aunt Octavia died and named me as her heir, I just hopped on the first flight I could get."

"Condolences."

"For what?"

"On the loss of your aunt."

I waved it away. "She was my great-aunt, and I barely knew her. I think I may have met her when I was a baby, when my mom was alive. Which is why I'm so shocked to find that she left everything to me."

"Forgive me, but I don't see what the problem is. Your fiancé left you, which is disappointing, but it seems like you've landed on your feet."

"That's what I thought, too." I was pleased that Father Calloway thought things were going well. "Even though I've never heard of New Bison, Michigan, I came anyway. I needed to get away, far away from anyone who knew me, so I could figure out how to regroup. I don't know anyone in New Bison. It's the perfect place to hide out for a while . . . and recover. You know, regain my dignity and social standing. Besides, New Bison . . . how bad can it be? It's less than a hundred miles away from Chicago, but . . . I'm starting to have second thoughts. I mean, there's not even an airport. I have to fly to Indiana and then rent a car and drive to New Bison. Do you think it's safe? Have you heard of it?"

"Actually, it's a very quaint town on the Lake Michigan shoreline. There are beautiful hills dotted with farms and vineyards."

"Vineyards?" I sat up. "Maybe it'll be like Napa or the south of France. I could live with that."

"What did your father think about your decision?"

I avoided eye contact. "I haven't told him yet. I thought it would be better to wait until I was there. Then I'd make a video and send it to him showing him what a great decision I made. Then, he'd have to be proud of me."

"I'm sure your father is proud of you anyway," he said quietly.

"I don't think so. My father is an admiral in the Navy. He makes decisions that affect tens of thousands of people in a split second. He never second-guesses himself, and he never makes mistakes that other people have to bail him out of."

He paused. "I'm sure your father makes mistakes. Everyone makes mistakes."

"Nope. He never does. He assesses the situation, weighs the pros and the cons, and then acts. My father is a man of action."

"I see. So, when the lawyer called, you . . ."

"Assessed my situation. Evaluated the pros and cons, and . . . here I am." I spread my hands. "Do you think it was wise? Did I do the right thing?"

"Only you can determine if this was the right decision, but I think you were very brave."

"You do?"

Talking to Father Calloway helped. I felt calmer than I had since I'd started my trek to the arctic north. I could completely understand why people talked to priests. They had a calming effect. Maybe it was the collar. Perhaps I should consider converting to Catholicism.

Before I knew it, we landed in Indiana. "Thank you for listening, Father." I wanted to give him a hug, but I wasn't sure if that was allowed. "Would you mind if I took a picture with you?"

Father Calloway didn't mind, and I whipped out my phone and snapped a few selfies of me and the father together. If my dad had any objections about New Bison, he surely couldn't object to a priest. On impulse, I posted the photo online. **#Catholic #LovingTheSimpleLife #LoveHonestMen**

Maybe hiding out wasn't the right course of action. Perhaps it would be better to let people see that I wasn't sitting home alone crying my eyes out over Elliott.

"You said you met your fiancé—"

"Former fiancé."

"Excuse me, former fiancé in college. Which college did you attend?"

"Stanford."

Father Calloway's eyes widened in a way that I'd seen many times before. "Stanford is an excellent school. You must be very smart. What was your major?"

"Art history with a minor in modern languages. I figured a doctor's wife would need to know about art. And one of the benefits of being a Navy brat is living in different countries. I picked up languages pretty easy. It was bound to come in handy sooner or later. Besides, Elliott barely spoke English."

Father Calloway tugged at his ear. "I have to admit I wouldn't have guessed you were into art history."

"I like art, but I don't know that I want to do anything with it. I just couldn't make up my mind, and eventually, they force you to pick a major."

"If I may offer . . . a piece of advice," Father Calloway said.

"Of course."

"Keep an open mind. New Bison won't be what you're accustomed to, but if you give the people and the place a chance, I think you may be surprised. In fact, I think you may find that it's exactly what you need."

After another torturous trip down the metal stairs of death, I made it inside what a small town in northwestern Indiana called an airport. There were only two luggage carousels and no porters to help me with my luggage. However, a college football team was arriving for a weekend game, and the players helped get my luggage onto a cart.

The rental car desks were near the luggage carousels. A gray-haired Black woman worked behind the counter. When I asked for something sporty, she told me I'd better go with something that was more suited for the climate. I envisioned a dogsled, but she didn't look like she had much of a sense of humor. In fact, she bore a striking resemblance to a drill sergeant I knew.

Determined not to let her put me in a *sensible* vehicle that would be a cross between a Sherman tank and one of my dad's Wasp amphibious assault ships, I tried again. "Okay, then I'll take a Mercedes."

She looked me up and down and then said, "Where are you from?"

"L.A."

"Never been to Indiana in the winter before, have you?"

"I've never been to Indiana, period."

She typed on her computer. "I'm going to put you in a nice luxury four-wheel-drive sedan." She looked past me at the luggage cart. "Is all that yours?"

I nodded.

She typed a bit longer and then handed me a set of keys. "I upgraded you to an SUV. You'll thank me later."

I sighed. It was a good thing I had practice driving everything from a dune buggy to a tank in the desert. Driving an SUV, even a luxury one, in the snow would probably be remarkably similar.

One of the football players actually took the keys and brought my car up to the door. The guys loaded my luggage. I took several selfies of me and the football players and posted them to social media. **#RealMen #LoveFootballPlayers #LovingTheSingleLife** *Take that, Elliott and Brandy.* They were all tall, handsome, and extremely fit—much taller than Elliott. *Eat your heart out, Brandy.* No one seeing those posts online would think I was sitting home, crying my eyes out and pining after him. Nope, I was hanging out with athletes.

The guys even sent me a text with their phone numbers before they left. Men in Indiana were very friendly. Maybe I could get used to life here, after all. I spotted Father Calloway leaving the airport and waved as I pulled away from the curb and out of the parking lot.

The rental-car drill sergeant hooked me up with a fully loaded, black Land Rover. I ran my hand over the soft leather seats. With the heat on full blast and the seat warmers going, the inside of the SUV was nice and cozy. As a military brat, I've lived all over the world, but mostly in warm, desert climates. The snow, ice, and cold of northwestern Indiana and southwestern Michigan would be a new experience. It wasn't something I was prepared for, and my wardrobe wasn't up to the challenge, but I didn't let that bother me. *I guess that means I'll just need to go shopping for warmer clothes.*

# CHAPTER 2

"What do you mean, I have to stay here? Why can't I sell the house and the business?"

Chris Russell sat behind a large, ornately carved mahogany desk with his glasses on the end of his nose. He was an older man with a bald head. He had brown eyes and a large brown mustache. He looked over the top of his glasses. "Those are the conditions of your great-aunt's will. You get the house, her bakery, and a small allowance to help with necessities, on the condition that you stay in the house and run the business for at least one year."

"What if I refuse?"

"Then all of the assets are to be sold and donated to charity." He leaned back in his chair. His office, which was in an old brick building, was lavishly appointed with dark wood-paneled walls and a thick carpet. One wall was fitted with floor-to-ceiling bookshelves filled with leather-bound books. Antiques were placed throughout the room, among them an old typewriter, a Victrola phonograph, and a collection of vases, which I recognized as expensive and most likely from the Ming dynasty. And my dad didn't think a degree in art history would come in handy.

He reached inside a large brown envelope on his desk and pulled out a rectangular object. "Your aunt made this for you. It should explain things better than I can."

He passed me the plastic rectangle.

I stared at it from multiple sides but gave up trying to figure it out. "What is it?

His mustache twitched but he got it under control. "It's a videotape." He rose from his chair and walked around the desk to an ebony-and-mahogany inlaid armoire that stood next to the bookshelves. He opened the doors to reveal a television. "Most people don't have these old VHS recorders anymore, not even me. I like antiques but I had to borrow this one from the local library. Octavia liked leaving notes. I guess this time she wanted it to be more personal." He held out his hand, and I gave him the box. He slid it into what looked like a mail slot. The face of an older Black woman popped onto the screen, and he took the remote and froze it.

"I'll leave you to watch alone, and then I'll be back." He handed me the remote and left.

I pushed play and watched.

The woman, Aunt Octavia, had skin the same color as mine. She had gray eyes and a head full of thick gray hair, which she wore in braids that reached her shoulders. She looked like an older version of my mom. Her eyes looked intelligent and kind. Her chin was firm. I'll bet she didn't have trouble making decisions.

*"Is this thing on?"* she asked someone I couldn't see. She must have received a positive response, because she continued.

*"Madison, if you're watching this video, then I must be dead. I'm sure you won't be too broken up about it. I haven't laid eyes on you in more than twenty years."* She smiled. *"Lord, the last time I saw you, you were just a chubby little butterball,*

*but your mama was so proud of you.*" She shook her head. "*When your mama died, your daddy . . . well, he was devastated. I offered to take you in and help, but he wouldn't hear of it. He knew his duty. Duty . . . what's duty got to do with raising a baby, I couldn't say. But he just shoved all his sorrow deep down inside and buried himself in his work.*" She paused. "*Anyway, I don't want you to think that I forgot about you. I checked on you. Your daddy sent me reports—not letters, mind you—reports on how you were doing. What you weighed and how tall you were . . . Lawdy.*" She shook her head and chuckled. "*That's men for you. You're smart. I told him I needed pictures. I needed to see for myself how you were. And I got 'em. He sent me pictures 'bout every month. 'Madison learning Morse code. Today, Madison took self-defense classes.' You looked more like your mama each year, more beautiful every time I saw you.*" She took out a white handkerchief and wiped her eyes. When she continued, her voice was gruff. "*Anyway, I could tell you were well fed, and you had plenty of money and clothes, but there was something else. . . . I could tell your daddy spoiled you. Expensive clothes, cars, and the shoes . . . Lawd have mercy, what's one woman gonna do with over two hundred pairs of shoes? And the prices? April tells me one pair of them Jimmy Shoes is two thousand dollars.*" She squinted. "*What? Chew? Oh, Jimmy Chews. Well, whatever they are, they was too expensive.*" She smacked her lips. "*That's when I knew something needed to be done. You're smart—too smart to waste your life buying shoes and posting stuff on the Internet. You graduated with honors from Stanford.*" She stuck out her chest. "*I used to be smart like that, too. Course I didn't go to no prestigious school, but I got a bachelor's in chemistry from Alcorn State.*" She paused, but then hurried on. "*You needed to get away and spend time with real people.*" She straightened her shoulders. "*So, here's the deal. I ain't got much, but what I have, I'm leaving to you on account of your mama. But you can't just sell my house and my business and buy more Jimmy Chews . . . although, there's plenty of folks that want to buy. Dem rich folks in Chicago done run out of property on Lake Michigan and come down to New Bison looking for more. Well, I ain't selling. I done told them over and over again that I ain't selling."* She pursed her lips and scowled. After a few moments she sighed. *"So, if you want to sell to them sadiddy big-city folks and take everything I worked my whole life to build just so you can buy more shoes . . . well, you gonna have to wait. You stay here for one year. That's all I ask—one year. You live in my house. Meet the people and see if it don't grow on you . . . that's all I got to say. Oh, and take care of Baby."*

The video went black.

"Baby?"

The office door opened and Mr. Russell walked in, leading a dark brown pony. "I almost forgot, Baby." He placed the reins in my hand.

"What am I supposed to do with a horse?" I stared from the beast to the lawyer.

"That's not a horse."

"Okay, a pony. But I don't—"

"Baby isn't a pony or any other member of the equine family. Baby's a dog—a mastiff, an English mastiff, to be exact."

"But I can't keep this . . . this . . ."

"English mastiff."

"Whatever. He's massive. Does he bite?"

"All dogs *can* bite, but Baby is a gentle giant."

"I can't keep some English mastiff."

"Baby isn't just *some* English mastiff. He's a champion show dog. Champion Crooner Ol' Blue Eyes, One for My Baby. Octavia really loved Frank Sinatra." He smiled fondly at the memory, then collected himself. "Baby's a champion with a string of initials behind his name for all of the titles he's won, which wasn't easy, considering Octavia had to work hard to prove he was purebred just to get his papers from the American Kennel Club. Baby was a lot more than a dog to your great-aunt. When she found him, he was just a tiny thing, the runt of the litter. Someone left him to die on the beach in the middle of winter. He was half-starved and nearly frozen. She fed him and nursed him back to health. She barely went anywhere without him. He became her protector and . . . her confidant."

I stared at the behemoth. "Did she ever find out who abandoned him?"

He paused so long I turned my gaze to him.

"If she did, she never said, but I think she had her suspicions."

"You know more than you're saying." I studied Mr. Russell for the first time since I entered his office. He was middle-aged and nondescript. From his tightly buttoned Oxford shirt to his tight lips, Mr. Russell was cautious. He wasn't the type to volunteer anything that could come back to bite him. I recognized his type. Not even flirting would loosen his lips. I know. I used to date a lawyer. Best to stick to facts. "He's got to cost a fortune just to feed."

"Actually, Baby's a champion stud dog." He rifled through a few papers until he found the one he wanted. "Yes, his stud fees average two thousand dollars, and there's a waiting list." He handed me a paper with a list of names.

I was stunned. "He's booked for the next two years?" This time when I glanced over at Baby, I had a bit more respect in my eyes, but I couldn't allow myself to get distracted by his big brown eyes and big . . . stud fees. "I don't know the first thing about dogs. I haven't had a pet since I was eight. It was a goldfish, and when I forgot to feed him, he died." I held out the reins to Mr. Russell. "I'm sure Aunt Octavia wouldn't want anything to happen to her dog."

He stepped back and held up both hands. "I'm sorry, Miss Montgomery, but those are the terms of your aunt's will. No Baby. No house. No store. No money."

I sighed.

"If it's any consolation, I can assure you that Baby isn't going to allow you to forget his feedings." He chuckled.

I wasn't amused. "What does it eat?"

"I'm tempted to say, *whatever he wants.*" He paused. If he had expected laughter from me, he was disappointed. After a few seconds, he straightened up. "Your aunt has large bags of food at the house. One of your neighbors has been going over and making sure that Baby had food and water since Octavia's death. Some of her friends tried taking him, but no matter what they did or where they took him, he managed to escape and made his way back home. Finally, one of the local vets said it'd be less stressful if we just let him stay at home, but they went by every day and made sure he was okay."

I glared. "What happens if Baby . . . oh, I don't know, ran away and got hit by a car?"

He frowned. "Miss Montgomery, animal cruelty is a crime, punishable—"

"Settle down. I can't even kill spiders."

He didn't look as though he believed me, but he must have realized he didn't have much choice. It was either trust me with the dog or take it himself. He handed over a set of keys and a paper with written directions to the house and Aunt Octavia's store.

I tossed the keys and the directions into my purse, stood, and headed for the door. Unfortunately, the beast had gotten comfortable and wasn't inclined to move. I tugged and pulled, but he merely looked up at me with soft brown eyes and yawned.

A guffaw left the lawyer's mouth, and he tried to cover it by coughing.

That did it. There was nothing I hated more than being laughed at. "Baby, come!" I ordered.

To both Mr. Russell's and my own surprise, Baby came.

I walked out of Russell, Russell, and Stevenson with my head held high, and my pony—ah . . . mastiff—lumbered behind me. Outside, both the backseat and the rear were piled high with luggage, as though the football players were masters of Tetris. I opened the front passenger door and commanded Baby to get in.

He put his front paws on the seat and then hoisted himself up and in. Once he was inside, I slammed the door. I hopped into the driver's seat and looked across at my passenger. Baby was huge, but there was something very appealing about his eyes as he perched next to me in the car. I snapped a picture of him and posted it online with the caption, *If you're looking for loyalty in a male, check out this big boy.* **#MovingOn #ChampionStud #EnglishMastiff**

"Well, Baby, I guess it's you and me." I looked into his eyes. He looked sad, and I wondered if he understood Aunt Octavia was gone. I stared at his giant muzzle. I certainly didn't want to say anything to offend him. I'd google later to find out how much dogs understood, just to be on the safe side. As I pulled away from the curb, something banged the hood of the car. I slammed on the brakes, and that's when I heard a string of expletives. I looked up and saw a man banging his fist on the car's hood.

A red-faced man with wisps of blond hair on either side of his head, but none on the top, glared at me. "Watch where you're going."

I rolled down the window. "I'm sorry. I didn't see you."

"Why not? Are you blind? I could have—"

I was so distracted by apologizing that I wasn't paying attention to anything else. However, the abrupt end to the man's tirade should have been my warning that trouble was lurking. It wasn't until I heard a low rumble that I remembered Baby. A split second later, two hundred fifty pounds of canine flesh landed in my lap, nearly knocking the air from my lungs.

Stunned, I worked to catch my breath and free my arms, which were frozen under the weight.

The man backed away from the window. His red face turned white, as all the color drained away.

"Baby, off," I commanded once I collected my breath.

I felt the growl growing inside the dog's belly and got my first sense of the power within the beast. One deep, guttural sound escaped, and every hair on my body stood up. Then, to my utter and complete surprise, he backed up to the passenger seat, never taking his eyes off the man.

"I'm terribly sorry. He's my aunt's dog . . . well, my great-aunt and . . . ," I babbled, but the man looked from me to the dog and then backed away.

Baby watched until the man was out of sight and then released the tension that made the hair on his neck stand up and eased his butt onto the seat. He looked straight ahead as if nothing had happened.

"I have no idea what that was about, but you're going to need to start anger-management classes if you don't calm down."

Baby licked his lips and drooled on the seat. Then he stared straight ahead as though he were the king of the world, ready to command his peasants. *Home, wench.*

I obeyed. I followed the directions the lawyer had given me to Aunt Octavia's house.

It didn't take long to get from the lawyer's office to the house. No interstate travel needed. One of the joys of life in a small town. The house was down a narrow road that ran parallel to Lake Michigan. Most of the properties looked as though they'd been built in the 1970s. Aunt Octavia's Georgian-style home looked older. It had probably been a stunner whenever it was built, but a lot of time had passed, and styles had changed. Unfortunately, this house hadn't. There was a single-car detached garage near the street and another two-car garage attached to the house. I pulled into the driveway and parked.

I looked over at Baby. "Let's go."

I walked around and opened the passenger door, shivering as I went. Baby got out and galloped toward a side door.

"Hey, where're you going?" I pointed toward the front door.

He didn't listen. Instead, he trotted to the side of the house, hiked his leg, and relieved himself. When he finished, he walked to the garage and sat down.

There was a numeric keypad beside one of the garage doors, and the paper I'd been given had four numbers. I recognized them as my mom's birthday. I punched in the numbers, and the garage door lifted like magic.

Baby gave me a look as though to say, *I told you so.*

"Oh, shut up. Nobody likes a know-it-all." I used my key and unlocked the door that led inside the house.

Baby went inside first, but before going inside, I rushed back to the car and pulled it inside the garage and lowered the door.

Aunt Octavia's house, now mine, was much larger than it appeared from the outside. It wasn't just the tall ceilings and views of Lake Michigan. There was a lot of room, and it sat on a bluff directly on the lakeshore. The back of the house was mostly windows, providing breathtaking views of the lake that went on forever. Lake Michigan was vast, and unlike the deep blue of the Pacific Ocean, it was light blue, white, and gray, but there was something appealing in its tumultuous white-capped waves. After a few moments, I turned my attention to the interior. I wandered from room to room until I had seen every square inch of the house. The furnishings were old and worn, but the house had a contemporary vibe. The only room that had been updated and brought into the twenty-first century was the kitchen, which was large, open, and airy. The cabinets were white, and there was a massive eight-burner gas range that was larger than my first convertible, a Fiat 500C.

The rest of the house had great bones. My favorite room was one of the bedrooms, which she had converted into a reading library and study. Floor-to-ceiling bookshelves and oversized furniture made the room look like a supremely comfortable place to curl up with a cup of tea and read. The only negative was the floral-print fabric that dated the pieces to the 1980s, but a nice throw would hide that until I could reupholster or replace them. A quick glance at the books indicated that Aunt Octavia's interests included English mastiffs, baking, and detective novels. The shelves were full of everything from Agatha Christie to Patricia Wentworth, with an abundant supply of Sir Arthur Conan Doyle's Sherlock Holmes. It was comforting to realize that Aunt Octavia and I shared a love of reading, but more important, we shared a love of mysteries.

As I perused the shelves and found old friends, I felt a connection to my great-aunt that I hadn't felt before. It was clear from the sheer volume of Sherlock Holmes editions that the private detective was one of her favorites, although I found Holmes cold, arrogant, and overly opinionated. He'd have done well in the military . . . if he were in command. Personally, I had a lot more sympathy for Dr. Watson, his tireless companion. I grabbed one of the Sherlock Holmes books and slipped it in my pocket, just in case sleep eluded me, and continued my tour.

By far, the most amazing thing about the house was the view. I stood at one of the windows and gazed out at the seemingly endless expanse of water. From my vantage point atop the bluffs, I noticed a set of stairs that led down to the beach. The wooden stairs were rickety and old, and didn't look very safe. Although it would be nice to have my own private beach access, I wasn't sure I wanted to risk those stairs. However, private beach access would be an attractive feature. Not for attracting a buyer. I couldn't sell the house, not yet anyway, but my tour had planted the seed that I might be able to generate additional income by taking in a renter. With a small amount of remodeling, the lower level would make a great rental. It had a full kitchen, a bedroom, a full bathroom, and a private side entrance. Plus, it might be nice to have someone else in the house. This was an awfully big house for one person. It was even large for one person and a large dog.

It took multiple trips for me to drag my luggage inside, but eventually I managed to get it all into the master bedroom.

Baby sat on the floor in the kitchen and watched the spectacle. With each trip, I was glad I'd decided to move the car inside the garage. It wasn't heated, but it was still warmer than the arctic blast that blew across the lake.

Hauling suitcases left me hot and sweaty and wishing for a moment I'd invited one of those strong football players to come help me. In the past, I'd always had men to help me with physical things like luggage. If it wasn't my dad or Elliott, then it was one of the thousands of sailors from the naval base.

*Woof.*

"You're right. I don't need my dad, and I especially don't need Elliott. I'm here to prove that I'm capable of taking care of myself. I'm responsible and independent. Independent women don't need men to bring in their luggage. They do it themselves, right?"

Baby gave one short bark and then stretched.

I showered and changed into my most comfy clothes: a pair of leggings and an oversized US Navy hoodie. Normally, I wouldn't be caught dead wearing anything like this in L.A., but New Bison was a million miles away, or at least it felt like it was. Besides, the hoodie was warm.

I debated going to check out Aunt Octavia's bakery and

store . . . my store. I should check it out, but it was so nice and warm inside. "Surely, the adult thing to do would be to wait until tomorrow, right?"

Baby got up and walked to the kitchen. He came back with the biggest dog bowl I'd ever seen.

"Now that you mention it, I'm rather hungry, too." I went to the kitchen. Just as I reached to open the pantry door, the doorbell rang.

At the front door, I looked around for some device that would allow me to see who was outside without opening the door. Either Aunt Octavia knew all her callers or didn't deem cameras worthwhile. I'd need to rectify that. I did notice a round circle, and when I moved closer, I saw it was an old-fashioned peephole. Considering I didn't know anyone in New Bison except Mr. Russell, looking outside didn't help.

Standing on the doorstep with a large bouquet of flowers was a young man with blond hair, green eyes, and a big smile.

"Who is it?" I asked.

"Bradley Ellison." He pulled a business card from his pocket and held it up to the peephole.

I recognized the logo as the same one I'd seen on yard signs around the neighborhood.

I hesitated. The responsible thing would be to not open the door to a stranger. That's one of the first things parents teach you as a kid: *Don't talk to strangers.* But that only applies to kids. Adults talk to strangers all the time. How else do you meet new people, right? However, as a single woman, opening the door and allowing a strange man to come in was probably not the responsible adult thing to do. I couldn't decide. "One minute," I yelled to the stranger, while I paced and weighed the pros and cons. He didn't look like a serial killer, but then I've never met one before, and when reporters interview the serial killer's neighbors, they always say they had no idea their neighbor was a psychopath. He looked and acted just like everyone else. I was just about to tell him to go away when Baby yawned. One glance at my two-hundred-fifty-pound housemate, and I knew he outweighed all the cons.

I opened the door. "Sorry for the delay, I . . . had to get dressed."

"No problem. You were well worth the wait." He smiled big and handed me the flowers, along with his business card. "I wanted to be one of the first people to welcome you to New Bison."

"Thank you." I took the flowers. "Please come in, Mr. Ellison."

"Please call me Brad. And you are?"

"Maddy Montgomery."

"A beautiful name for a beautiful lady."

"Thank you." I stuck my face into the large bouquet to hide the fact that I was blushing like a schoolgirl. "These are beautiful. I'd better put them in water."

I went to the kitchen, followed by Brad and Baby. I opened half a dozen cabinets before I found one that had a large crystal vase. I filled it with water and the flowers and then put it on the island.

Brad Ellison had hopped up on one of the barstools and made himself comfortable.

"Are you part of New Bison's welcoming committee?" I asked to break the awkward silence.

He chuckled. "No, but I have to admit, ever since Octavia's unfortunate accident, I have been looking out for you."

"Really?"

"Yes, you see I'm extremely interested in buying your aunt's property. I made Octavia several, very generous offers, but . . . she wasn't interested in selling. When I heard that her legatee was a young woman accustomed to big cities, I thought it might be worth trying again."

I stared. "I don't understand how you heard about me?"

"Well, you're a lot smarter than—" He flushed and gave a nervous laugh.

He didn't say, *smarter than you look*, but I could tell that's what he'd intended.

"In all transparency, I went down to the courthouse and checked the probate documents. That's how I found out your name." He held up his cell phone. "It didn't take long to find you online. You're very popular on social media."

He didn't say that he knew about my failed wedding, but if he found out about me on social media, then he knew. I could feel myself flush. I had hoped that New Bison was far enough off the social-media-inner-circle grid that I'd be able to hide, but that wasn't going to be an option. Good thing I'd already decided to play the *I've moved on, look at me moving on with my life* angle on social media.

"Okay, you've found me, and if you've read my aunt's will, then you know that I can't sell."

"You can't sell for one year, but when the year is up, I'd like the inside track. I want to buy this property, and I'm willing to wait for the opportunity. I already have a buyer who's extremely interested. In fact, I've already talked to them about your situation, and they feel confident that they could break your aunt's residency requirement."

*My situation?* "How?"

He avoided eye contact and rushed on. "We could prove your aunt was nuts. You'd have to be nuts to pass up this kind of money." He reached inside his jacket and pulled out a stack of papers. "I could arrange—"

I held up a hand to stop him. "Mr. Ellison, I've only been in New Bison a few hours. I may not have known my aunt Octavia, but I'm also not prepared to have her declared crazy. Now I think maybe you should leave."

The smile on his face froze. I could see the wheels inside his head spinning as he quickly tried to regain ground. "Maddy, you're right. I'm sorry. I meant no disrespect to Octavia and no offense to you. I'm just really excited about this deal, and I let my excitement run wild. I'm truly sorry. Can we start over?" His eyes pleaded. "Please? Maybe you'd let me take you out to dinner. I could show you around New Bison. It's a small town, but there are some great little restaurants and a few decent wineries." He laughed. "They might not be up to California standards, but they're starting to get noticed by some of the important magazines and gaining traction."

Brad was the first young person I'd met, and it would be nice to have someone show me the best restaurants. Plus, it would be nice to have someone to talk to besides Baby. Besides, he'd photograph well for social media. "Sure. I'd like that."

He looked relieved, and I was about to ask him if he wanted to grab a pizza or something when my phone rang. One glance at the picture on the screen, and my stomach muscles tightened.

"I have to take this."

He promised to stop by in a day or so and then left.

I took a deep breath. "Hi, Dad."

The Admiral was in full-blown command mode, firing questions at me at the speed of a rifle. Was I out of my mind? What was I thinking? How could I just pick up and move to some godforsaken hick town in the middle of nowhere without consulting with someone first? Of course, by *someone*, he meant him. When he was in this type of mood, nothing I said or did would matter. He wasn't listening. I put the phone on speaker and let him rant. I could tell he was winding down when he started using words like *irresponsible, impulsive,* and *immature.* After more than a quarter century of The Admiral's tirades and countless hours talking to shrinks, I'd developed a thick shell to protect my emotions. The next part was always the hardest. "Honey, I'm sorry. I don't mean to yell at you. It's just that sometimes you make decisions without thinking them through. You don't *weigh the pros and cons* before you leap.

That was fine when you were a kid, but it's time to *act like a responsible adult.*"

I'd heard this spiel so many times before, I mouthed the highlights along with him.

"It's a dangerous world. I know, I've seen the worst of it. A single woman like you will be prey for some con man or worse. Now, I checked the airlines, and you can book a flight back home first thing tomorrow. The next flight—"

"I'm not coming home."

"What?"

"I'm not coming home. I inherited Great-Aunt Octavia's house and her business and . . . her dog." I glanced over at Baby. "I met with her attorney and I intend to live here and . . . and run her business . . . my business."

"Honey, how are you going to run a business? You can't even balance your bank account. Now, I understand that you're upset about Elliott, but that's no reason to go off half-cocked and get yourself in over your head with some two-bit store and a rat-infested shack in the middle of nowhere. But if it'll make you happy, I can call my lawyer the first thing Monday morning, and he can offload everything for you. Maybe you'll even clear enough to pay for a new pair of those expensive shoes you like. Now—"

Obviously, he'd never seen Aunt Octavia's house, or he'd know it was far from a shack. I hadn't seen the business, but she had managed it, and I was determined to do the same.

Baby placed his huge head in my lap and stared up at me. His soulful eyes instilled courage in me. "Dad, I'm not coming back . . . not yet anyway. Aunt Octavia entrusted me with her greatest possessions. She believed in me. It's time I believed in me, too."

He was silent for a long time while he prepared for his final assault—the calm before the storm. "Sweetheart, you need to be practical. It's dangerous for a young, attractive woman to be living alone with no one to look out for you. You don't even know how to defend yourself. I blame myself for that."

"I took self-defense classes on base. I'm perfectly capable of defending myself if I had to." I tried to remember the self-defense classes he'd insisted I take. Was it SING? Or SIGN? Or . . .

"I should have forced you to learn to shoot, but honestly, I always assumed you'd get married, and your husband would do that."

"Well, I'm not married, and I don't need a husband to take care of me." *Or a gun.* "I'm perfectly capable of defending myself, but I appreciate your concern. Now, I have to go, but I'll give you a call in a few days." I hung up.

I didn't realize I was crying until Baby gave my face a big lick. "Ugh."

Undeterred, he continued licking me until I was lying on the sofa laughing and trying to fend him off. Finally, I sat up. "Baby, *no*."

Surprisingly, he was a total gentleman. He leaned back on his haunches and stared.

I took out my phone and snapped a couple of quick pictures and posted them. **#PerfectGentleman #NoMeansNo #KnowsHowToMakeMeLaugh #LoveEnglishMastiffs**

Baby nudged my leg and brought me back to the present. "Dinner, right."

I scoured the freezer. It was crammed full of meat, vegetables, and something Aunt Octavia had labeled STOCK. She even had an ice cream tub with Baby's name on it. However, she must not have been a fan of quick meals like pizza, because in that respect, it was barren. I opened the refrigerator. It was crammed with giant containers and ziplock bags full of something that looked like chicken stew. On the label, she had written CHICKEN AND RICE WITH SWEET POTATOES, BROCCOLI, AND GREEN BEANS. "Hmm, must be chicken soup. Maybe I'll heat it up." I placed the bag on the counter and started for the pantry when I heard the garage door rolling up and froze.

Baby's ears perked, and he stared at the door.

My dad's voice rang in my head, but I refused to let him be proven right. I looked around for a weapon and grabbed a marble rolling pin. I scurried behind the door and raised the rolling pin, prepared to club whomever came through that door. My heart beat so fast, I thought I might pass out. Instead, I took a deep breath, closed my eyes, and tensed my stomach muscles.

The door slowly swung open. Weapon raised, I was ready to strike when Baby got up and ambled over to the door where he sat and whined with his tail swishing across the kitchen floor.

Seconds before I clubbed the intruder, a downy-haired white head popped through the door. "Baby, you decent?" She laughed.

Baby stood up, and his tail wagged.

I put down my weapon and hid it behind my back. "Hello."

The woman stopped petting Baby and turned to look at me. "You must be Madison." A petite woman with curly white hair, blue eyes, and glasses extended her hand. "I'm Alma Hurston. I live down the street. I've been coming over to make sure Baby was okay."

"Pleased to meet you. I'm Madison Montgomery, but you can call me Maddy."

"You're Leah's daughter." She tilted her head forward and gave me a good glance over.

"Did you know my mom?"

She shook her head. "Not really, but Octavia talked about her so much, I felt like I did."

Baby barked and stood on his hind legs and put his paws around Alma's neck. Fully extended, he was at least a foot taller and about one hundred fifty pounds heavier, but she didn't seem to mind.

"Baby, off," she commanded, and he complied. "I'll bet you're hungry."

He turned around in a circle and barked.

"I was just about to feed him, but I didn't know where . . ."

Alma opened up one of the pantry doors that I hadn't gotten to yet and pulled out a larger industrial-sized scooper. She opened a bin, which I assumed held potatoes, and put two large scoops into his bowl. When she finished, she returned the scooper and pointed to an index card taped to the inside of the door. "Octavia was always leaving notes all over the place. Baby gets two scoops of dry food twice per day." She grabbed the bag that I'd placed on the counter for my dinner and dumped it in Baby's bowl. "She made up large batches of Baby's special food about once a month. I'm sure if you check the freezer, you'll see she's stocked up for several weeks."

"That's dog food? I had no idea. I was going to eat it."

"It wouldn't hurt you." She took a spoon and took a bite. "Cold, but I don't think Baby minds that." Alma laughed. "It's all perfectly natural, organic, human-quality food." She mixed the human food with the dog food and placed the bowl on the floor by a huge container of water.

We stood by and watched as Baby gobbled down the food.

"I'm sure if you check around, you'll find the recipe. Octavia was always leaving notes around the house and the store."

He ate half of the bowl in record time.

"Is there anything for humans to eat in this house?"

"Octavia loved to cook, but she wasn't big on what she called 'instant food.' She had the butcher drop off meat for her and Baby, and when it's warm, she had arrangements with some of the local farmers for fresh produce deliveries."

"Great, but I don't have the time to defrost and bake a chicken." *Not to mention the knowledge.*

"Well, we do have restaurants in New Bison."

"Can you recommend a pizza parlor." I pulled out my cell phone and made a few swipes. "Normally, I don't consider a restaurant with less than a thousand five-star ratings, but I don't know if New Bison has that many people."

Alma smiled. "I think there were about eighteen hundred at the last census, but Papa Luigi's makes good pizzas with fresh ingredients, and the place is so clean, you could eat off the floor."

I hoped I wouldn't need to eat off the floor, but I appreciated the recommendation. "If you'd care to join me, I'd love the company."

Alma checked her watch. "Well, I can stay for a bit, at least until your pizza arrives. My daughter will be home soon."

We went to the sunroom. It was a rectangular space with glass on three sides, but there was a comfy sofa and a wood-burning fireplace. Alma turned a key, which caused a hissing sound, and then took a long match and lit the pilot, which started a flame. I watched carefully as she fed pieces of wood from a nearby basket and then closed the door. Within minutes, the room was warm and cozy.

When she finished lighting the fire, she flipped on a lamp and sat on the sofa overlooking the lake. "This was Octavia's favorite spot. This and her library." She shook her head. "She loved her mystery novels."

I reached into the pocket of my hoodie and pulled out a book.

"She especially loved Sherlock Holmes," Alma said. "That woman read and reread those books so many times, and she seemed to get as much joy out of them every time she read them."

"I never knew her. What was she like?"

"She was strong, independent, and stubborn as a mule." She chuckled. "When she got something in her head, she didn't let it go." She frowned. "That was part of the problem. Octavia read all those crime novels, and she started seeing sinister plots and evil villains everywhere."

"What do you mean?"

She was silent for several moments. "I probably shouldn't

even be telling you this, and don't think I didn't love and respect your aunt, because I did. I'm not saying anything to you I didn't say to her face when she was alive." She paused. "But Octavia had it in her mind that there was something wrong going on in this town. If she saw that young real estate developer having lunch with the mayor, then, according to Octavia, that proved that the mayor was involved in the conspiracy. They must be in cahoots. I told her they might just be having lunch. It's a small town. There doesn't need to be any type of conspiracy behind two people sharing a meal, but she wouldn't listen."

"Was she a bit . . . you know . . . mental?" I whispered. *Maybe Bradley Ellison wasn't wrong about her being nutty.*

"Good Lord, no. There was nothing wrong with Octavia's mind except too many crime novels mixed with stubbornness."

Baby must have finished eating because he moseyed into the room.

Alma rose and opened one of the doors and let him go outside to take care of the call of nature. When he was done, she let him back inside.

"How did she die?"

"Octavia fell, down there." She pointed toward the staircase from hell. "My daughter found her when she was walking on the beach."

Like a bad wreck on the I-405 where you don't want to look but can't turn away, I stared down at the stairs.

Alma left just as the pizza arrived. She promised to swing by to check on me.

The pizza arrived still hot, and I gulped down two slices before I remembered I'd left my laptop upstairs. I wanted to document my ideas for updates to the house and start journaling my first days in New Bison while everything was still fresh. I ran upstairs to grab it and came back in time to see Baby standing up on his hind legs eating the rest of the pizza that I'd foolishly left on the counter. I stared at the mammoth dog. *This is going to take a lot of getting used to,* but I decided to make the best of the situation and snapped another photo. **#PizzaThief #PizzaItsWhatsForDinner #StillLoveMyEnglishMastiff**

In bed, my dad's words rolled around in my head like gravel in a huge cement tumbler. I tossed and turned . . . well, as much as I could with a huge English mastiff taking up more than his share of the bed. After a few hours, I gave up on sleep and decided that I really did want to get a look at the building. I was certain my dad was wrong. It might not be Microsoft, but surely Aunt Octavia's business wasn't a *two-bit store* that would need to be offloaded. I couldn't rest until I went and took a look for myself. After all, it was my inheritance.

I hopped out of bed, threw on the clothes I'd stripped off earlier, and pulled my hair back into a bun. No need to bother reapplying my makeup. I glanced at the time. Chances that I'd run into anyone at eleven at night were slim to none. Besides, no one in New Bison even knew me.

"Baby, come."

Had it been only a few hours earlier that I hadn't wanted anything to do with the giant dog? Now I had to admit there was something very comforting about having this powerful beast by my side, especially when wandering into unknown territory.

Baby was resting comfortably, and it didn't look as though a late-night trip were among his top twenty-five plans for tonight. After a bit of coaxing on my part, which involved bribing him with the promise of a steak from the freezer, he eventually climbed down and followed me to the car.

I followed the directions I'd gotten from Mr. Russell and headed for downtown New Bison.

If I hadn't been looking for downtown, I'd have missed it. There were roughly three blocks of storefront businesses. A brick building on the corner of Main and Church had a sign, BABY CAKES BAKERY AND STORE.

I pulled up to the front of the building. It was a bakery and kitchen store. "How cool." I snapped a picture. **#NewVenture #NewLife #EntrepreneurLife #BabyCakesBakery**

I drove around the corner, taking in my new building from three of its four sides. In the back, I pulled up behind the building into one of two parking spaces.

I hopped out and hurried around to open the door for Baby, who wasn't nearly as impressed as I was. He climbed down and moseyed to a dumpster that was nearby, hiked his leg, and peed, while I unlocked the door.

The keys Mr. Russell had given me did the trick, and soon Baby and I were inside.

It was dark, and I fumbled to find the light switch. Behind me, Baby growled.

"I'm trying to find the lights," I said. "Hang on." Did people talk to their dogs? Regardless, it was comforting, even if he didn't speak back. I felt around until I found the switch and flipped on the lights.

Baby growled again, and the hair on my arm stood up. He took several huge strides and hurled himself forward.

I stood frozen for several moments, but when I didn't hear a commotion that sounded like he'd ripped an intruder's throat out, I whispered, "Baby, come."

After a few seconds, he came.

I looked at him as though he could tell me what had set his fur on end, but he merely shook himself and sat.

"What was that about?"

He didn't answer.

I shook myself in the hopes that it would calm my nerves, just as it had his, but apparently a full-body shake worked only for dogs. I was fully prepared to tuck my tail between my legs and make a hasty retreat. I got as far as the back door before I stopped.

"No. This is *my* store. I'm an adult." I glanced at Baby. "How can I prove to my dad that I'm capable of making my own decisions? Or prove to Elliott that I don't need to marry a doctor? I'm an independent woman. Successful, independent women don't run just because a dog growls when we enter an empty store, right?"

Baby stared.

"Right." I looked around for a weapon.

The kitchen was to the right. I flipped the switch and found a large wooden knife block full of blades that looked capable of slicing through a Volkswagen. I grabbed the largest one but immediately put it back. "I need something more lightweight and easy to wield." I picked a medium-sized blade instead. Cell phone in one hand and samurai dagger in the other, I crept around the corner.

Half of the building was a bakery with glass display cases. The other half held shelves with bakeware, kitchen utensils, gadgets, and various other instruments that I'd seen on YouTube but couldn't identify for the life of me.

I put the sword on a table and snapped a few pictures of the space with my phone. The bakery area was small but efficient. It had tall ceilings, with heavy oak beams suspended below and mounted into the brick walls. The beams gave the building a rustic character. The store could use a bit of help. The gadget wall looked as if it hadn't been touched in decades, and the bakeware was strewn on shelves and looked more like a rummage sale than a high-end baking specialty store. Just because I couldn't cook didn't mean I hadn't seen the inside of a Williams Sonoma. With a bit of rearranging, Baby Cakes Bakery could be a store Ina Garten would be proud to frequent and, with any luck, film. I allowed my thoughts to drift to dreams of the Barefoot Contessa sipping expensive coffee and commenting on the flakiness of my . . . well, something or other.

Baby must have gotten bored because he goosed me, and I nearly jumped out of my skin. "All right, I'm ready."

I flipped off the lights, locked the door, and Baby and I left.

The remainder of my first night in New Bison was uneventful. My highlights included having my pizza stolen and then waking up in the middle of the night with a two-hundred-fifty-pound dog snoring in my face. The sunrise over Lake Michigan was a thing of beauty, and I woke up eager to start adulting and proving to my ex, my dad, and myself that I was capable of being independent, making good decisions, and standing on my own two feet.

I hopped out of bed. "Come on, Baby. Let's go outside."

Upon hearing his name, Baby opened one eye. However, upon realizing it was just me, he closed it and went back to sleep.

I pushed and shoved but he refused to budge. "I'm going to need a shower and coffee." Maybe Baby would be willing to move after a couple of more winks.

It took several attempts before I found the outfit that said, *successful business owner*. At least, that's what I thought it said. In the meantime, rather than merely taking up half of a king-sized bed, Baby had turned horizontally and was now enjoying the entire bed.

He was massive, but he had a sweet face. I took my phone and snapped another photo. I quickly uploaded it online. **#WakingUpWithMyBaby #HeSnores #LoveMyBigCuddlyBaby #LoveEnglishMastiffs**

Before I put my phone away, I checked the other pictures that I'd uploaded. *Shut the front door. This can't be right.* The pictures of Baby I'd uploaded yesterday had gone viral. In less than twenty-four hours, he had two hundred thousand likes and forty thousand people had shared the photo. "You're trending. Holy macaroni. You're freakin' trending on social media."

Baby yawned and stretched. He may not have been impressed, but I sure was. Even when I'd posted my wedding dress, I didn't get two hundred thousand likes. I quickly scrolled through my phone and smiled. "Brandy Denton never got that many likes, either." I reached over and gave Baby a hug. "You're awesome." He yawned, and I nearly passed out. "Note to self, no pepperoni for you." I sat up and smacked his backside. "Okay, let's go."

This time, Baby stood up. He climbed down from the bed and shook himself. Then he followed me outside to take care of the call of nature.

I waited on the bluff for him to finish.

"Are you Maddy?"

I jumped back and nearly tripped over a shovel that was propped against the side of the house. I grabbed the shovel and held it like a bat. "Baby, come."

Baby took several giant strides. When he was inches from the stranger, he stood up on his back legs, put his giant paws around the man's neck, and proceeded to lick every inch of his face and head.

"Ack. Baby, you got me right in the mouth." The man struggled to detangle himself from the dog's embrace. He freed one hand, reached into his rear pocket and whipped out a large bone. He raised the bone overhead and then flung it away.

Baby abandoned his lovefest with the stranger and galloped after the bone. When he found it, he lay down on the ground and gnawed on it.

"Hi, I'm Leroy Danielson." He extended a hand. "Would you mind lowering your shovel?"

He was about five feet ten, thin with shoulder-length dark, wavy hair. His brown eyes were hidden behind a pair of thick black-rimmed glasses. He looked harmless enough, and Baby obviously knew him, but my dad's words from last night had me on extra-high alert with all strangers. "Who are you?"

He frowned. "Leroy . . . Danielson."

"I heard you the first time. I mean, why are you here?"

"I work at the bakery, and Mr. Russell told us that Miss Octavia's niece was going to be taking over. When you didn't arrive this morning, we were worried. Miss Hannah suggested I come and make sure you were okay."

"Oh, you work at my great-aunt's bakery?" I scrutinized him more closely now that I was relatively certain he wasn't a psychopath intent on murder. At least, I was fairly sure he wasn't. If he was, he was the most well-mannered psychopathic killer ever. I grew up surrounded by platoons of young white men who didn't realize that older Black women were insulted when they called them by their first names. It was just as insulting as Black men being called "boy." Leroy had what my dad referred to as "home training." I lowered my shovel and extended my hand. "Madison Montgomery, but you can call me Maddy."

We shook.

"Is your name really Leroy?" I asked.

Of course if it wasn't, he wouldn't be likely to tell me, but it seemed odd.

"What's wrong with Leroy?"

"Nothing. It's just ... I haven't met many men named Leroy who weren't ... oh, well ... you know ... a bit ..." I struggled to find the right words, but couldn't and rambled on to hide my confusion. "I mean I've met a lot of men, well not a *lot* of men ... it's just my dad was in the Navy and there are lots of men in the Navy. They have women, too. It's not just for men, but there are still a lot more men than women." I could feel the blood rushing up my neck and knew that I was not only rambling but oversharing, but I couldn't stop myself. Thankfully, Leroy took pity on me.

He laughed. "It's okay. I know Leroy is an old-fashioned name. I was named after my grandfather."

I took a deep breath. "I'm sorry. I didn't mean to offend you."

He waved away my apology. "No apology necessary, but we should probably head into the store." He tapped his Apple watch and noted the time.

"I was just going to the store but needed to let Baby . . . well, you know." He was still gnawing on the bone but had already devoured one corner. "Do you know what my aunt did with Baby during the day while she was at the . . . bakery . . . ah, store?"

"She brought him with her. Miss Octavia said if anybody had a problem with Baby, then they didn't need to patronize her store." He chuckled. "He just climbs in his bed and sleeps all day anyway."

I breathed a sigh of relief. I could only imagine the trouble he would get into left to his own devices, although the idea of a huge dog in a bakery didn't seem like such a good idea, either. But what did I know? "Great, then maybe I could follow you."

"Sure thing." He turned to go but then turned back. "Miss . . . ah, Maddy, are you sure you want to wear that?"

I examined the outfit I'd stressed about. "What's wrong with it?"

He shook his head. "Nothing. You look real nice. It's just that . . . well, it's a bit . . . *much* for a bakery, and those shoes don't seem like something you'd want to stand around in all day."

I considered my pumps. I struggled to envision what environment Louboutin wasn't appropriate for, but my imagination failed. "What would you suggest?"

"Jeans and a sweatshirt. You're bound to be covered in flour by the end of the day. I'd recommend comfortable shoes. Tennis shoes or something . . . flatter."

I balked at the idea of taking fashion advice from someone who looked like he wouldn't know the difference between silk and polyester. However, when in Rome . . . or New Bison . . . I hurried back upstairs. I went through all the clothes I owned and decided against blue jeans, opting for the leggings I'd worn last night with a silk blouse and ballet flats. It wasn't the *I'm the proprietor* statement I'd hoped to make, but it was still somewhat professional.

Leroy must have agreed, because when I came back downstairs, he gave me a thumbs-up. Although there was still something in his eyes that indicated he thought another change was needed, but he was smart enough to keep his mouth shut.

Outside, I thought about the interior of the rental and realized I needed protection if I intended to cart around a massive dog who already had a drooling problem along with his supersized bone. The rental company would charge me a fortune if he damaged the seats. I glanced at Leroy's beat-up pickup truck, which appeared to be leaking something onto the driveway. "Ah . . . would you mind taking Baby with you?"

"No problem." He opened the passenger door. "Baby, get in."

The mastiff stood, picked up his bone, loped over to the truck, and hoisted himself inside.

I hurried to get my purse and then hopped in the rental. Unfortunately, daylight didn't do much to improve my opinions of New Bison's downtown. It was still small, and there wasn't a Neiman Marcus or Saks Fifth Avenue as far as the eye could see. I followed Leroy as he pulled around behind the brick building where I'd stopped the night before.

There were two parking spaces next to a large dumpster. The one closest to the door had a sign I hadn't noticed last night, OWNER, DON'T EVEN THINK ABOUT PARKING HERE! Leroy parked in the other space, so I pulled my SUV in front of the sign. A shiver went up my spine, and I couldn't help smiling at the thought that I was now the owner. I pulled out my phone, snapped a picture, and uploaded it before I got out. **#Business-Owner #LivingMyBestLife #LovingLifeOnTheLake**

While Leroy opened the back door, Baby, still holding his bone, hiked his leg on the same dumpster he'd used last night. For a big dog, I had to admire his balance.

We all went through a small hallway. I noted a powder room on the left and a storage area on the right that I hadn't noticed last night. Next, there was the kitchen. Similar to Aunt Octavia's kitchen at home, this was modern and new, with shiny stainless-steel commercial appliances and sparkling white tiles. It was massive. Beyond the kitchen was the store and bakery. Rather than the empty cases I'd seen last night, this morning they showcased cakes, pies, pastries, cookies, and lots of other amazing-looking goodies. There were four bistro tables against the side wall of the bakery, and each table was full. In fact, the small bakery was packed. The smell of sugar, cinnamon, and chocolate was heavenly. I closed my eyes and inhaled the delicious aroma.

"Wow. Looks like Baby Cakes is doing well." I snapped pictures of the crowd and uploaded to Instagram. **#BabyCakes-Bakery #Yum #BakedWithLove**

"Yeah, but we're running low on inventory. We closed for a couple of days after Miss Octavia's death, but we didn't want the things that were already baked to go bad. It felt wasteful, and Miss Octavia hated waste. We asked her attorney, Mr. Russell, and he said we could sell the things that were already baked. After he talked to you, he told us you were coming, and he thought it would be okay if we opened up when you got here. We had to pull everything out of the freezer to take care of today's crowds. Saturday is our busiest day of the week. If we don't do some massive baking, we won't have enough to open on Tuesday. So, you wanna bake or take care of customers?"

"What? You're joking, right? Why would I want to bake?"

He hesitated as though waiting for the punchline. When none came, he spoke slowly as though he thought I'd lost my senses. "You're the owner. This is your shop. Miss Octavia did most of the baking. After all, it's *Baby Cakes Bakery*."

"But . . . surely, there was someone else?" He couldn't possibly expect me to bake.

"I helped out with some of the baking and so did Miss Hannah." He pointed to an older woman who was taking orders.

"She helps with the baking when she's . . . well." He leaned close and whispered, "She has dementia. Most days she's okay to bake, but someone has to keep an eye on her. She and Miss Octavia were best friends for over sixty years. She comes and works every day she's able."

"Who's that?" I pointed to an older Black man behind the counter.

"Garrett. Garrett Kelley." Leroy smiled. "Miss Hannah referred to him as Miss Octavia's beau. Garrett had a crush on her for . . . well, for as long as I've been alive. He owns a bookstore across the street."

Hannah looked up from behind the counter and spotted Leroy and me chatting. "You two just gonna stand there yapping all day or you gonna help?"

"I don't . . . I've never . . ." I felt like every eye in the store was staring at me.

I leaned close to Leroy and whispered, "I can't cook."

For about thirty seconds, he just stared at me with his mouth open. Eventually, he closed his mouth, shook his head, and swallowed the shock. He handed me an apron he picked up from a nearby hook. "Then I guess you better help serve." He looked at the glass cases that were practically empty. "I'll make some cookies and apple turnovers."

There was a large mattress-sized dog bed in a corner, and Baby had curled up with what was left of his bone and was already asleep. This dog led a cushy life.

I walked around the counter and plastered a fake smile on my face, and hoped it would mask the fear that I felt inside.

Hannah pointed to the cash register. "You know how to run that thing?"

"No, but if someone is willing to give me a crash course, I'm a fast learner."

Garrett waved for me to come over. "I've got to get back across the street to my own store, but when I saw the line and

Hannah in here alone . . . I thought I'd see what I could do to help." He quickly showed me how the machine worked and watched while I ran a cash and then a charge sale. When he was confident that I had the basics down, he scribbled down his phone number on a scrap of paper in case of an emergency, and then squeezed past me and hurried back across the street.

The point-of-sale system was easy enough, and apart from a blip when I ran out of paper for receipts and had to change the roll, all went smoothly. Once I knew what I was doing, I went on autopilot. I barely noticed the faces.

"You seem to have acclimated very well."

I glanced up, and it took a few seconds for my mind to connect the face with a name, but recognition hit. "Mr. Russell. Yes . . . Leroy and Garrett got me started and . . . here I am."

He smiled. "I'm sure Octavia would be proud."

I noted that Mr. Russell used my aunt's name without adding the respectful title, but I chalked it up to ignorance and shook it off. Besides, I felt good. For some reason, knowing that someone was proud of me made me happy, even if the person was a dead great-aunt whom I'd barely known. "Thank you."

Mr. Russell took his pastries and left, and I got back to the line of customers waiting to check out.

"Hello. I thought I'd find you here."

I looked up into the smiling face of Bradley Ellison.

"Mr. Ellison, what a surprise."

"Everyone in town knows Baby Cakes is the best bakery in New Bison." He grinned.

"Given the size of New Bison, I'm going to go out on a limb here and guess that Baby Cakes is the *only* bakery in New Bison."

"Not true. There's a bakery at the grocery store."

The idea of grocery-store baked goods sent a shiver up my spine.

He chuckled. "Don't tell me you're a bakery snob?"

"Well, I do own a bakery. At least, I have for almost twenty-four hours."

"True."

Miss Hannah swiped my butt with a tea towel. "Are you two just going to stand there grinning at each other all day? Snap out of it. We've got customers."

Bradley Ellison gave me a grin, swiped his credit card to pay for his pastries, and then gave me a friendly wave as he left.

I watched him as he walked away. He had a nice . . . walk. Just as he reached the curb, another man beckoned for him to come over. Before Brad could comply, Garrett Kelley ran outside. Garrett looked mad enough to spit nails. You didn't need to read lips to know that he was livid, but I wasn't sure which of the two men had angered him.

"Hey, you gonna work or stand there daydreaming all morning?" Hannah said, bringing me back to reality.

I put my head down and got back to work.

"You want a break?" Leroy asked.

I checked the time. "It's been three hours. Wow! That went by fast. Are things always this busy?"

"You should see it around the holidays." He put a tray of tiny cookies about the size of a quarter into a case.

"Those look amazing, and I'm starving. What are they?"

"Miss Octavia's thumbprint cookies. They're one of our best-selling items." He stood up. "Why don't you grab a sandwich in the kitchen and take a break. I'll take over for a bit." He leaned close. "And there's a tray of thumbprints cooling on a rack in the kitchen."

"What about Miss Hannah?" I whispered.

"Today is one of her good days. I'll keep an eye on her. When she gets tired, she'll go upstairs and lie down."

I was just about to head to the back when the door opened and the red-faced man I had nearly hit the day before walked in.

Leroy groaned. "Here comes trouble."

"Who is that man?"

Before Leroy could answer, the man forced a smile that looked like a grimace on a gargoyle and stuck out a hand. "You must be Octavia's niece. I'm Jackson Abernathy, but you can call me Jack."

I reached over the counter and shook his hand, which was warm and greasy and left me wanting to wipe my palm, but I resisted. "Mr. Abernathy, I—"

"Jack. You and I are going to be good friends." He looked around. "Perhaps your worker there could cover so we can go somewhere quiet and talk business."

Something about the way he said *worker* made me want to correct him. I made an impulsive decision. "Leroy isn't just a worker, he's the head baker, now that my great-aunt Octavia is gone." I could feel Leroy's surprise at my announcement, and I hoped he was okay with his sudden promotion. "Leroy, would you mind?"

He stood straight and tall. "Not at all."

I walked around the counter and led Mr. Abernathy back to the kitchen. When we were away from the crowd, I turned. "Mr. Abernathy . . . ah, Jack. I want to apologize for yesterday. I truly didn't see—"

He waved away my protest. "Water under the bridge."

"Really? Well, Baby behaved abominably, and I'm terribly sorry. I think he was just trying to protect me."

Again, he waved away my apology. "Baby is a great dog . . . a prince among English mastiffs, but . . . he is a lot of dog for a little lady like you."

I bristled at the implication that I couldn't handle the English mastiff, even though he was probably right.

"A big, strong dog like that needs a firm hand and experience. I should know, I breed English mastiffs. In fact, I was just on my way to see Mr. Russell about putting in an offer to buy him when we . . . ran into each other." He chuckled. "I've wanted to buy Baby for years, but Octavia . . . she was a stubborn woman. She'd grown attached to the dog, and once she got something in her head, you just couldn't change her mind."

I wondered what it must have been like to have that much confidence and assurance. Jackson Abernathy called her stubborn, but to me, she sounded like a woman who knew her own mind. Even though I didn't know Aunt Octavia, I felt suddenly resentful of his insinuations.

"Now, you seem like a rational woman, and I'm confident that you and I can come to terms on a fair price for the dog." He flashed a smile that didn't reach his eyes.

"Baby isn't for sale."

The smile froze, and his eyes hardened. "Perhaps you should hear my offer before you reject me." He tossed out a six-figure number that left me staring with my mouth open.

I quickly closed it. That much money would allow me to go back to warmer weather with the ability to show my father that I didn't need him, Elliott, or anyone else to be successful. It would prove to my dad that I was responsible. I could even pay him back for the money he'd lost from the non-wedding, but . . . something didn't feel right. "I'll admit that I don't know anything about champion English mastiffs, but that seems like quite a bit of money. Why so much?"

"Well, Baby's young, and I factored in the income from his stud fees. Octavia treated him like a person and barely scratched the surface of what he could earn." He shook his head. "Why, a dog like that could sire twice as many offsprings if your aunt hadn't been so picky and just scheduled appointments with anyone willing to pay the stud fee. Plus, modern technology means we don't need to wait for a bitch to go into heat. We can collect the sperm, freeze it, and generate more than double the income your aunt had arranged. He's a dog. No need for him to enjoy the process. This is business." He shook his head. "Now, if you're in agreement, then I can take him off your hands today."

My mind raced. I could hear my dad's voice in my head

screaming, *Take the deal!* I kept seeing Baby's big, soft brown eyes and goofy expression. My phone vibrated. I glanced down and saw that the last picture of Baby that I'd snapped of him asleep with his bone had surpassed half a million likes. "No."

"Excuse me?"

"No. Baby isn't for sale."

"Now, you listen here. That's a fair offer. You don't know the first thing about caring for a champion stud dog. You've got to feed him properly and get him to exercise." He sneered. "I saw that picture you posted . . . only an idiot would feed pizza to a prize stud dog like Baby."

My initial reaction to this tirade was shock, but when I recovered from that, I felt anger build up inside, which was even more surprising. "Get out!"

He sputtered. "What?"

"You heard me. Get out. You are not welcome in *my shop.*"

"You can't do that."

"If you're not out of my shop in ten seconds, I'll make sure you regret ever stepping foot in here. Now, *out!*"

Abernathy heaved, and his face had moved beyond red to purple. He slammed his fist down on the counter, sending a tray of thumbprint cookies crashing to the floor. He took one step toward me, but only one. Two seconds later, Baby stood by my side, his teeth bared and drool pouring like a waterfall from his jowls. A growl rumbled deep inside him.

Abernathy stared from Baby to me. "If that dog attacks me, I'll sue you for every dime you have."

"Baby, sit," I commanded with more authority than I knew I had. To my utter and complete surprise, he sat. Yet he was careful not to take his gaze from Abernathy, and I could feel his muscles, like a spring, ready to uncoil at any second.

Abernathy skirted around the kitchen and inched his way to the door. When he made it to the doorway, he stopped and glared. "You're as nutty as that aunt of yours. Well, you haven't heard the last of this."

Baby rose, and Jackson Abernathy turned and ran.

A few seconds later, Leroy poked his head around the corner. "Everything okay?"

"Yes . . . no . . . I don't know." I paced. "That man . . . he was horrible. Did you hear him?"

"I think we all heard it."

I stopped pacing and turned to stare. "You don't mean . . . ?" I pointed toward the front.

"Yeah, you two were pretty loud, and then Baby ran through the shop like a bull ready to attack." He glanced down at Baby, who was now finishing off the thumbprint cookies from the floor. "Looks like his allegiance has shifted."

"What do you mean?"

"Miss Octavia raised him from a puppy. She saved his life, and he knew it. He's a mild-mannered goofball ninety-nine percent of the time, but if anybody even thought about bothering her, Baby turned into a raging beast. Looks like he's turned his protective instincts toward you."

I watched while Baby licked up every crumb from the floor. "Why? Why me? Do you think he knows that Octavia was my great-aunt and that she left him to me?"

"No idea. Maybe it's in your blood or DNA or maybe he just knows you control the food. Either way, I think Miss Octavia would be pleased."

I stared at Baby a while longer and felt myself getting misty over a great-aunt I hardly knew and a massive dog I never knew I wanted. "I need some fresh air." I marched out of the kitchen. In the store, the noise level was considerably less than it had been earlier. I ignored the stares and walked outside.

It was cold, but my anger kept me warm until I made it to the end of the block. Unfortunately, it didn't take long for the wind off Lake Michigan to cut through my anger and my totally-inappropriate-for-the-Midwest-in-the-winter clothes. I turned and noticed a small clothing boutique, and on impulse I went inside.

The store was small but neat. The wooden shelves were filled with brightly colored handmade sweaters, scarves, and hats. I picked out a red beret and matching scarf set, along with a soft black cashmere turtleneck and a multicolored hooded jacket. It was a banded patchwork of maple, brick red, gray, and black tweed yarns and reminded me of the woven jackets I'd seen in South America. As soon as I slipped it on, I felt warm, and I couldn't stop rubbing my hands over it. "It's *sooo* soft." I checked the price tag and gasped.

"It's alpaca imported from Peru." A man with dark hair, vivid blue eyes, and a small frame poked his head from behind the counter.

I rubbed the sleeves. "It feels silky. I would have expected alpaca to be rough."

"Not at all. Alpaca fibers are rarer than cashmere and warmer than wool. That's baby alpaca, and they say the silky-smooth textures were so fine and so rare that they were once reserved for Inca royalty. It's also hypoallergenic. I call it part of my Peruvian period. I was inspired by a trip I took to the Andes. That pattern took me over a year to make." His face radiated pride. He smiled. "I could probably take ten percent off."

I turned to see my discount giver. "I'm not one to pass up a discount, but the price is already a lot less than what I would have expected for a handmade original jacket. Are you sure?"

"You must not be from here." He stared at me more closely.

"What was your first clue?"

"Ah . . . the way you're dressed. The fact that you didn't run screaming when you saw the price tags, and the fact that you've just plunked down a credit card to pay for nearly a thousand dollars' worth of winter wear without trying to convince me to give you a bigger discount."

"You already offered me a discount on the jacket." I stared. "Was I supposed to barter? I'm not good at that."

"No bartering, but it's what the people around here expect." He completed the sale and handed me back my credit card. "Do you want a bag?"

"Nope. I'll wear it." I wrapped the soft, warm scarf around my neck and went to admire myself in a mirror, still rubbing my hands up and down the sleeves.

"I'm Tyler Lawrence." He extended his hand.

"Maddy Montgomery." We shook. "I just moved here. My great-aunt died and—"

"Oh, you're Miss Octavia's niece?"

I smiled. Here was another well-mannered young man. "Great-niece."

"I'm so sorry. Miss Octavia was a wonderful woman. She never flinched at my prices and used to commission gifts for Christmas presents. I'm really going to miss her."

"You do commissions?"

"Sure." He waved his arm around the shop. "Most of these items started off as commissions that customers changed their minds about."

"You should make them pay up front. That way they can't back out."

"I've tried that, too."

"Do you mind if I take some pictures and post them online?"

He hesitated. "Not in the least."

I pulled out my phone and snapped pictures of myself and then took pictures of some of the best pieces. **#HandMade-Originals #ImportedYarn #ReasonablePrices #LoveAlpaca #TylersHandcraftedKnits**

I picked up a large basket-weave afghan that was the color of vanilla ice cream. It was soft and fluffy, and I could imagine myself curled up in it with a big cup of tea while I read and looked out over Lake Michigan. This would be perfect for covering the floral-print furniture in the study. "I'll take this, too." I placed the afghan on the counter.

"Great choice. This is merino wool. It's natural, soft, and luxurious. Took over ten pounds of yarn to make an afghan that size."

I thought about Baby. "Can I wash it?"

"Hand-wash and lay flat to dry."

He smiled as he rang up the afghan and wrapped it. "Thanks to you, I've just had my highest single-day sales total."

"Great." I picked up a similar afghan that was smaller. "This one doesn't feel as soft as mine."

"That's because you have excellent taste and chose the merino wool. The gray is acrylic. It's about half the price as the merino wool, but it isn't quite as soft. Although the acrylic is machine washable."

"I'd put this in the front window, and if you have another one in that merino wool, you should put it up there, too. They're stunning and with the weather as cold as it is, folks will want to snuggle up in these. I'll bet it's gone by the end of the weekend."

"Are you a marketing guru?"

"No, but I do know a bit about social media. Well, I need to get back. Thanks."

This time when I went outside, I was warm and cozy in my new winter weather gear. Nothing like a new outfit to improve your mood.

"I see you found Tyler's Handcrafted Knits," Hannah said.

I took off my jacket and scarf and laid them on top of one of the shelves in the kitchen area. "He's really talented. I could get in big trouble if I spend much more time in there."

It was late afternoon and most of the people had left, and the noise level was down to a low rumble. Baby was asleep in his dog bed, and the bakery smelled lemony and sweet.

I inhaled. "What's that amazing aroma?"

"Smells like Leroy made lemon squares. We can freeze them until next week." Hannah glanced in my direction. "I suppose we should be formally introduced. My name's Hannah Portman."

Hannah and I shook hands. "Maddy Montgomery."

"Leroy tells me you don't cook."

I bit my lip and made sure no one was listening. "Not really, no."

"Leroy's a good baker. He's almost as good as Octavia. She taught him everything she knew, and I'm pretty good, too. I didn't go to college to learn to bake, but I been cooking and baking my whole life. Octavia thought it was good enough, but you may want someone from one of those fancy French schools. But if you're staying, I can help." She stared down her nose. "You staying?"

She was certainly direct. I'd need to get used to that. "I'm sure you're a great baker, and I'd love for you to stay. I can use all of the help I can get." I smiled. "As to whether I'm staying . . ." The front door opened, and a middle-aged man with gray hair, glasses, and a smile that would have been perfect for a toothpaste commercial waltzed in. He was the same man I'd seen earlier arguing with Brad and Garrett Kelley in the street.

He scanned the crowd and then made a beeline for me.

"Darn it," Hannah muttered.

"You must be Octavia's niece who we've heard so much about." He reached inside his pocket and pulled out a business card and handed it to me. "I'm Paul Rivers. I own the hardware store next door, and I'm also the mayor of this fine town."

"Maddy Montgomery."

"Welcome to New Bison. Is there someplace we can go to have a private talk?"

I'd been in town less than twenty-four hours and this was the second person who wanted to have a private talk with me.

Business must really be booming here in this small town. I led him to the kitchen and prayed he didn't want to buy Baby, too.

"I don't believe in beating around the bush, so let me just say that I want to make an offer for this shop. I want to expand my hardware store, and I need this building to do so. Now, I'm prepared to make you a fair offer for the property." He held up a large envelope.

"Mr. Rivers, I—"

"Paul." He smiled.

"Paul, I hate to be the bearer of bad news, but I have no intention of selling. In fact, I can't—"

"Let's not get hasty. You haven't even heard my offer yet."

"I don't need to hear your offer. The bakery isn't for sale. This belonged to my great-aunt—my family—but I couldn't sell even if I wanted to."

"Now, I know about the terms of Octavia's will, but I'm sure we can work out something that will be mutually beneficial." He grinned. "Besides, it's not like she kept this place up. It's in horrible shape. The wiring isn't up to code, and it's just an accident waiting to happen."

"It looks fine to me," I said without the slightest amount of confidence. What did I know about the wiring? It was an old building, and he lived next door, so he might be right. I made a mental note to call someone to come out and take a look at the wiring. I passed back the envelope.

"Hold on there," he said. "Perhaps we can sit down and talk things over like responsible adults. You don't want to make an impulsive decision that could lead to financial disaster and ruin your aunt Octavia's good name in the process."

I could feel the blood rushing to my face, but before I could respond, Hannah was standing behind me holding a rolling pin.

"You heard her," Hannah said. "She ain't interested, you dirty, low-down murderer."

I turned to face Hannah. "Did you say 'murderer'?"

"I did, and I didn't stutter when I said it." She waved the rolling pin. "He murdered Octavia, just as sure as I'm standing here."

"She's crazy." He glanced from Hannah to me. "You're all crazy."

"Go on. Get out of here before I beat you to a pulp."

He pointed at me. "You mark my words. You're going to wish you'd sold." He turned and marched out.

After he left, I said to Hannah, "What do you mean, he murdered Octavia?"

But Hannah was gone. Physically, her body was still there, but when I looked in her eyes, no one was home.

"Hannah?" I reached out my hand to take the rolling pin.

"Who are you?"

# CHAPTER 3

At the rear of the bakery, there was a door that led upstairs. I helped Hannah up the stairs to the bedroom so that she could lie down. She was fast asleep and snoring almost from the moment her head hit the pillow.

I looked around at the small, one-bedroom apartment. The living area was large enough for the necessities: a sofa, coffee table, and a comfy chair. The living room opened onto a tiny kitchen with open shelves, a hot plate and countertop oven that served as a stove, a dorm-sized fridge, a sink, and not much else. There was a bathroom with a walk-in shower, sink, and toilet, and a bedroom that was large enough for a twin-sized bed. In cities like New York and Paris, this tiny little space would be labeled a bachelor's apartment or a pied-à-terre and would fetch a lot of money, but I couldn't imagine that it would bring in much money here in Michigan. The space had been painted and, despite its size, was bright and inviting. There was no private entrance, which was probably why my aunt hadn't rented it.

When I came back downstairs, the bakery was practically

empty, apart from a couple of teenagers and what appeared to be a family. A gray-haired older woman, a younger woman with the same blue eyes and high cheekbones, and an adorable little girl with curls and even bluer eyes and rosy cheeks sat enjoying thumbprint cookies. Three generations of the same vibrant blue eyes painted a picture that would make great advertising for small-town life.

I walked over to the group. "I'm the new owner—"

"Oh, you must be Octavia's niece." The older woman extended her hand. "We were so sorry to hear about her passing. We've been coming here for years. She was a wonderful woman and a fantastic baker. She'll definitely be missed."

Her daughter nodded. "Best thumbprint cookies I've ever had."

"Thank you. I was wondering if it would be okay if I took a few pictures. I'd like to do some promotions for the bakery."

The older woman looked at her daughter, who shrugged.

"Thank you." I quickly snapped a few photos and uploaded them. **#BestThumbprintCookies #ThreeGenerationsOneBakery #BabyCakesBakery #NewBisonMichiganBakery**

When I finished, I joined Leroy in the kitchen.

"Wanna help?"

I glanced around. "You talking to me?"

"You see anybody else around who owns a bakery but doesn't know how to bake?" He smiled but then looked serious. "Look, I know you were probably just trying to get that old windbag, Abernathy, off your back, but were you serious about me being the head baker? Because if you weren't, it's okay."

"Of course, I was serious. It makes sense. You worked with Aunt Octavia and you know how to bake, which is more than I can say for myself. I was hoping we could partner together. You do the baking, and I'll handle the marketing, promotion, and the store."

"Really? Great. Yes, but . . ." He grinned. "Does the promotion include a raise?"

I frowned. "Honestly, I don't know. I haven't looked through the books yet, but I'll try."

"That's okay. I mean, a raise would be nice, but I love baking, and just knowing that I get to stay here and bake is great. I was afraid you'd sell and then I'd have to find something else."

I watched while he poured ingredients into a huge mixing bowl and mixed up a dough.

"Wanna give it a try?"

"I thought we agreed I'd stick to the non-baking parts of the business?"

"Miss Octavia used to say many hands made light work."

I wasn't sure my great-aunt was right, but it wouldn't hurt to learn a couple of things. I grabbed an apron and put it on over my new black cashmere turtleneck sweater.

Just as we were about to start, we heard the bell from the front door. I reached around to untie my apron, but Leroy was quicker.

"I'll get it." He handed me an index card with an ingredient list. "You put the ingredients in the mixer, and I'll be right back."

"Piece of cake." I measured out flour, baking powder, baking soda, and salt and put them into the bowl of the giant stand mixer. The card indicated to *Mix to combine.* I waited for several seconds for Leroy's return, but when he didn't, I thought I'd move on without him. I flipped the slide on the mixer to the highest setting. The next moment, the mixer rumbled, and flour was flying everywhere, like a windstorm in the desert.

I must have screamed because Leroy came running into the kitchen. "What the—"

He flipped the mixer off, and the white dust that had been airborne just seconds earlier descended and coated every surface of the formerly sparkling kitchen, including me and my brand-new black cashmere sweater.

Leroy stared at me, and the corners of his mouth twitched.

"Don't you dare laugh."

He fought it for several seconds, but eventually he lost the battle and laughed long and hard. Every time he tried to stop, he glanced at me and started up again.

I marched out of the room into the bathroom. One glance at myself and I knew why he couldn't stop laughing. I was covered from head to toe in white flour.

"Maddy."

"What?" I turned just as Leroy snapped a picture of me with his cell phone. "If you post that picture, I'll . . . I'll . . ."

"Fire me? You can't afford to fire me. Besides, I think it'll be great for business. Everyone will want to come see our new owner."

That's when an idea struck me. "Wait. You know, that's not a terrible idea."

"Wait. What?"

"People love outtakes."

"What are outtakes?"

"You know, the bits that get cut out of videos and movies. They used to call them bloopers. Come with me." I grabbed him by the hand and led him to the store section. "This area could be redesigned, and we could do cooking classes. I could videotape you demonstrating the proper way to . . . I don't know—combine ingredients in a stand mixer or roll out dough or something. What do you think?"

He stared at me. "You think people will pay for something like that?"

I thought for a few moments. "I would."

I had him send me the photo, and I gritted my teeth for a few seconds but eventually uploaded it. **#LearningToBake #DontTryThisAtHome #BakingClassesComingSoon**

I cleaned myself the best that I could, and Leroy and I worked together in peaceful harmony to clean up the kitchen. When the last customer left, he flipped the sign from OPEN to CLOSED and locked the door.

It wasn't until I flopped down in a chair that I realized how tired I was. I racked my brain but couldn't remember ever working that hard. I hadn't had to work hard before, not physically. Growing up on military bases, I always had access to plenty of strong men to take care of any physical labor, or my dad's money to pay for it. However, there was something satisfying in working hard for something that belonged to you.

"How about an apple turnover?" Leroy asked. "I put a couple aside when I replenished the case."

"Absolutely. You get the turnovers, and I'll get the coffee." I hoisted myself up and headed to the small coffee maker at the back of the shop and poured two cups of coffee. We could use a larger coffee station, perhaps one that made espressos and lattes. I made a mental note to look into the costs of a coffee bar and perhaps a barista. I needed to talk to Mr. Russell to see if my allowance would extend to the renovations to the store and a coffee upgrade.

I woke from my daydreams when a tall, handsome man knocked at the door. I focused on not spilling my coffee as I made my way back to the bistro table.

The stranger pounded louder and pointed to the knob.

I shook my head and pointed to the sign indicating we were closed.

Unfortunately, he merely pounded louder.

"We're closed," I yelled.

"What's all the noise?" Leroy hurried from the back. He took one look at the stranger and hurried to unlock the door.

"What're you doing?" I said. "We're closed?"

Leroy ignored me and unlocked the door.

The stranger rushed inside. He blew on his hands and glared in my direction. He was ruggedly handsome with dark skin, light gray eyes, and a five-o'clock shadow. He and Leroy did a manly half hug and then knuckle-punched.

Leroy turned to me. "Maddy, this is Dr. Michael Portman, Hannah's grandson."

"Sorry, I had no idea." *Not another doctor.*

"Michael, meet Madison Montgomery, Miss Octavia's great-niece and our new owner." He finished the introductions and then headed upstairs. "I'll go get your grandmother. She's upstairs resting."

Michael walked over to the table and extended his hand. "Condolences. Your great-aunt was an amazing woman."

"Thank you. I didn't really know her, but from what I've heard, I'm sorry I didn't get a chance to know her better." I pointed to a chair. "Dr. Portman, would you mind having a seat. I'd like to talk with you if you have a moment."

He raised an eyebrow but took the seat opposite mine and waited. "Please call me Michael."

"Michael, I know your grandmother is . . . well, according to Leroy, she has dementia."

"Early stages, but yes. She's on medication, and most days she's able to function well. She has a few memory lapses, but . . . she's able to remember most things." He tilted his head and stared. "Was there a problem? Miss Octavia never minded, and we all felt it was good for her to continue doing the things she loved for as long as she was able."

"No problem, but something unusual did happen today." I quickly explained my visit from the mayor and Hannah's reaction. "I asked a neighbor how my aunt Octavia died, and she said she fell. She never mentioned murder. So, when your grandmother accused Mayor Rivers of killing her, I was shocked. I was wondering if there was any particular reason why she would say that?"

He released a breath. "Please ignore that. Your aunt Octavia fell on the bluffs behind her house. She was, we assume, outside with Baby and lost her footing. If you're staying in the house, you've seen that the stairs leading down to the beach are old and, in the winter, the spray from the lake freezes and makes them very slippery."

I had noticed the stairs and could easily imagine someone slipping and crashing to their death against the large boulders.

"Gram doesn't like Paul Rivers. He's tried many times to buy this building, but Miss Octavia wouldn't sell. She and my gram were close—closer than sisters. She took her death hard. I guess she's decided that anyone who caused her friend trouble . . . was an enemy. I'm sorry if she worried you."

"Thank you. I was sure it had to have been a mistake, but for a moment when she spoke, she looked so . . . I don't know. She just looked serious. Then, the next moment, she was gone. I just wondered where she got such an outlandish idea."

Leroy came downstairs with Hannah. She was well rested and looked back to normal. "It's 'bout time you got here."

Michael kissed his grandmother's cheek, helped her on with her coat, and walked her toward the door. Before she left, she turned to me. "Tomorrow's Sunday, so the bakery's closed for the next two days. I've got to go to church tomorrow, but I'll bake some bread, cookies, and sweet potato tarts on Monday, so we have something to sell on Tuesday morning."

"Thank you."

Leroy locked the door behind them, and we sat and ate our apple turnovers.

Baby got up and stretched as though he'd just worked a twelve-hour shift on a chain gang.

I stood and stretched, too. "I'd better take him home before he eats the few items we've got left."

"I'll just finish cleaning and lock up. We're missing one of the knives." He pointed to the knife block on the counter.

I'd taken one of the knives the night before. I retraced my steps from the previous night, but it wasn't on the shelf where I'd left it. "Sorry, I thought I left it right here."

"It'll turn up. They always do." He looked at everything except me. Clearly something was on his mind. "I might be a little late . . . you know, baking. Mind if I crash upstairs?"

"Of course not."

He released a breath and smiled. "Miss Octavia let me stay there sometimes. Ever since the developers started buying up all the land, rent in New Bison has gone up so much, I had to get an apartment thirty miles away to find something I could afford."

"I noticed there's no alarm." I thought of the noise that had sent Baby racing through the shop last night.

Leroy chuckled. "No need for an alarm in New Bison."

I wondered if he was right. Anyway, I let it go. Whatever had captured Baby's attention last night was long gone now. I tried to take comfort by telling myself it was probably a mouse, but that didn't bring me peace either. I would prefer a two-legged burglar over a four-legged rodent any day of the week. Besides, rodents were bad for business.

I wrapped myself in my new knitwear and got in the car. I stopped for fast food on my way home and ate it in the car, not giving Baby a chance to beat me to dinner tonight. By the time we made it home, I was exhausted. I wasn't exactly new to the workforce, but my previous jobs were brief and involved more mental exercise than physical. I hated to admit it, but Leroy had been right about the shoes. I made a mental note to order a couple more pairs of flats and even a pair of sneakers. Did Jimmy Choo make sneakers? I'd have to look.

I filled Baby's food and water dishes and let him outside to take care of the call of nature. Then I took a shower and washed the flour out of my hair and went to bed.

Baby climbed in after me.

I stared at the large dog. "Tomorrow's Sunday. The bakery's closed, and I plan to sleep late, so don't wake me."

He yawned and stretched.

It felt as if I had just closed my eyes when I was jerked awake. The doorbell rang, and someone was pounding on the front door.

Baby barked and then rocked the bed as he leaped down and raced to the door.

I grabbed my phone and a robe as I hurried to follow the mastiff. I looked through the peephole and quickly unlatched the door when I saw two policemen on the front porch.

"Can I help you?" I said through a crack, which I used more to keep Baby from getting out than to prevent the police from coming inside.

The uniformed officers held up badges. "New Bison Police. Are you Madison Montgomery?" One of the officers was round and pudgy and reminded me of the Pillsbury Doughboy. The other one looked about twelve with a face full of acne.

"Yes." I was wide awake now. It was never good when policemen knew your name.

"We're going to need you to come with us." Doughboy held up a flashlight, and I had to squint to keep from going blind.

"Come with you? What time is it? What's happened?"

"There's been an incident," Doughboy said. "We need you to come with us."

"An incident? What kind of incident? I don't understand. Where was the incident? Where do you want to take me?"

"Ma'am, we just need you to come with us."

"I don't know. I don't think I should. How do I know you're real policeman? I don't even know anyone here. This sounds fishy to me, especially when you won't tell me why you need me to go with you." My heart was pounding in my chest. I'm not sure where I got the courage to refuse, but I've heard horror stories about bad things happening to minorities, especially in small towns. And there were several articles that I remembered going around the Internet about killers who pretended to be policemen and then kidnapping women and selling them as sex slaves.

Doughboy looked incredulous. "Ma'am, there's been a fire and a murder, and we need to ask you a few questions."

"Murder? Who was killed? Why do you need me?"

"We'll explain everything when we get downtown." Dough-boy was persistent, if not helpful.

"Okay, but why me? I just got into town a day ago. I barely know anyone here. Who's dead?"

There was a substantial pause, but I was a champion at playing chicken. Eventually, the officers must have realized we were at a stalemate, and Acne Face said, "Mayor Paul Rivers."

"The mayor's dead? Wow. I just met him today."

"We understand you two argued," Acne Face said.

Doughboy shot him a look that indicated he'd shared too much, and Acne Face quickly shut down. "Would you come with us?"

My nerves went into hyperdrive, and I babbled and shared too much information, but I couldn't stop myself. "We didn't really argue. We had a disagreement, that's all. He wanted to buy the bakery, and I didn't want to sell. Well, I'm not sure if I want to sell, but, regardless, I can't sell even if I wanted to, but he didn't want to listen."

"Ma'am, we'd like your cooperation in our investigation. Now, I'm asking you to come along peacefully, but if I have to, I can get a warrant."

"I'm more than willing to help, but I don't understand. Why me? I can't be the only person who had a disagreement with the mayor."

Doughboy gave me a steely stare. "Maybe not, but the body was found in your bakery, and your fingerprints were found on the murder weapon."

# CHAPTER 4

Doughboy and Acne Face waited outside while I went upstairs and dressed. My mind raced around in circles. *The mayor killed in my bakery and my fingerprints were on the murder weapon. How could that be? I've only been in town a little over twenty-four hours. I'd only met the mayor once. Surely, they didn't . . . couldn't think . . . well, they certainly wouldn't be here if they didn't think I had something to do with it. My fingerprints were on the murder weapon.* I pulled on a pair of leggings and a sweater, which took very little time, and spent the next few minutes pacing.

"Maybe I should call my dad and arrange for a lawyer to be with me. What do you think?" I stared at Baby as though he were going to reply.

Baby rolled over on his back, his underbelly exposed for the world to see. He wiggled his body from side to side.

"No, you're right. I can't call my dad. I can't expose my weakness like that. He'll just say he was right. I'm not mature or responsible enough to be on my own, but what am I going to do?" I paced.

With his itch abated, Baby did a big-dog version of the downward-facing dog yoga position that ended when he sat. Even though I was standing and taller than him, it looked as though he were staring down his nose at me. The look lit my memory.

I pulled out my phone. "Mr. Russell, he's an attorney. He'll know what to do." I tapped the number I'd saved in my phone for him and waited what felt like a lifetime for him to answer.

"Hello," he said groggily.

"Mr. Russell, this is Maddy Montgomery, I'm Octavia Baker's—"

"I know who you are, Ms. Montgomery. Do you know what time it is?"

"Mr. Russell, the police are here. They said the mayor's been murdered and my—"

"*What!*"

"Look, this will go a lot faster if you'd stop interrupting and just let me tell you what's happened." I hurriedly told him about the police on my doorstep waiting to take me . . . I don't know where, to answer questions. "I need advice. I didn't kill the mayor or anyone, but I think it might be good to have a lawyer, and you're the only one I know in New Bison."

He was moving and sounded a little breathless. "You're right. Go with the police, but don't answer any questions until I get there."

Knowing that I wouldn't have to face the police alone had a calming effect. I grabbed my purse and headed downstairs.

The two policemen were on the front porch, right where I'd left them. When I opened the front door, Doughboy released a breath and his shoulders relaxed.

"Shall I follow you?" I held up my car keys.

They exchanged glances.

"That way, you don't have to drive us home."

"Us?" Acne Face asked.

"Baby and me. I can't leave him here alone." I paused. "I mean, it's not like I'm under arrest, am I?" I smiled.

The officers glanced at Baby just as what looked like a quart of drool fell from his mouth.

It's no surprise that, given a choice between riding with a two-hundred-fifty-pound English mastiff with drool hanging like tinsel on a Christmas tree from his jowls or allowing me to follow them in my own car, they decided it would be perfectly all right for me to follow them.

The drive to the police station was short and uneventful, but for a split second, visions of Thelma and Louise crossed my mind. However, things didn't end well for them, and I doubted that Baby and I would fare much better, so I pushed all thoughts of flight from my mind and followed the police, careful not to exceed the speed limit or violate any of the rules of the road. My high school driver's education teacher would have been proud.

The New Bison Police Station was a newer building with a nautical theme. It was blue and white with a lighthouse dome and looked more like a bank branch than a garrison for law-enforcement officers. The parking lot was also larger than I would have thought necessary for a town this size, but then maybe the citizens of New Bison visited the police station frequently. There weren't many cars in the lot at this time of the early morning, but there was a gray-and-blue Jeep with a hitch towing a khaki-colored boat with MARINE PATROL painted on the side. I guess that explained the lighthouse-themed police station.

I grabbed the towel that I'd designated as Baby's for handling drool and gave his face a wipe. When I finished, he shook his head and flung the remaining drool across the dashboard. "When the rental company finishes charging me for cleaning this car, I could have bought it."

Baby put his paw on the dashboard and barked.

"You really think I should buy this car?" Baby nodded . . . well, it looked like a nod. "If I'm not arrested, maybe I'll consider it. Now, let's go."

We followed the two policemen into the station. Inside, the space was open and airy. Not at all what I expected. I'd never been inside a police station, but I expected it to be dark and gloomy.

We walked into the main area under the dome. There stood the most beautiful woman I've ever seen. She was wearing a uniform, which indicated she worked here, although she looked as though she would have been equally at home draped in designer clothes on a catwalk in Paris or Milan. Nearly six feet tall with gray eyes and dark, wavy hair pulled back into a bun, she looked stunning, despite the beige uniform.

She stood under the dome with her hands at her side, legs wide like a Wild West gunslinger.

Her facial expression was dead serious. I followed the angle of her line of sight, which ended with Baby. To my utter surprise, Baby held her gaze.

Sensing a catastrophe in the making, I tugged on the dog's leash, but to no avail.

The woman counted. "One. Two. Three."

On three, Baby took off toward her, dragging me on the end of his leash and me yelling for him to stop.

Baby charged.

The woman pulled her hand from her holster and pointed a finger at Baby just as he leaped into the air.

"Bang."

From midair, Baby stopped and then dropped to the ground, inches from the woman.

"What just happened?" I stared from the gunslinger to the prostrate dog on the ground.

After a few seconds, the other officers who had come out to watch applauded. The woman got down on her knees and started rubbing Baby's belly, while he rolled around on his back with his tongue hanging out and drool falling from his mouth. When the lovefest was over, the woman stood up and extended a hand. "Hello, I'm Sheriff April Johnson."

"Madison Montgomery." I shook her hand. "Obviously, you already know Baby."

"Oh, yes. Miss Octavia and I were good friends. I really miss her." Her eyes filled with water, and she choked up, but she swallowed it. "I'm very sorry for your loss."

Baby nudged her hand with his nose.

"Did you teach him to play dead?" I asked.

She shook her head. "I wish I could take the credit for it, but that was all Miss Octavia. She taught him a ton of tricks, but the best one was watching them dance."

"Dance?"

"Your aunt loved Frank Sinatra, and she and Baby would dance around the house. She said Baby was the best dance partner she ever had because he wasn't always trying to take the lead." She chuckled.

She knew Octavia was my great-aunt, not my aunt, but I was getting tired of correcting people. It was easier to let it go, so I did. "I wish I had known her."

"She was an amazing lady." She took a deep breath. "But you're not here in the middle of the night to listen to me prattle on about Miss Octavia, bless her heart."

*Oh, I don't know. I'd certainly prefer that to spending the night locked in a cell.*

"Let's go back to my office." She gave Baby a pat, turned, and walked around a desk.

I walked past an officer who was looking at a video of Baby's performance on his cell phone. "Would you mind sending me the video?" I scribbled my telephone number on a scrap of paper I found in my purse, handed it to him, and then quickly followed Sheriff Johnson.

There was a metal detector like in airports, but she took Baby and me around the side and through a door that led back past a few cubicles. In the back, there was a door with her name on it. She held it open for Baby and me to pass through before she closed it. "Coffee or tea?"

I shook my head.

She moved behind the desk and sat. "Now, did the officers tell you why you're here?"

"They said Mayor Rivers was murdered in my bakery and that my fingerprints were on the murder weapon, but I don't understand how that can be. I barely knew the man."

"I know. You didn't get to town until the day before yesterday and just met him. Although he had the power to infuriate most women in record time with his condescending remarks, I doubt that he had enough time to irritate you enough to stab him."

"Is that how he was murdered?"

"I probably shouldn't have told you that, but Miss Octavia always told me I should trust my gut, and my gut tells me that you're not the killer."

I stared. "Then why did you have me picked up and brought here?"

"Because he was found in your bakery after it was closed. I was hoping you could tell me why he was there. Plus, it's one of your knives. I recognized it at once. When we dusted it for prints, the only ones on it were yours."

"I have no idea why he was in the bakery after hours. I certainly didn't let him in." I paused. "Wait. Where did you get my fingerprints?"

April smiled. "That was easy. With your dad in the Navy, I figured you'd probably have had a summer job on some military base. Sure enough, there you were."

"But why? What made you think they were my fingerprints?"

"Miss Octavia used to always say, the easiest route was usually the best route. The knife had Baby Cakes engraved on the handle, so I started with everyone connected to the bakery first. That meant you, Leroy, and Hannah. I tried you and Leroy first, and sure enough, I got a match. Although it was a bit challenging with the fire—"

"Fire? What fire?"

"I'm sorry, I should have told you about the fire. Whoever killed Mayor Rivers started a fire, probably in an attempt to destroy the evidence."

I stood as panic gripped my heart. "Leroy. He was going to stay—"

"Leroy's fine. He has trouble sleeping—insomnia. He knew I was working third shift, and he brought me a coffee and some of that delicious Lemon Zucchini Bread."

I flopped back down into my chair. "Thank God."

"Leroy ran into Tyler Lawrence on his way back to the bakery. Tyler forgot something in his shop and headed back downtown. That's when they noticed the flames coming from Baby Cakes. Garrett Kelley must have seen the flames, too, because they found him trying to drag the mayor outside, but it was too late. If they hadn't arrived when they did, Garrett, too, would be dead from the smoke."

It took a few moments for the shock to wear off. "Are they okay?"

"Tyler called nine-one-one while Leroy dragged Garrett out, but it was too late for the mayor. Leroy and Garrett went to the hospital, but they should both be okay."

Her phone rang. She listened for a few moments before frowning as she covered the phone with her hand. "Chris Russell is outside demanding to be present while you're questioned."

"Oops." I'd forgotten all about him. "I called him when the two cops—ah, I mean, police—showed up at my door in the middle of the night demanding that I come with them."

She sighed and then spoke into the phone. "You'd better send him back."

The Chris Russell who marched into the office wasn't the same prim, proper attorney who sat behind his desk with his starched Oxford shirt, dark suit, wispy hair, and wire-framed glasses. This Chris Russell's shirt was wrinkled, and peeking out from his coat collar was the edge of a pajama top. In his haste, he'd misbuttoned his trench coat, causing the coat to bunch at the bottom, and he had a bad case of bed head that caused a section of his hair to refuse to lie flat. "I hope you haven't been questioning my client without legal counsel present."

"I really wasn't questioning her at all, not really. Please have a seat." She indicated a chair. "Would you like coffee?"

"What? No . . . thank you. Are you arresting my client?"

"Mr. Russell, I'm sorry that you came all the way down here for nothing, but Miss Montgomery isn't under arrest. We just wanted to talk to her. I'm afraid my deputies may have been a little overzealous when I asked them to bring her. I didn't mean to imply that she was wanted for anything more than to help us fill in some gaps." She gave a big dazzling smile. "But since you're here, why don't you sit down?"

Mr. Russell consulted his watch and flopped down in the chair.

"Now, I wanted to ask Maddy—"

"Wait," I said. "You told me there was a fire at the bakery."

"It looks like whoever killed Mayor Rivers tried to destroy the evidence. Thankfully, it looks like Garrett Kelley arrived fairly soon after the fire started. The fire department put the fire out quickly, but . . . the majority of the damage came from smoke and water. You won't be able to open again for quite some time."

I groaned.

"I'm sure Octavia had insurance, but I'll look through the

papers tomorrow." Russell's glasses slipped down his nose, but he pushed them back in place and ran his hand over his head.

April continued, "I was telling Madison that I recognized the weapon used to murder the mayor. It was one of Miss Octavia's knives and had Baby Cakes engraved on the handle." She must have sensed that Chris Russell was revving up for a battle because she quickly added, "However, since it was from the bakery, and we know that she owns the bakery, it would make perfect sense that her fingerprints would be on it."

Mr. Russell's shoulders relaxed, and he sat back in his chair. "Then why?"

"Madison's only been here a couple of days. I know she had an argument with the mayor, but most people in town have fought with him at one point or another, including you." She smiled.

Chris Russell bristled, but said nothing.

April turned to me. "Can you tell me what the argument was about?"

"Don't answer that." Chris Russell scooted to the edge of his seat.

"I don't mind. I have nothing to hide. I didn't kill Mayor Rivers."

Chris Russell stood up. "Sheriff, I'd like a word with my client alone."

"Certainly, why don't Baby and I go see what we can find to snack on in the break room."

I don't know if it was hearing his name or the word *snack* that did the trick, but Baby, who moments earlier had been asleep, roused himself, and with nary a backward glance at me trotted behind April out of the office.

"Miss Montgomery, I know you don't think you have anything to hide, but let me caution you that anything you say can be used against you in a court of law. Sheriff Johnson is trying to catch a murderer. Many innocent people are lulled into a false sense of security by the police, and they end up say-ing things that can get them arrested, prosecuted, and impris-oned or . . . worse."

"But I didn't murder Mayor Rivers."

"That doesn't matter. Why don't you tell me what happened and let me guide you? After all, that's why you called me in the middle of the night, isn't it?"

My guilt inflamed my cheeks. "I'm sorry, I've never had the police come to my house before. I was scared, and I didn't want to call The Admiral—my father."

"You were right to call me, but you need to listen to me. Now, what happened?"

I told him about the altercation we had at the bakery. "I'm pretty sure I never touched those knives. . . . At least . . . I must have touched them, but not when the mayor was there. I mean, Leroy is going to teach me to cook, but I don't think I touched . . . oh . . ."

"What? You remembered something. What is it?"

"It's just that the first night when I arrived, after I went to the house, later that night, I went to the bakery."

"Was the mayor there?"

I shook my head. "No one was there . . . well, I didn't see anyone, just me and Baby, but that must have been when I touched the knife. Baby was acting funny . . . like he heard something, and he ran off barking, and I grabbed a knife to de-fend myself."

"Against whom?"

I shook my head. "No idea. I just got into town, and I didn't know anyone. I grabbed a knife, and then Baby came trotting back like nothing happened, so I put the knife down. No one was there. At least, I don't think anyone was there."

"Where did you put the knife?"

I thought for a moment but shook my head. "I just laid it down on one of the shelves in the store, but it wasn't there today—I mean yesterday. Leroy mentioned one of the knives was missing, but we figured it would turn up."

"Did anyone see you while you were at the bakery?"

"I don't think so. It was late."

April knocked on the door. "Is it okay for us to come in?"

Baby didn't wait. He bounced into the room and greeted me by putting his paws on my shoulders.

April took her seat behind the desk. Upon getting a nod from the lawyer, she turned to me. "Now, would you mind telling me about the argument you had with the mayor?"

Mr. Russell granted his approval, so I repeated what I'd just told him about checking out the bakery on my first night in town and picking up the knife and then the argument with the mayor. She asked me to describe the knife.

"It was a knife. I honestly wasn't paying a lot of attention, but it wasn't the biggest knife in the block. It was medium sized with a whitish handle."

"Sounds like our murder weapon, all right."

"Anyone could have taken the knife. You don't have anything to hold my client on."

"I agree." She smiled. "I have no intention of arresting Madison."

"So, she's free to go?"

"Absolutely."

April got up and shook hands with Mr. Russell and me and then gave Baby a big hug. She spoke baby talk to him, which made his tail wag and his butt shake. Then she gave him a pat and promised to bring him a special treat when she saw him again.

Outside, Mr. Russell reminded me not to talk to the police unless he was present and then surprised me when he climbed into a Pacific-blue McLaren Spider. Honestly, I wasn't that into cars and had never heard of a McLaren, but Elliott, my ex, had been obsessed with British sports cars. He could drone on for hours about dihedral doors and carbon ceramic brakes. This expensive sports car was going to be his gift to himself upon graduation from medical school. Back then, I took my fiancée responsibilities seriously and looked at brochures, oohed and aahed at the appropriate places, and feigned interest, as was my duty. I wasn't an expert, but New Bison didn't seem like the place for a three-hundred-thousand-dollar sports car, especially in the middle of the winter. However, who was I to judge? If I'd shelled out more than a quarter of a million dollars for a car, I'd probably drive it every day, too.

I opened the passenger door to the rental and glanced down in time to see Baby relieve himself on the tire. When he was done, he hopped up into the car. *I'm really going to need to buy a seat cover.*

When I got behind the wheel, my phone chimed. One glance showed me that the video of Baby and the sheriff had arrived. I took a few moments to watch it before I posted it to social media. **#GunfightAtTheNewBisonPolice #NoMastiffs-WereInjuredMakingThisVideo #WhoKnewEnglishMastiffs-WereSuchHams #EnglishMastiffDramaQueen**

# CHAPTER 5

I argued with myself about driving by Baby Cakes tonight, technically this morning, but the sun wasn't up yet, so as far as I was concerned, it was night. Sheriff Johnson told me I couldn't go inside because it was a crime scene. Plus, she said I should wait until later, when the sun came up, especially since there wasn't anything I could do. Besides, everything looks better when the sun is shining. However, I couldn't resist. I had to see what was left of my inheritance.

When I pulled up in front, I knew I should have listened and skipped this visit. Even though sunlight wouldn't make a difference. The glass was broken in the front windows. The brick was black from smoke damage, and whatever display cases weren't damaged by the fire or smoke had been finished off by the firefighters. Sitting in the car, I was overwhelmed by the devastation and placed my head on the steering wheel. *It had taken me only forty-eight hours to destroy the business Aunt Octavia had built. How would I bounce back from this? What would happen now? The details of Aunt Octavia's will stated I had to run the business, but there was no business left for me to* run. *I'd have to call Chris Russell after he looked up my insurance. My dad would tell me to come home. How could I argue with him?*

I nearly leaped out of my skin when someone knocked on the window. I turned and saw Leroy and hurried to roll down the window. "You scared me. Are you okay? What happened? Are you injured? What are we going to do?"

He held up a hand wrapped in white gauze. "Hold on. You're firing questions faster than lightning. Give me a chance to breathe."

"I'm sorry. How are you?"

"I'm fine. I just cut my hand." He held up his bandaged hand. "They gave me oxygen for the smoke. Wanted me to stay overnight, but no point in that. Besides, I need a shower and to get out of these clothes." He sniffed his T-shirt.

He reeked of smoke. Granted, the entire street smelled of smoke, but up close it was overpowering. I must have scowled.

"Yep. I stink." He took a step back.

I thought about lying, but I'm a terrible liar. "You do smell bad, but I'm glad you're okay. How's Garrett Kelley?"

"I think he's going to be fine. He got a lot more smoke in his lungs than I did, so they're keeping him overnight. Plus, his hands have cuts and burns."

"He's going to be okay . . . isn't he?"

"I think so."

"Maybe I should swing by the hospital tomorrow. I don't really know him, but he dated Aunt Octavia, so . . . I suppose it's expected . . . unless you think that I shouldn't?" I looked eagerly at Leroy, hoping he could tell me the right thing to do.

"I'm sure he'd like flowers. I mean, that's what most people do." He coughed like a five-pack-a-day smoker until he hacked up a wad of something that probably should have stayed inside. When he was done, he burst out laughing. "I'm not contagious. The doctor said I'd probably have a cough for a few days."

"What do you mean?" I lied, and forced my brows to unfurl and my facial muscles to relax. "I wasn't worried that you were contagious."

"You're a horrible liar."

"I know. Are you sure you're okay? I think you should go home and get in bed and . . . just stay there. You sound awful."

"Thanks, but Baby Cakes doesn't provide health insurance, so . . . I need to work." He looked at the building. "Well, when we reopen. We are going to reopen, aren't we?"

"Of course . . . I mean, I'm sure we . . . I need to find out what insurance we have, but I don't think we'll be able to open until the police finish investigating."

He coughed.

"You go home and get some rest, and we'll talk later. Uh, do you need a ride?"

Leroy shook his head. "I need to air out as much as possible, but I'll see you tomorrow."

I watched Leroy walk away and wondered if I should have insisted that he get in the car. Although, insisting wasn't exactly my strong suit. "He would have said if he wanted company, right?"

Baby yawned.

Before I left, I pulled out my phone and snapped pictures. **#BabyCakesBakery #ClosedUntilFurtherNotice #Smoking HotBakedGoods #DownButNotOut**

I posted the pictures and hoped that the last part was true.

I drove home as the sun rose above the trees and painted the morning sky with a bright show of orange and golden yellow over the green, red, and amber-colored treetops. I expected to be tired, but when I pulled into the driveway, I realized that rather than exhaustion, I was energized. I took a quick shower to get the odor of smoke out of my hair, skin, and clothes and then slipped on a pair of skinny jeans and a silk shirt. Nothing like silk to make you feel refreshed and special. I hoped that special feeling would spark brain waves to help me figure out what to do about the bakery, the fire, Baby, and my dad. That was a lot to expect from one little silk blouse, but it was a really cute blouse and I never underestimated the power of silk.

I glanced at Baby, who was stretched out on the kitchen floor with his food bowl between his paws.

"I'm hungry, too." I copied what I'd seen Alma do and pulled a bag of Baby's special mixture from the refrigerator and replaced it with a bag from the freezer. Then I filled his bowl with both the dry and wet food. I mixed the two and took a whiff. "This actually smells pretty good." I got a small spoon and took a taste. "Actually, if it had a little salt, it would be pretty tasty."

Baby got up on his hind legs and placed his paws on the counter.

"All right, I just took one taste." I placed the bowl on the floor.

He went to work on the mountain of food.

I took out my phone and asked Siri, "What's the easiest food to make?"

She came back with a list that confirmed that her idea of "easiest" and mine were drastically different. Then I latched onto one item—scrambled eggs. I opened the fridge and found some eggs. "I've seen people make scrambled eggs on television. How hard can that be?"

Baby looked up from his bowl and tilted his head as though my question required a great deal of thought. After a few moments, he returned to his bowl.

I stuck my tongue out at him and took the carton of eggs to the counter. I dropped the first two eggs on the floor. By the time I got the paper towels and came back to clean it up, the mess was gone, and Baby was licking the floor with bits of eggshell stuck to his nose. I whipped out my phone and asked Siri, "Are eggs harmful to dogs?" Siri said eggs were not harmful. Baby seemed perfectly fine, but to be safe, I asked about raw eggs and eggshells. Apparently, raw eggs and even the eggshells contain several vitamins that are good for both dogs and humans, and the risk of salmonella is low. I wiped the eggshells from his nose, but he was now sitting by my side, apparently waiting for any other goodies that I dropped for him. "Who knew there were so many nutrients in eggshells?"

Baby licked his lips as though to say, *Yep, you should have asked me.*

I was more careful with the next two. This time, they made it into the bowl. Unfortunately, not just the innards but most of the shell made it into the bowl. Despite all of the nutritional benefits, I decided against his eating the shells and tossed them down the sink. The next two made it into the bowl with a minimal amount of shell, which I was able to scoop out with a spoon. I found a wire whisk in a drawer. I was sure I'd seen chefs on television using them to beat eggs. So, I vigorously beat the eggs with the whisk. That was when I learned that I'm a lot stronger than I thought. My vigorous whisking left me with eggs in my hair, eyelashes, and on the front of my shirt.

Sensing that I needed cleaning as much as the floor did, Baby got on his hind legs and licked the eggs from my face and hair.

"Baby, *off*," I ordered.

He took one last lick and then got back down on all fours.

I set the bowl on the counter, got a paper towel, and moved to the sink to clean myself up. When I was clean from the eggs and dog spittle, I turned back around and found that the bowl with the remaining egg mixture was now on the floor . . . and empty. I scowled at Baby. "Bad dog."

He licked his lips.

I put the bowl in the dishwasher.

"I own a bakery. I'm going to need to learn to cook and learn quickly. I can't let myself be defeated by eggs."

The next two eggs made their way to the bowl with even less of the shell. I lowered my muscle power from tornado strength to a gentle breeze. This time, all of the mixture ended up in the skillet, and I felt as if I'd just climbed Mount Everest. I did my happy dance and turned the knob on the stove. Nothing happened. There was a clicking noise, and I smelled gas, but no flame. I turned the knob off and tried again, but the results were the same. After a third try, the smell of gas was so strong, that despite the cold artic wind blowing off Lake Michigan, I opened a window. The last thing I needed was for Baby and me to die from carbon monoxide or natural gas or whatever killed people. I stood at the sink and stared at the massive stove.

My stomach growled, and a tear ran down my cheek. My father's voice played in my head. *A man is dead, and you're standing there crying over eggs? Suck it up, sailor. You can't even turn the stove on, how are you going to learn to run a bakery? This is ridiculous. You might as well pack it up and come home.*

I might have actually listened to the voices if Baby hadn't nudged me with his head and broken the trance. I reached down and scratched behind his ears. "If I left now, what would happen to you, big boy? There's no way my dad would let me bring you home."

Baby snorted, and I laughed. "Yeah, that's what I think of that arrangement, too."

The doorbell rang, and I started toward the front door until I noticed Baby headed to the back. Based on the way his rear end wagged, he smelled a friend on the other side of the door.

I looked through the peephole and was surprised to see Sheriff April Johnson balancing a casserole dish and a drink carrier with five cups of coffee.

Before opening the door, I ushered Baby into the garage.

"Sorry, I had to get Baby out of the way."

"That's perfect. I love Baby, but he's a whole lotta dog. One push and I would have been wearing this casserole instead of getting ready to eat." She rushed into the kitchen and put the casserole on the counter. "I sure hope you're hungry. I didn't know how you took your coffee, so I just got black. I figured you could doctor it up the way you wanted."

"Thank you." I took the cup she extended to me and took a sip.

April went to a cabinet and removed a tray. She stacked plates and then reached in a drawer and loaded silverware and napkins onto the tray. When she was done, she picked up the pot holders and her casserole and headed to the dining room. "You wanna grab the tray?"

I was too surprised to do anything except comply, so I put my coffee on the tray and followed her into the dining room.

She placed the casserole on the sideboard and then started to set the table.

I stood and watched for a few seconds before I got the nerve to ask, "May I ask what you're doing? Are you expecting visitors?"

She stopped and stared. "Oh, I'm sorry. I thought you knew."

"Knew what?"

"Well, your great-aunt was a brilliant woman. She baked, she ran her business, and she . . . solved problems." She blushed and looked down.

"What kind of problems?"

She took a deep breath and sat down. "My ex-husband used to joke and say, 'You sure are pretty, but you're not the sharpest crayon in the box.'" She paused. "Only he wasn't joking. He meant it. I never was one for books, not like you and Miss Octavia, who went to college. I graduated from high school by the seat of my pants. My dad said high school was all the *book learning* any girl needed."

"Wow. He sounds like . . ."

"A Neanderthal? You can say it. It's the truth. According to him, God made women for cooking, cleaning, and . . . well, you know."

"That's awful, but I don't understand what that has to do with my great-aunt." *Or me.* "You've obviously proved everyone wrong. You're the sheriff."

"Thanks to Miss Octavia." She wiped a tear away and took a sip of coffee. "She was the first person who ever believed in me. She convinced me that I could do whatever I wanted. I used to come to Baby Cakes every day around closing time just to sit and listen to Miss Octavia talk about all of those books she's read. Eventually, we got to be friends. One day, the old sheriff was in there, and he was being . . . crude." She paused and turned red. After a few moments, she continued. "Miss Octavia wasn't having none of that sexist, male-chauvinist talk. She stood up for me. She told him that I had more smarts in my little finger than he had in his pea brain, and if he didn't watch out, I just might take his job. You should have heard the laughter that followed that announcement. That's when I decided to do it. I would run for sheriff."

"Was that something you wanted?"

"I didn't know I wanted it until I started campaigning." She shook her head. "I was so scared, but Miss Octavia said if that pea-brained half-wit could be sheriff, then I could, too. Plus, I had something that he didn't."

"What?"

She smiled. "Her on my side. Well, after being in pageants since I was old enough to sit up, I knew how to campaign and win votes. I've never lost any contest I've ever entered, so we made posters and flyers. I smiled and passed out buttons, and Miss Octavia donated the pastries at my events." She smiled. "I think more people came for the food than to hear me. Before long, here I was."

"Don't you have to have been in law enforcement to be the sheriff?"

April shook her head. "Surprisingly, no. Law-enforcement experience was preferred, but not required. In fact, in most parts of the country, the requirements are really basic." She held up her hand and ticked them off. "You need to be a US citizen, eighteen years old, live in the county for at least one year, have a high school diploma or GED, and you must be physically and mentally fit."

"I would have expected them to require previous law-enforcement experience."

"Honestly, so did I, but Sheriff Harper didn't have any experience, either. He ran for office and was elected. When the Association for Sheriffs tried to tighten the regulations and require law-enforcement experience, he used his connections to get an exclusion for New Bison. Most sheriffs serve the county. New Bison is the exception, serving only the town. I guess he assumed he'd continue his reign." She shrugged. "After I was elected, I attended the twelve-week police academy program. It was hard work, but I learned a lot."

"Do you like being the sheriff?"

"Most of the time I do. I don't like the paperwork. Some of the men used to make fun of me . . . heck, they still make fun, but thanks to Miss Octavia, I've solved some cases that made them sit up and take notice of me for more than my looks." She sat up straighter.

"That's great, but I'm afraid I still don't understand why you're here."

She chuckled. "Oh, listen to me rambling on. . . . Well, after that—the elections—we started coming here every week. She called us her Baker Street Irregulars. We talked through tough cases and worked out a plan for figuring out *whodunit*, as Miss Octavia used to say."

"That's great, but . . . Aunt Octavia's dead, and I'm no great detective. In fact . . . wait, who's 'we'?"

The doorbell rang.

"That'll be the rest of the Irregulars." She hopped up and continued setting the table.

Even without Baby's help, I knew to go to the back door. Leroy came in carrying a platter filled with pastries, croissants, and scones, which was covered in plastic wrap. He still had a slight odor, but it was more the smell of a heavy smoker rather than of a man who'd been in a building fire.

"Hmm, that looks and smells good." I put my nose near the plastic and took a big whiff.

"I wasn't sure if we would be meeting given everything that's happened, but then I saw April's car." Leroy had shaved and was wearing a white shirt and starched jeans and after-shave, which probably masked some of the smoke.

"You look very nice. April didn't tell me this was a formal occasion."

Leroy avoided eye contact and turned away. "I don't know what you're talking about."

"Is there something going on between you and April?"

He nearly dropped the platter. "No, you must be kidding. She's . . . not interested in someone like me . . . an assistant baker."

"Head baker, you've been promoted, remember?"

"Assistant baker, head baker, none of that matters. April is so far out of my league. I wouldn't stand a chance with someone like her."

I touched his arm to get him to look at me. "I don't know April very well, but she seems pretty down to earth. Have you told her how you feel?"

He shook his head. "No, and please don't you tell her, either. The only person who knows—knew—was Miss Octavia, and she said I would tell her when I was ready."

"Sounds like she was a wise woman."

He took a whiff of himself. "Do I stink bad?"

"Barely noticeable, but how's your hand?"

He held up his bandaged left hand. "Not bad."

"What's going on in here?" April came in and Leroy turned away, so his back was to her.

"I made a pastry platter. I'm just going to add some whipped butter and preserves to the tray."

"Sounds delicious. Your croissants are always so flaky, I think yours might have been even better than Miss Octavia's."

Leroy flushed. "I wish. Nobody made pastries like hers."

The doorbell rang again.

With two other people here and Baby in the garage, I decided to forgo my security procedures and left the door unlocked.

"Come in," I yelled.

Hannah Portman entered, followed by her grandson and Tyler Lawrence.

"Take that bowl of fruit into the dining room," Hannah ordered.

Michael Portman nodded and followed her directions.

Tyler Lawrence had a hand-knit shoulder bag with a southwestern design. There were two bottles coming out of the top, and he held a platter that smelled like bacon. "Hmmm. Tyler, right?"

He smiled, pleased that I'd remembered his name. "Yes, and let me tell you, you're amazing. I've sold more in the past twenty-four hours than I have in weeks. I've got orders coming in from all over the world."

"I'm so pleased, but I can't take the credit. It's your beautiful knitting. I just helped people find you."

"I brought champagne. We're going to celebrate." He smiled and walked into the dining room.

"We brought champagne, too." Hannah placed a large bag on the counter and pulled out two large bottles of champagne and a large container of orange juice. "You got the flutes for mimosas?"

April intervened. "I'll get them."

She opened a cabinet and pulled out several beautiful fluted glasses, which she carried into the dining room.

Leroy and Hannah followed her with the remaining food. After a few moments, Michael returned. "Where's Baby?"

"I was afraid he'd eat all of the food, so I put him in the garage."

"He's surprisingly well behaved . . . at least, when he wants to be."

He leaned against the counter, and I got a good look at him for the first time. He had on a gray sweatshirt with US ARMY emblazoned across the front, sweatpants, and running shoes.

"Were you really in the Army? Or are you one of those guys who think they can impress women by wearing military gear to make them think you work out?"

He smirked. "Are you impressed?"

"Not with the Army."

He crossed his arms over his chest and gave me a hard stare. "You don't look like an anti-military hippie."

"That's because I'm not. My dad's an admiral in the Navy. I've spent my entire life on naval bases surrounded by sailors. So, it's going to take a lot more than a sweatshirt to impress me."

"Squids," he muttered.

"Excuse me?"

"Nothing. You just don't look like a military brat."

"Because I don't walk around in camo and combat boots? That's not my style, but I wouldn't take you for a dumb Joe."

"Oh, it's like that, is it?"

I drummed my fingers on the counter.

After a beat. "Is that Morse code?"

I stopped my nervous drumming. "It's tap code . . . but I guess the Army wouldn't know anything about that. I learned it when I was a kid and used it to communicate with my friends in class."

"Oh, the Army knows about tap code. I'm just surprised you know it."

"Why, because I'm a woman?"

"No, because you're a civilian. Oh, and for the record, I am *not* a dumb jerk."

I tapped a response that would have gotten me grounded in middle school.

It took him a few minutes to decipher, but when he did, he glared for a few moments, but then shook it off. "After I graduated from Princeton, I served four years' active duty while I decided what I wanted to do with my life. And I'm training for a marathon, so I do work out."

I was impressed by the marathon, but I made sure my face didn't show it. Instead, I focused on the other parts of his life. "Four years in the Army sent you to medical school?"

"Four years in the Army sent me to veterinary school."

"You're a vet? I thought you were a real doctor—I mean—"

"I know what you meant, and, contrary to what *some* people might believe, I am a real doctor. I just have patients who aren't human."

"I'm sorry. I didn't mean to offend you. I just had a bad experience with a doctor, so I'm not a big fan."

"I haven't had any complaints from my patients."

"Let me try this again. So, four years in the Army led you to *veterinary school.*"

"I lucked out. I was an animal-care specialist. That's what helped me realize that I loved animals, and I knew what I wanted to do with my life."

Hannah came back in the kitchen. "You two going to stand there jabbering all day? We're hungry."

"Yes, ma'am," Michael said.

"And when you get finished exercising Baby, bring him in

so I can get my hug in." She turned and walked back into the dining room.

"Is she always that . . . pushy? Wait, what did she mean about exercise?"

"Miss Octavia liked to make sure Baby stayed in shape, so I usually took him for a brisk walk, although he's only good for about twenty minutes and then he's content to lie in the shade while I work out. That is, unless you want to exercise him."

"No . . . that's fine. I'm not much into . . . exercise."

"You're not really dressed for working out anyway."

I looked down at my clothes. "What's wrong with this?" Men in New Bison sure had a lot of opinions about clothing. I'd pulled on a silk blouse and skinny jeans.

"Nothing. It's just a bit . . . fancier than what most people around here wear for a Sunday morning, that's all." He grinned. "You'd better get in there for your meeting. If you think she's pushy now, you don't want to see her when she's hangry. I'll take care of Baby, and you and the Irregulars can get busy solving your mystery."

I searched for the right words. "But . . . I'm not Aunt Octavia. I don't know anything about solving mysteries. I mean, I enjoy *reading* mysteries. In fact, I've read a ton of them, but I haven't actually solved a mystery before."

"I think this Baker Street Irregulars stuff is just an excuse for them to get together."

"You really think so?"

"Sure. Miss Octavia was a smart woman, but she really wasn't some female version of Sherlock Holmes who could identify one hundred types of tobacco based on the ashes."

"It's one hundred and forty different types of tobacco."

He raised an eyebrow. "I stand corrected."

"I've read the Sir Arthur Conan Doyle books, but I was never a huge Sherlock fan. I mean, I liked Agatha Christie's Hercule Poirot with his *little gray cells* a lot better. It's been years since I've read a Sherlock Holmes novel," I whispered like a kid admitting to eating the last cookie. I knew I was over-sharing, but . . . I couldn't help myself.

"Well, you probably shouldn't tell them that. Just listen and nod a lot." He smirked. "No one would expect a squid brat to solve a murder anyway."

My head knew he was joking, but something inside wanted to prove him wrong. I straightened my posture, pulled my shoulders back, pivoted as I'd seen countless sailors drilled to do, and marched out of the room. He didn't believe I could do it. He thought I was just a pretty face with no brains. Most of the time I was okay if men saw me that way. That's how my dad saw me. Elliott certainly treated me that way. Well, I had enough of that. I may not know how to identify one hundred and forty types of tobacco ash, but I was determined to prove this GI wrong, even if it meant I had to solve a murder to do it.

# CHAPTER 6

Righteous indignation and sheer determination propelled me to the dining room door, but it evaporated before I entered. I stood just outside of the room and took several deep breaths. I tried to channel my father. *What would The Admiral do?* I stood tall, pushed my shoulders back, and took a long, deep breath. I knew beyond a shadow of a doubt that my dad would not show fear. He wouldn't let on that he didn't know anything about Sherlock Holmes, cigar ashes, or solving a murder, but he would do it. He would find the killer, and I was determined to the do the same thing.

My mental pep talk worked well. I almost convinced myself that if I couldn't solve the murder, I could at least fake it enough so that they all believed I could.

"Hooyah!" My stomach growled, and I went in.

In my brief absence, the group had set the table, and everything looked and smelled delicious. "This looks fantastic." I pulled out my phone and quickly snapped some photos. **#Baby CakesBakeryNotConfinedToABuilding #NoBuildingNoProblem #DeliciousBakedGoodsUnlimitedPossibilities**

I took a deep whiff. "What is that wonderful aroma?"

Leroy smiled. "You must mean April's breakfast casserole. She uses maple sausage, and it's delicious." He stole a glance at her.

"Well, I'm starving."

I sat down and piled food onto my plate. Hannah smacked my hand.

"Ouch."

"We haven't said grace."

"Oh, I'm sorry." I put down my fork and waited. After a few awkward moments, I looked around.

Hannah sighed. "Usually, Octavia led grace, since it was her house, but I'll do it."

A quick wink from Tyler made me feel better.

Hannah said a prayer. After which we all mumbled, "Amen."

This time, I waited until I saw others digging into the food before I followed suit. I was so hungry I could have eaten a pair of my Jimmy Choo boots, and I love my Jimmy Choos. Not surprisingly, everything tasted fantastic. Leroy and Hannah were excellent bakers, so I expected good things from them, but April's breakfast casserole was delicious, too. It was sweet with a little kick. However, my favorite had to be the croissants. Leroy's croissants were soft, buttery, and flaky. "These are fab. Do we sell these in the bakery?"

Leroy grinned. "Miss Octavia made croissants occasionally, but we mostly stuck to sweets."

"Well, we should be selling them every day."

"Do you really think people would be interested?" Leroy asked.

"Let's see." I picked up my phone and uploaded the pictures I'd snapped of the pastry tray. **#FlakyButteryCroissants #Scones-ToDieFor #BabyCakesBakery #MoreThanSweets**

"She's really good with social media," Tyler said. "My sales have been *amazing* since she posted about my store. So, Leroy, you better get busy baking." He shoved a croissant into his mouth, closed his eyes, and moaned. "They're like crack. I can't stop eating them."

Leroy smiled. "I was going to do some baking later if you're okay with that. Maybe I'll whip up a few dozen croissants."

"Absolutely, but . . . I mean there's no hurry, right? It's not like we can sell them anyway."

"Why not?" Hannah asked.

I wondered if she was having one of her episodes, but her eyes looked clear. "Because of the fire at the bakery. I thought you knew?"

"Pshaw. Of course I knew about that. This is a small town, and Leroy smells like a chimney."

Leroy turned red and took a whiff of his shirt.

"Oh, I know you can't help it," she said to ease the sting of her words. "Besides, you're a hero. If it weren't for you, Garrett Kelley would be dead."

This time, Leroy's flushed complexion was due to the adoring stares he received. He mumbled something, lowered his head, and shoveled food into his mouth.

Hannah returned her attention to me. "The bakery caught fire, but I don't see why that should stop us from selling anything."

"The building is in bad shape. Anything that wasn't destroyed by the fire and the smoke, the firemen soaked. There's no way the health department will let us bake there. It reeks, and—"

"I'm not talking about the building. I know we can't bake there, but I don't see why that has to stop us. We'll just go back to what we used to do."

"I don't understand."

"Before Octavia bought that building downtown, she baked here. This is where Baby Cakes started." She pointed a finger in the direction of the kitchen. "That kitchen is a commercial cook's dream."

"But . . . you mean people just came here and bought pastries?"

"Well, not here," Leroy said. "She just baked here. People would go to the garage to buy stuff."

"The garage? Where did she park?"

"Oh, good grief, girl. Didn't you notice that detached garage near the street?"

"I did, but I thought it was just . . . I mean, I didn't think . . . it just looks like an old garage."

Tyler chuckled. "It was, until Miss Octavia converted it. There's a studio apartment upstairs. She didn't want strangers traipsing through her house to use the bathroom. Plus, she"—he made a slight inclination of his head in Hannah's direction—"liked having a quiet place to relax. You should check out the inside. It's nice. In this part of Michigan, there's lots of farms, fruit stands, and barns where people sell jams, jellies, baked goods—everything. Compared to some of those places, that garage is a palace."

"We'll use the house kitchen and do most of the baking and sell them out of the garage like we used to," Hannah said. She peered over her glasses at me. "You can get the word out on that phone and let people know Baby Cakes is open for business. If they know we're open, they'll come. Folks are addicted to Baby Cakes by now, and a few extra miles won't matter."

"I had no idea."

"Octavia was a smart businesswoman. She talked about turning this place into one of those bed-and-breakfasts on the weekends during football season. Hotels near the stadium fill up fast, and they charge an arm and a leg for rooms. Plenty of folks rent out their homes during football weekends to make extra money. It's only a thirty-minute drive to campus, and those rich city folks will pay just about anything for a comfortable room."

My mind wandered a bit during Hannah's speech. I remembered thinking about all the extra space in the lower level. It would make a great B&B, and I could probably generate a nice bit of income. The only problem would be that second *B*. I could provide the bed, but, judging from my efforts to scramble eggs, I would need help with the breakfast part. I took a bite of April's breakfast casserole and wondered if I could coerce her or Leroy to help with that. My musings were interrupted when Hannah reached across the table and swatted my arm.

"Wake up."

"I'm sorry. I was just thinking about . . . the bakery and the opportunities."

"Well, good. We'll clean the cobwebs out of the garage and get it ready for business before we leave, but that can wait. Now, let's get down to the important business. We need to get this meeting started."

I shoveled a scone into my mouth. No one could expect me to talk with my mouth full.

April took a deep breath. "Miss Octavia always said we needed to start with the facts. So, here's what we know for sure. Mayor Rivers was murdered. He—"

Tyler pulled out a notebook and was writing furiously. "I hope no one minds if I take notes." He looked around, and everyone shook their heads. "Good. Miss Octavia always took notes, but I can do it if that's okay with Maddy."

I waved him on and then shoveled more food in my mouth.

"How was he killed?" Leroy asked.

"Most likely stabbed with one of the knives from Baby Cakes," April said. "I recognized the engraved handles."

"Lord, what a waste," Hannah said. "Octavia paid a fortune for those knives. Looks like the killer could have used one of those cheap knives we take to catering jobs. Or, better still, why didn't he use his own knife? That's just downright rude if you ask me."

Leroy and April exchanged a quick glance, but something

Hannah had said actually got my wheels turning. "That's interesting. I wonder why the killer took one of our knives."

Tyler pointed his pen in my direction. "Good point. Let's follow that." He turned his notepad sideways and drew a straight line. Then he drew branches off the main line. "Before I opened my shop, I used to be a corporate accountant, and they used to make us take Lean training. This is what they called the Five Whys. Now, why did the killer use one of the Baby Cakes knives?"

"Because it was convenient," Leroy said.

Tyler wrote *Convenient* on one of the lines. "Why was it convenient?"

"Because it had Maddy's fingerprints on it," Leroy said.

"Why did it have Maddy's fingerprints?" Tyler asked.

"Because it's her freakin' bakery and her knives," Hannah said with a huff.

"True, but Maddy just got here two days ago. How did the killer know that the knife had Maddy's fingerprints on it?"

"Maybe the killer saw her using the knife," April said, "so he knew it would have her fingerprints on it."

"That can't be. Maddy can't cook—" Leroy clasped his hand over his mouth. "I'm sorry."

"It's okay. Everyone's bound to find out sooner or later." I reached across the table and squeezed his hand.

"So, why were Maddy's fingerprints on the murder weapon?" Tyler asked.

I felt everyone's gaze boring holes into my skin like lasers.

"Well, I certainly didn't kill him. I barely knew the man."

April wiggled in her seat but took a deep breath. "What about when you and the mayor had your argument?"

"Now, don't you start with her, April Renee Johnson," Hannah said. "Maddy didn't kill that man."

"Thank you." I smiled at Hannah, grateful that someone had faith in me.

"I didn't say she did. I'm just wondering if that's when she picked it up. It was the middle of the day, and there were people in the bakery. Maybe someone saw her with the knife and decided it might come in handy."

"That's possible. Mayor Rivers had made plenty of enemies in New Bison. I can believe that easier than believing that Maddy had anything to do with murdering him."

"Thank you." I smiled in Hannah's direction again.

"Besides, nobody related to Octavia would have been stupid enough to have left their fingerprints on the murder weapon." Hannah patted my hand. "Even if she can't cook, she'd have to be completely addlepated to use a knife from her own bakery and then leave her fingerprints on it. Every idiot knows enough to wipe off their fingerprints or wear gloves."

I wasn't sure if Hannah was defending me, insulting me, or both. I decided to give her the benefit of the doubt. "I'll take that as a compliment."

Tyler took a sip of champagne to hide the smirk that had broken out across his face.

"Where does that leave us?" Leroy asked.

"Trying to explain why Maddy's fingerprints were on the murder weapon," April said.

I thought back and triggered a memory. "The first night I got here, I decided to swing by the bakery." I explained how Baby started barking and I grabbed a knife for protection. "But no one was there."

"What did you do with the knife?" Leroy asked.

I thought back. "I don't know. I think I just left it on a shelf in the store."

Leroy groaned.

April's eyes got big, and she looked frightened.

"What?"

"Don't you see? The killer must have been in the store."

"Baby would have attacked." I looked from one to the other. "Wouldn't he?"

"Not necessarily," April said slowly.

"When Jackson Abernathy yelled at me, I thought Baby was going to rip his throat out."

"Baby never liked Abernathy," Hannah said. "Octavia always thought he was the one who left him out on the beach to die." She muttered some words that I was rather surprised to hear she even knew.

"Why didn't she have him arrested?" I asked.

"No proof," April said. "Just because Jackson Abernathy breeds English mastiffs and Baby is an English mastiff doesn't mean that Jackson Abernathy was Baby's owner. Besides, he's been trying to buy Baby from Octavia. If he abandoned him, then why would he try to buy back his own dog? He could have just demanded that she give him back."

"Because then he'd have to admit that he abandoned him in the first place," I said, but no one seemed interested in Jackson Abernathy or Baby's breeder. So, I dropped it and zeroed in on the other flaw in that theory. "Anyway, I find it hard to believe that if the killer had been in the bakery, Baby didn't attack."

Silence sucked the air out of the room, and I waited for someone to explain.

After a long pause, April took a deep breath. "Baby would attack if someone threatened his human, but . . ."

"But?" I whispered.

"He wouldn't attack if the killer was someone he recognized, someone he considered a friend."

# CHAPTER 7

Awkwardness settled over the room like a blanket. We looked around at each other while trying not to look like we actually were.

April broke the tension by laughing. "That's bound to be a New Bison first. Apart from the fact that it's ridiculous to think that one of my friends was a killer, can you imagine if I showed up in court and all my evidence was based on the fact that Baby *didn't* attack an *alleged* intruder? I'd be laughed out of town."

We chuckled. Although it sounded strained, even to my ears.

Hannah surprised me by saying, "April's right. Octavia always said we had to stick to facts. That's what Sherlock Holmes would do. Now, remember that quote Octavia always used?"

They smiled and recited the famous Sherlock Holmes quote: "Once you eliminate the impossible, whatever remains, no matter how improbable, must be the truth."

"Now, what's the impossible?" Hannah asked.

"It's impossible that I killed Mayor Rivers," I said.

Tyler wrote it in his notebook. "It's impossible that any of us would kill him, especially by setting up Maddy to take the blame."

"So, we're back where we started." I sighed.

"No," April said, "we know whoever killed Mayor Rivers had to be someone who was in the bakery either Friday night or Saturday morning."

"On television, the medical examiners can never pinpoint the exact time of death," I said. "How can you be sure about the time?"

"Our coroner's the same way. He can give us a range based on temperatures, rigor mortis, and a lot of other icky things I won't talk about while we're eating."

"Thank you," I mumbled.

"Plus, it's too soon. He hasn't even started the autopsy. I just mean we know what time you and Baby went to the bakery. We also know what time Leroy got there to open up." She looked at me and smiled. "Now, I'll admit, I don't know you well, but you don't strike me as the type of person who would pick up a bloody eel knife?"

"What kind of knife?"

April exchanged a knowing glance with Leroy. "Mayor Rivers was murdered with an eel knife."

"What's an eel knife?" I asked.

"It's pretty much what it sounds like," Leroy said. "It's a knife with a very distinctive shape that is ideal for preparing eel. It has a single, thick beveled blade. The flat heel of the blade is used for chopping, and the angular tip is used for filleting."

"Why would a bakery need an eel knife?" I asked.

Hannah snorted. "We don't, but nothing would satisfy Octavia. She had to have the best knives. Claimed she was going to sell more than baked goods one day. Octavia loved to cook, although I know she never made eel a single day in her life. She wanted to do all types of cooking on the store side of the building, maybe even classes. She spent a fortune on those knives. Ordered them all the way from Japan."

"I think cooking classes would be a great idea." I exchanged a glance with Leroy.

Hannah snorted again. "I guess you really are related to Octavia, although you obviously didn't inherit her gift for baking."

I shook off the insult and settled in on the compliment. I didn't know anything about cooking or baking, but if Aunt Octavia thought cooking classes was a good idea, then I wasn't completely off base, and my confidence skyrocketed. I turned to Leroy. "What else can you tell us about the murder weapon?"

He sat up straighter, and his eyes flashed. Talking food was his passion. He bored us for a few minutes as he talked about the quality of the steel and the handle construction. My interest picked up when he mentioned that the knives were made by a company in Japan that had been making knives for over six hundred years and was originally famous for making samurai swords. "Miss Hannah's right about one thing, the knives were expensive. That one knife cost over twelve hundred dollars."

Tyler had just taken a sip of champagne and nearly choked. "Twelve hundred dollars for one knife?"

Leroy nodded.

"Is that a lot?" I asked.

Based on the looks I received, I got my answer.

Tyler finished dabbing at the champagne he'd spit onto his sweater, picked up his pen, and wrote. "Well, that rules out Hannah and Leroy."

"Why? Not that anyone would ever seriously consider either of them as suspects." I quickly added.

"Because, if we were going to stab Mayor Rivers, we wouldn't have been stupid enough to use a twelve-hundred-dollar knife from Japan when a nine-ninety-five utility knife from Walmart would have done the job just as well," Hannah said. "Besides, it would have been less mess to just grab one of those cast-iron skillets from the pantry. That skillet would have done the job just fine, with no cleanup."

"Why run the risk of ruining the blade or damaging the handle?" Leroy said. "I know it sounds callous, but twelve hundred dollars is a lot of money."

"Whoever used that knife either didn't know its value or didn't care," I said. "Who wanted Mayor Rivers dead?"

Hannah snorted. "Anybody who met him."

"That can't be true. Everybody couldn't have hated the man. How did he become mayor? I mean, was he a Democrat or a Republican?"

Leroy shook his head. "Neither."

"Independent?"

Tyler shrugged.

"Well, he must have run on some party ticket or platform."

Finally, April said, "Mayor Rivers changed his views based on whichever way the wind was blowing. Honestly, I'm not sure what party, if any, endorsed him. Our last elections were a bit . . . unusual. New Bison generally tends to be very conservative. There were two strong conservative candidates who split the vote, and the Democrat was so far left that he wasn't even a consideration. Paul Rivers just slipped under everyone's radar."

"That's the truth," Hannah said. "Who would have thought that slick-talking, double-dealing hardware salesman would be running our town?" She puckered her lips as though she'd just eaten a lemon.

"Paul Rivers was a fast talker," April said. "He reminded me of a used-car salesman. Once those rich folks from Chicago discovered New Bison, they started buying up all the lakefront property, and Mayor Rivers was like a kid in a candy store."

"Aunt Octavia mentioned something about that in the video she left me." I made a mental note to watch the video again. I'd look around the house to see if she had a VCR, or I could check one out from the library, as Chris Russell had done.

"Most folks around here were opposed to the developers

coming in, snatching up all the land," Hannah said. "Locals who were born and raised right here can't afford to live here anymore."

"I can attest to that," April said. "My landlord is going up on my rent, and I'm having to find a new apartment by the end of the month, but there's nothing in New Bison I can afford."

"Most of us have to move farther away from the lake or south to Indiana, but even that's getting expensive now," Leroy said softly. "I'm thirty miles away."

"I can't even do that. I'm the sheriff. My contract requires me to live in New Bison."

Hannah drank her coffee. "It's a crying shame if you ask me. First, there was the casino coming in and buying up all of the farmland and bringing strangers to town, but that's Indian land. You can't do anything about that. Plus, I kind of like being able to go play the slots."

Bradley Ellison had mentioned a casino, and it had to be the same one. New Bison was too small to have more than one. I decided against mentioning Brad to this group. However, I glanced at the flowers he'd brought me, which were in a crystal vase on a sideboard, and I couldn't help smiling.

"The casino brought a lot of traffic to town," Leroy said. "Weekend sales at Baby Cakes skyrocketed."

"Sales aren't the only thing that increased," Hannah said. "Traffic increased. Crime increased. And accidents, too, with those folks speeding up and down the roads like they're in the Indianapolis Five Hundred. Isn't that right, April?"

April shifted in her seat. "We have noticed an uptick in alcohol-related crime and accidents."

"If Mayor Rivers was in favor of development, who was opposed to it?" I bit my tongue and didn't add, *other than Aunt Octavia and the folks around this table.*

"When she was alive, Miss Octavia was pretty outspoken about her opposition to the developers," April said. "And, of course, Garrett Kelley. He loved Miss Octavia and would agree with anything she wanted."

"Baby definitely knows him," Leroy said.

"Who else?" I asked.

After a moment or two of awkwardness, Leroy took a deep breath. "Most of us at the table."

Tyler put his pen down and glared. "What's that supposed to mean?"

Leroy glared back. "You know what it means. Most of us were opposed to those rich folks from Chicago coming in and snatching up all the waterfront property, but not *all*. You certainly weren't."

"I own a business, and I need those rich Chicago folks to stay in business." Tyler crossed his arms across his chest and took several deep breaths. "I guess that eliminates me from the list of suspects, since I was *not* opposed to the development."

I wasn't sure that I followed, but I wasn't going to be the one to add fuel to an already flaming topic. "We have Garrett Kelley as a possible suspect, but there are a lot of reasons that people murder each other, aren't there?"

"Miss Octavia always said the primary reasons were money, love or lust, and vengeance," Hannah said.

"Did Mayor Rivers have a family?" I asked. "Who gains from his death?"

"He's divorced."

Hannah snorted. "Twice."

Based on the looks on everyone's faces that was a surprise. Hannah obviously liked a bit of gossip. She took a sip of her mimosa before continuing. "His first wife, Marjorie, was a beautiful wisp of a girl. Sweet as cherry pie, just like April." Hannah gazed off into space as though she were looking back in time.

April smiled at the compliment. "What happened?"

"I always thought she'd marry . . ." Hannah shook her head and snapped back to the present. "She could have had any man in town. I never could understand why she married Paul Rivers, but she did. Everybody thought maybe some of her goodness would rub off on him, but . . . that's not how things work. It only takes one rotten apple to infest the whole bushel, and that's what happened. Poor Marjorie just seemed to shrivel up inside. Her personality changed, and instead of the vibrant girl that he married, after a couple of years, she just withered up, and the light went out of her eyes."

April whispered, "What happened to her?"

Hannah paused. "No one knows. One day, she just up and left. Word on the street is she ran off with Garrett Kelley's son, David."

"Wait, Garrett Kelley has a son?" Tyler leaned forward with his mouth open. "I thought he spent his entire life pining after Miss Octavia, and if you tell me that he and Miss Octavia had a love child that she never mentioned, I'm going to faint."

"You stop that foolishness. You know good and well Octavia never had any children." Hannah swatted his arm.

Tyler fanned himself. "Well, up to a few minutes ago, I didn't know Garrett Kelley had children, either."

"I have to admit, I never knew Garrett Kelley had children, either," April said. "What's the scoop? Spill it, Hannah. You can't just leave us hanging." She fought to keep from smiling, but her eyes twinkled.

Hannah was the center of attention, and she sipped her mimosa and took her sweet time answering. "It's true Garrett Kelley always had a crush on Octavia. God knows he asked her to marry him plenty of times. When he graduated from high school, he asked her to marry him, but she wouldn't. He went off in a huff and joined the Army. When he came back four years later, he was married with a small boy. He had been stationed in Japan. His wife was a nice woman. She died giving birth. Garrett was tore up inside. He had her body shipped back to Japan to be buried with her ancestors. David, his son, spent most of the year in Japan with his relatives there, but always spent his summers here in New Bison. One year, he spent the summer as usual, but he never came back. That was the same year that Marjorie disappeared."

We waited, but she simply sipped her drink.

"Is that it?" Tyler asked.

"That's it. Just because the boy didn't come back, doesn't mean Marjorie ran off with him, but folks around here don't like coincidences, and that was a coincidence," Hannah said.

We exchanged glances.

"Did anyone ever ask Mayor Rivers what happened to her?" April asked.

"Or did anyone ask Garrett Kelley?" Tyler asked.

"Garrett said his boy didn't like New Bison and moved back to Japan. For a few years, he made trips to visit. Well, that's where he said he went." Hannah gave a knowing look. "Later, he got a letter that David was killed in a car accident."

"That's it?" Leroy asked.

"That's it," Hannah said.

I brought the conversation back to the murder. "What about his second wife?"

"About five years ago, Mayor Rivers married Candace Hurston," April said.

"Hurston? I know that name." I snapped my fingers. "Is she related to Alma Hurston, my next-door neighbor?"

"Candace is Alma's daughter. She's a waitress at the New Bison Casino."

"*Pshaw.*" Hannah snorted. "You call what that girl does waitressing?"

April narrowed her eyes and gave Hannah a hard look. "Now, Mrs. Portman, you know Miss Octavia didn't take kindly to women putting other working women down."

Leroy snickered, but a sharp glance from April put a cork in his merriment, and he bowed his head sheepishly and mumbled an apology.

"Waitresses take orders and deliver *food*," Hannah said. "I have nothing but the highest respect for waitresses, but those scantily clad women at the casino are not waitresses."

"She can't pick the uniform," April said.

I leaned over to Tyler and whispered, "What do they wear?"

"Basically, tattered rags. The casino has them dress like Native American squaws from a bad B-rated movie."

Even though Tyler and I whispered, April heard us. "Which is sad. It's bad enough that Hollywood has created this negative image of Native Americans as bloodthirsty savages with those awful movies, but they also portrayed Native American women as little more than ignorant baby machines." She leaned forward. "I read in the FBI crime report that the number of crimes against Native American women is fifty percent higher than crimes against other women."

"Hollywood has a lot to answer for," Hannah said, "but you'd think the casino would try to change the perceptions rather than continuing it by having those girls prancing around the floor wearing little more than scraps."

"Is the casino owned by a Native American tribe?" I asked.

"It's run by the Pothanowis," Leroy said. "They're a small band, but they were able to prove that they are indigenous and got their federal recognition. They bought a ton of land and built the casino."

"Pothanowis . . . have you ever seen any of them?" Hannah said.

"I once met a really old guy who was a Pothanowi," Leroy said. "He was sitting in the lobby."

"I think it's mighty strange that people from around here have never seen or heard of the Pothanowis, and I think it's mighty funny that no one from New Bison ever heard of them before they came down and bought all that land and opened the casino," Hannah said.

I picked up my phone and typed in *Pothanowi*. "You don't think they're a real tribe?"

"I'm not saying there were never Pothanowis. Of course, they're a real tribe . . . or they were until they were just about wiped out by the government. I'm saying they weren't here in New Bison."

"I don't suppose there's any law that says they can't move and settle wherever they want." I shrugged.

"It's those Chicago developers. They're behind them. That's how they got their claws in New Bison. They found some Native Americans who were just about dying out and threw some big-city lawyers with shiny shoes behind them and got five hundred acres of land. Then they thought they could just waltz in here and buy up all the land on Lake Michigan and build condominiums," Hannah said.

She said *condominiums* as though it were a bad word, and I struggled to keep from laughing. "So, you think the Chicago developers are behind the casino?" I looked at Hannah.

"Of course, they're behind it. They're behind all of this, and Octavia was on to them. She figured out what they were doing and was going to stop them when they took her out."

Tyler groaned.

"Are you saying the Chicago developers killed Aunt Octavia?" I asked.

"That's exactly what I'm saying. Those developers bought the land for the Pothanowis. They scooped up as much lakefront land as they could. They bought the mayor and the entire city council, but they met their match with Octavia. They couldn't buy her or this land, so they killed her."

# CHAPTER 8

Hannah was upset, and her eyes flashed. Then, in an instant, it was over. Moments earlier, her eyes were bright and fiery, but a light went out and she was gone.

"Miss Hannah, maybe you should rest," April said. "It's been a long morning." She stood and helped Hannah to her feet. "Would it be okay if I helped Miss Hannah to the spare room?"

"Of course." I stood up to help, but April waved me back down. "Don't trouble yourself."

April guided Hannah down the hall. As they left, Hannah asked, "Aren't you nice. Who did you say you are again?"

The mood in the dining room was somber, but I couldn't help asking. "That's the second time she's implied . . . well, downright accused someone of killing Aunt Octavia."

"She and Miss Octavia were like sisters," Leroy said. "I guess she's finding it hard to accept that her friend is gone."

When April returned, we chatted a bit, but then we headed outside to the garage to take stock of what needed to be done to prepare for opening in two days.

The four of us marched out to the garage, and it wasn't until we were standing in front of the building and everyone turned to stare at me that I realized I didn't have the key. Thankfully, Leroy walked around the side of the building and picked up a fake rock, pulled a key from underneath, and opened the door. "Miss Octavia always liked to plan ahead."

From the outside, the single-car garage looked old and weathered. However, once we were inside, I saw that the building was quaint and functional. There were wood-and-glass display cases along the back wall and a large chalkboard on which someone had written the daily features and prices. Against one wall, there was a counter with a wooden base made from reclaimed wood. A glass display shelf covered about two-thirds of the countertop. The last third held a cash register. The lighting had been updated so that the space was bright and cheery. It reminded me of the quaint boulangeries and patisseries viennoise in Montreal, Paris, and throughout Europe with a shabby-chic American flare.

We swept the floors, dusted the cabinets, and cleaned all the glass so it sparkled. Many hands made light work, as Aunt Octavia used to say, and we were finished in record time. Once the space was cleaned, I snapped photos and posted them online to let patrons know that Baby Cakes would be open for business on Tuesday morning. **#DownButNotOut #BabyCakesOpenForBusiness #NewLocationSameGreatPastries #TastyTuesdayBuy2Get1CroissantSpecial**

Leroy raised an eyebrow. "Croissant special?"

"It'll be a great way to get people hooked. Plus, no one is going to want three croissants. If it's a couple, then they'll want an even number. So, they'll buy four and get two free."

He stared with something that resembled respect in his eyes. "I guess I'd better get busy baking."

We worked out a menu, which April wrote on the blackboard, along with prices that would be easy to calculate in our heads without requiring me to rely on the antique cash register.

The bakery was still a crime scene, which meant we couldn't access any of our supplies, so Leroy wrote out a grocery list and said he'd take care of it. I was thankful, since I didn't have the slightest idea where to pick up groceries. I offered money, but he waved it away, saying he'd just have them put it on our account. Wow! We had an account.

A glance around showed the only thing missing was the food. Leroy, and hopefully Hannah, would take care of that before Tuesday morning. With nothing left to do, we closed everything back up and went back inside the house.

Leroy opened a door to a large pantry and took stock of things like plastic bags, gloves, and brown paper bags. With his list in hand, he and April left together.

In the kitchen, Michael and Baby were dripping with sweat and guzzling water when we returned. Well, Michael was dripping sweat. Baby drooled, but the effect on me was the same.

"Is the game afoot?" Michael said with a grin. "Have you solved the case and figured out who shanked the mayor?"

"Not yet, but we will." I pushed by the veterinarian and tried not to notice how muscular his arms were. "Are you sure exercise is good for Baby? Should he be panting this much?"

"He's a big dog and while he can't run like a greyhound, he still needs exercise. I'm careful not to overtire him, but he needs to stay active." He grinned. "Especially if he's going to be eating things like pizzas."

I felt heat rush up my neck, but I wasn't sure if it was from the shame of being called out as a bad pet parent who allowed her dog to eat pizza or because he'd read my posts, which meant he was following me online. I was glad he didn't know about the eggs and eggshells Baby had consumed just a few hours before.

The doorbell rang, and I was grateful for an excuse to get farther away from Michael Portman.

I opened the door and was pleasantly surprised to find Bradley Ellison standing there with more flowers. "Hello, beautiful.

I heard about the fire and wanted to give you something to brighten your day."

I smiled and accepted the bouquet of yellow roses, even though roses weren't my favorite flowers. "Thank you. They're beautiful, but you already sent flowers."

"Ah, but those were I'm-sorry-for-getting-off-on-the-wrong-foot flowers. These are totally different." He grinned. "These are I-think-you're-beautiful-and-want-to-get-better-acquainted *flowers.*"

"You're right. That's totally different." I smiled. I stepped aside for him to enter and then closed the door. "Let me get these in water." I walked to the kitchen and wasn't surprised when he followed. When we got to the kitchen, Michael Portman and Baby were still leaning where I'd left them. I tried to remember where the vases were as I opened cabinets. "Do you two know each other?"

In some type of male-dominance exhibition, they glared at each other but didn't speak. Michael grunted, and Bradley nodded. Even Baby seemed affected. He never lost eye contact with Bradley.

I found a vase in an upper cabinet and reached up to get it. The vase tipped forward and would have fallen if Brad hadn't rushed up behind me and caught it.

I turned around to thank him, and we were inches apart. I could feel his eyes smoldering, and the heat on his skin made my breathing heavier. When I spoke, my voice had a Lauren Bacall huskiness. "Thank you."

We stared into each other's eyes for several moments until a low rumble from Baby broke the spell.

Baby growled. When he barked, I knew he meant business. A split second later, he lunged toward Bradley Ellison, who quickly moved so he was behind me.

"Baby, no!" I yelled.

Up until now, Baby had been obedient and listened whenever I commanded. However, this time, he ignored my order and lunged forward. He would have attacked if Michael hadn't grabbed him by the collar and pulled him down. He then dragged Baby out the back door and into the garage.

I was so stunned by Baby's behavior that for a few moments I was frozen. When I recovered, I turned to apologize. "I'm so sorry. He's never behaved like that before . . . well, once, but that was a different situation. He thought I was being threatened. He was just protecting me. He's never disobeyed me before." I babbled on, in my nervousness sharing more than was necessary, but Brad Ellison wasn't listening.

The blood drained from Brad's face, and he looked like a ghost.

"Are you okay?"

He took a deep breath. "That dog's vicious."

"I don't know what came over him. He's usually so laid-back and calm." I wondered if I should go to the garage and check on Michael, but the growling had stopped, and I felt confident that Baby wasn't feasting on his flesh. Besides, Michael Portman was a vet—in every definition of the word: profession, experience, and military. If anyone could handle the eighth-of-a-ton dog, I felt confident he could. Although he had been gone for quite some time. "Maybe I should check—"

Michael came in and quickly closed the door.

"Are you okay?" I asked.

"I'm fine. Although it seems that Baby doesn't care much for Mr. Ellison." He folded his arms across his chest and stood up taller and straighter than he had before.

"He must be jealous," Brad said. "I hear sometimes male dogs can get very possessive of the females in their lives, especially if they think some other male is moving in on their territory." He reached over and caressed my cheek. He then took a strand of hair that had fallen free from its band, tucked it behind my ear, and gazed into my eyes.

I would have considered the gesture very intimate if I hadn't suspected that it was done more to prove his point with Michael than as an act of care for me. However, I had noticed that I'd become a lot more cynical where men were concerned since Elliott had abandoned me at the altar.

Michael laughed. "Really? I must have missed that in veterinary school."

Both men glared, and the tension was so thick you could have cut it with a knife. Fortunately, Hannah came in.

She looked more alert than she'd been earlier, but she still seemed a bit hazy. "There you are. I thought I heard your voice. I must have dozed off. Have you and Baby had your run?"

Michael helped his grandmother outside, leaving Bradley and me alone in the kitchen.

I put water in the vase and arranged the roses primarily to give myself something to do.

"How about dinner?" Brad said.

I stifled a yawn. "I'm sorry, but I've been up since two this morning, and I think everything has finally caught up with me. How about a rain check?"

Like a wave, a second yawn formed in my mouth and forced its way outside, but this time I wasn't able to stop it. "I'm so sorry."

"No need to apologize. You get some rest, and I'll call you tomorrow." He stared at me and for a half second, I thought he was going to kiss me. He must have thought better of it and caressed my cheek instead.

When he was gone, I suddenly felt exhausted. I opened the garage door, and Baby came inside. He took a few laps around the kitchen island and then trotted into the living room. Satisfied that he was the only male in the house, he sat down next to me and proceeded to lick himself.

"Ugh. Males."

I marched off to bed.

# CHAPTER 9

Monday morning, I had every intention of sleeping late. However, one thing about growing up on military bases is that you learn early that sleeping late wasn't tolerated. The Admiral prided himself that by six in the morning, he would have accomplished more than most men did in an entire day. My dad got up at four every morning, rain or shine. He worked out, showered, ate the same breakfast every day, and by six he was working. I wasn't as regimented, but I was a light sleeper, and it wasn't easy to remain asleep with all the activity that took place on a military base.

By now, I was getting accustomed to the snoring coming from the other side of my bed. Baby was fully stretched out with his head on my pillow. The snoring was cute. The drool that soaked the pillow was *not*.

My cell phone vibrated, and Baby lifted his massive head and looked in my direction.

"I'm so sorry, my liege. I didn't mean to awake you." I reached for the phone.

Noting it wasn't anything of importance, Baby lay back down and returned to sleep.

It was a text from Leroy.

*U up?*

NO

*Be there in 15. U want coffee?*

*Where? Yes2coffee*

*There. Cream and sugar?*

*Y? Yes*

*We have a lot of Baking 2do*

That's when it all came back to me. The bakery was a burned-out crime scene. So, if we were going to open tomorrow, he'd need a large commercial kitchen in which to bake. I growled but forced myself out of bed.

*K.*

Baby opened his eyes but didn't bother to lift his head.

"No need to get up. You continue your nap. Don't let me disturb your beauty rest."

Sarcasm was wasted on him. He closed his eyes and was snoring again before I made my way to the shower.

The warm water pelted my skin, and I felt invigorated. By the time I was clean, dry, and dressed, I was almost ready to tackle the day. Baby was now sprawled horizontally across the entire bed. I pulled out my phone and quickly snapped a few pictures and uploaded them, then I gave his rear a smack. **#SleepingIn #LoveEnglishMastiffs #BabyCakes**

The smack worked wonders, and he was up in no time, looking around as though he had no idea what just bit his bottom.

"Come on, let's go outside." I motioned for him to follow, but he needed to do his yoga stretches first. I thought I knew what would get him moving. "Let's go outside, and then we'll get breakfast."

No response.

"Food."

Still no movement.

"Treat."

Bingo! That did it. Baby practically leaped to his feet and

galloped out of the room. I filed that information away in my brain for future reference and followed him.

By the time Baby finished his business, Leroy's truck pulled into the driveway. It was packed full and took multiple trips for us to get everything in the kitchen.

Inside, I took care of Baby's needs first. Mainly because I didn't want him eating everything Leroy baked.

Leroy handed me the coffee. I held it in my hands, took a big whiff, closed my eyes, and let the nutty aroma of Colombian coffee beans fill my soul before I took a sip. When I opened my eyes, Leroy was staring with a smile on his face.

"What?" I asked.

"Nothing . . . I wasn't judging. We all have our vices."

I wondered for a split second what his were but didn't think we knew each other well enough to ask. "Okay, well, I'll just leave you to it." I turned to go in the library, intent on reading the Sherlock Holmes book I'd grabbed a few days ago.

"Where do you think you're going?"

I stopped. "To the library to read, although I might just go grab some breakfast first. I'm starving."

He stared at me as though I'd suddenly sprouted another head. "You're not leaving me to bake everything by myself."

It was a statement, not a question, so I didn't feel a need to answer. Instead, I stared back. "Have you forgotten? I don't know how to cook. I tried to make eggs yesterday and I couldn't even figure out how to turn on the stove."

For close to ten seconds, he stared at me and struggled to keep a straight face. However, the effort was too much, and he burst out laughing.

"I'm glad you're amused. At least you can understand why I'm not going to be much help with the baking."

He shook his head. "Oh, no, you don't. You're not getting out of this that easily. You're an intelligent, independent, resourceful woman."

"Where are you going with all this horse pucky?"

"It's not horse pucky. It's the truth. You're a college-educated woman who is a marketing and social media genius. Plus, you're now the owner of a highly successful bakery. Are you trying to tell me that you're not teachable? That you can't be taught to whip up batter or roll out dough?"

I squinted and frowned. "Has anyone ever told you that you're really good at manipulation?"

He grinned. "I might have heard that I can be persuasive."

"I'll bet."

"Besides, wasn't it you who told me that you wanted to have cooking classes?"

"Yes, but I'm not the one who's going to teach them."

"Would you like some cheese to go with all of that whine?"

"Now you sound like my dad." The fact that he was right didn't help.

"Have you taken a look at that post I uploaded of you covered in flour the other day?" He pulled out his phone and swiped until he found what he was looking for.

"Holy macaroons. I've gone viral." I stood with my mouth open and stared at him.

"You're hot." He blushed. "I mean, you're hot on social media. That's not to say you aren't hot . . . I just meant—"

"I know what you meant." I thought for a few moments. "So, you're thinking we take pictures of you teaching me to cook and that will inspire people to want to give it a try themselves?"

"I was just thinking a few fun pictures of you learning to bake might make people want to come by the bakery and see what you've made." He grinned. "Or the guys will come by to see the hot girl covered in flour."

I punched his arm and couldn't help thinking how quickly Leroy and I had gotten comfortable with each other. I'd always wondered what my life would have been like if I had a sibling. Hanging out with Leroy was what I imagined it would be like if I had a brother. I wondered what The Admiral would have thought of Leroy. I gave him a hard, critical glance. His hair was pulled back into a ponytail. He was wearing a Captain America T-shirt and loose jeans. I didn't think The Admiral would have approved of his easygoing personality, and I doubted that Leroy would have liked the regimented life of the Navy. And I had no doubt that any son of Admiral Jefferson Augustus Montgomery would have been forced to serve in the Navy. No, he wouldn't have approved of Leroy, but it didn't matter. I liked him.

"Why are you looking at me like that?" he said. "Do I have something on my face?" He looked at his reflection in the glass of the microwave.

"No. I was just thinking. We could have a special section for people to buy my samples . . . provided they're edible." That might actually be a good marketing ploy.

"Good. Plus, I need a sous-chef. Hannah will bake plenty if she's up to it. But normally there would be three of us baking. I'm going to need help."

"Good point." My stomach growled. "But I'm going to need breakfast first."

"Let's try those eggs again." He grinned and moved over to the refrigerator. He took out butter and eggs and put them on the counter.

I watched carefully as he got a bowl and cracked the eggs against the side and allowed the insides to drip into the bowl. When he was finished, he handed me a bowl and two eggs and watched while I tried the same thing.

My efforts weren't nearly as bad as they had been on Sunday. All of the egg made its way into the bowl. Unfortunately, a bit of the shell did too. However, Leroy simply got a spoon and fished them out, just as I'd done.

Next, he showed me how to turn on a gas burner by turning the knob until I heard the clicking sound, which he told me would ignite the pilot, and then turning the knob to medium-low. He melted butter while I beat my eggs. He put a splash of milk in the bowl and told me to keep beating. Then, he instructed me how to pour the mixture into the skillet. He took a block of cheddar and a grater and quickly grated cheese into the eggs. Then he took a pinch of salt and pepper and sprinkled it over the mixture. Leroy was a patient teacher, and in short time, he was showing me how to plate my eggs. He took parsley and sprinkled it over the top, which gave the simple dish an air of sophistication. I took out my camera and snapped a few pictures. **#BabyCakes #MoreThanSweets #BestEggsEver**

It might have been my imagination, but those were the best scrambled eggs I'd ever eaten.

"Hmm. These are delicious."

He grinned.

"What?"

"It's just eggs. They taste good because you made them yourself."

"Maybe, but I don't know. I think you sprinkled something on top that made these eggs special, but I'm glad I won't be forced to eat Baby's food."

At hearing his name, the mastiff, who had lain down on the rug and taken another nap, looked up.

Once I was fortified with scrambled eggs, coffee, and toast, it was time to work.

Leroy made various stations around the kitchen. Most of my tasks involved measuring dry ingredients, mixing, rolling out dough, and cleanup. Periodically, Leroy or I would stop to take pictures and upload them. **#BabyCakesBakery #BakedWithLoveAndButter #MeltInYourMouth #TurnoversCookiesAndCroissantsOhMy**

By the time we finished, we had six dozen croissants, twelve dozen thumbprint cookies with various fillings, two dozen apple turnovers, two dozen Danish, and something twisty that Leroy called cinnamon twists.

I flopped down in a chair. "I'm exhausted. I couldn't roll another pastry if my life depended on it."

"You're out of shape." He must have noticed the steam coming out of my ears because he quickly added, "I didn't mean to imply that you're not in good physical shape, but baking uses a lot of different muscles than you use when you're working out. You're standing on your feet for long periods of time, and rolling dough is tough." He held up his arm and showed his bicep, which was rather impressive.

Every flat surface was covered in baked goods. "Do you think we have enough?"

"Who knows? If Miss Hannah is feeling up to it, she'll bring some things, too. Miss Octavia used to say, when we run out, it's time to close the doors."

"We should get a lot more traffic tomorrow. People are nosy. They'll swing by just to see what happened and maybe pick up a bit of gossip." I sighed. "We just need to make it work for our benefit."

He didn't look as though he believed me. "We'll need to keep up with the inventory and do this again tomorrow."

"Ugh."

He chuckled. "Maybe we shouldn't have done the buy-two-get-one-free promo. If you're right, we'll sell out faster."

"Now you tell me."

Hours earlier, Baby had given up on waiting for us to drop something and lain down and gone to sleep. Now he sat up, and his ears perked like antennae. After a moment, he gave a bark, stretched, and then moved to the back door. By the way his tail was wagging, I knew that whoever he heard wasn't a threat.

After a few seconds, there was a brief knock on the door.

"Come in," I yelled.

Alma Hurston got two steps inside before Baby launched

himself at her, got on his hind legs, wrapped his paws around her waist, and licked her face.

I forced myself up and hurried to prevent him from knocking her over with his exuberance. "Baby, off."

I need not have worried. Despite his size and enthusiasm, Baby was gentle and careful not to overpower the smaller woman.

"Thank you, Baby. I never get a greeting like that from my husband." She chuckled. "That's why I brought you a special treat."

She spoke the magic word—*treat*.

Baby got down on all fours, spun around in a circle two times, and then, using all his willpower, forced his butt down and waited while his tail swept the floor like a metronome.

Alma reached in her pocket and pulled out a large bone. I didn't think Baby's tail could wag faster, but I was wrong. Not only did his tail speed increase, but his drool went into overdrive, and the effort to stay grounded proved overwhelming. His butt inched up, then down. Staying seated was a battle, and he was losing. Thankfully, Alma didn't keep him waiting long. After a few seconds, she handed him the bone. Baby snatched it and trotted over to his favorite spot, lay down, and proceeded to gnaw on it.

Alma took a look around. "It looks like you two have been busy. If I'm interrupting—"

"We're done for the day. Please, come in and have a seat. We were just taking a break."

"I just wanted to see how you were doing. I read about the fire." She turned to Leroy. "Are you okay? That was very brave of you. Everyone's saying you were heroic to go into a burning building to save Garrett Kelley."

Leroy blushed and mumbled, "I'm no hero. I just did what anyone would do. I didn't even think."

"Well, I can tell you that everyone at church thinks you are—especially the women." Alma grinned.

Leroy turned away, but not before I saw his flush deepen.

"Would you like a cup of tea and one of Leroy's buttery, ultra-flaky croissants?" I said. "I'm pretty sure we can spare a few."

"That sounds lovely, and your kitchen smells delicious. Can I help?"

"Let me get things ready," Leroy said. "You two sit down." He opened a cabinet and pulled out a teakettle. Obviously, he knew where everything was, although I was sure he volunteered more to have something to do.

I picked up a tray of croissants and put three teacups and plates on the table.

It didn't take long for the tea, and within a few moments, we were all seated at the dining room table. Like a hawk, Leroy and I watched Alma take her first bite. When she closed her eyes and smiled, we knew they were a success.

"Oh, my word," Alma said. "Those are scrumptious." She used her wet finger to pick up bits of the flaky pastry that had fallen onto her plate.

"I planned to come by later and give my condolences," I said between bites of croissant.

Alma stopped chewing and looked at me. "Condolences?"

"On your son-in-law's death," I said softly. "I thought someone told me that your daughter was married to Mayor Rivers, but I must have gotten it wrong."

Alma rolled her eyes. "Oh, that. They've been separated for months, and the divorce was almost final. I don't think Candace is shedding a tear."

What do you say to that? I had no idea, and an awkward silence fell over the table. Leroy sipped his tea, and I tried to figure out what to say.

Alma must have sensed the awkwardness. "I'm sorry. I know you're new here, and I didn't mean to make you uncomfortable. Marrying Paul Rivers was the biggest mistake of Candy's life. She was over twenty years younger than him and flattered by the attention he paid her. We tried to tell her that she was making a mistake, but when girls are at that age, they won't listen." Alma stared at me, and even though I had never met her daughter, I knew by the embarrassed expression that raced across her face that Candy and I were close in age. "Oh, I'm sorry. I didn't mean any offense . . . I didn't intend . . ."

"No need to worry," I said. "No offense taken."

She released a long breath. "It's wrong to talk bad about the dead, but Paul Rivers was a smooth-talking snake in the grass. He painted a picture of a life filled with mansions, luxury yachts, and trips to the governor's mansion and even the White House." She shook her head. "They weren't married six months before she started to see what he was really after."

I waited a beat, but when no explanation came, I asked, "What was he after?"

"He wanted her to try to get me and Octavia to sell to that Chicago developer. Octavia was Candy's godmother. I guess he thought she could influence her. Well, I can tell you Octavia wasn't having any of it, and he left with a bee in his ear. Now, my property isn't as big or as nice as Octavia's, but when he saw he couldn't smooth-talk me into selling, he tried to get Candy to convince me to sign my house over to her in some shady real estate maneuver he claimed would reduce inheritance taxes . . . later." She took a sip of tea and gave me a hard stare.

"Why?" I asked.

"I have no doubt that he thought that I'm just a dotty little old lady, and when I kicked the bucket, then he could finagle it away from Candy."

I frowned. "But why was it so important to him?"

"I'm sure he promised more than he could deliver, and I have no doubt that there was something in it for him. Paul

Rivers never did anything if it didn't benefit him somehow. You mark my words."

Alma certainly wasn't shedding a tear over her son-in-law's untimely death, but that didn't mean she killed him. I racked my brain trying to think of a subtle way to ask if she and Candy killed him. Leroy came to the rescue.

"I sure hope she wasn't working at the casino when she found out," he said. "Even though they were separated, I can't imagine finding out something like that while I was working."

I had to admit that was a good lead-in with the appropriate level of concern. His voice rang with sincerity.

Alma must have thought so, too. "That's very kind. She wasn't working, thank goodness. She was home in bed when the police came by to tell us he was dead. Martin and I were getting ready for church, but Candy was still asleep. She'd worked a double shift and was exhausted when she got home. She didn't even take off her uniform. She just fell asleep right where she was."

Candy had worked a double shift, so there were probably tons of people at the casino who could vouch for her, but that left Alma and her husband, who might have wanted to kill their son-in-law.

Alma stayed long enough to eat three croissants and throw more shade on her deceased son-in-law. Then she bought two dozen thumbprint cookies and four more croissants.

After she was gone, Leroy smiled. "Maybe I'd better make a couple dozen more croissants for tomorrow."

"I told you they'd sell."

He stood taller and straighter. Praise works wonders for great posture. "What did you think about what Alma Hurston said? Do you think she or Candy could have killed Rivers?"

"Maybe, but I just can't see either one of them stabbing the mayor." He swallowed hard. "That knife was pretty deep. No matter how sharp that eel knife was, I can't see that Alma

Hurston would have the strength or the stomach to do it. She may not have liked Paul Rivers, but killing him is an entirely different matter."

I wasn't sure about that. I'd seen a lot of petite women in the Navy who could crawl under barbed wire, scale walls after jogging twenty miles carrying fifty pounds on their backpacks, and still have the energy to toss a grown man over their shoulders. Alma may not have been in the military, but I'd learned not to underestimate anyone. "What about Martin Hurston? I haven't met him yet. I suppose the neighborly thing would be for me to take some baked goods next door and introduce myself, right?"

"Actually, I think they're supposed to bring you the baked goods. You're the new person. But I'd say absolutely not for Martin Hurston."

"Why not? And don't tell me because he's old. That's ageism, and it's wrong. You can't discriminate against someone just because they're older. Although, I don't think this is exactly what the law intended. Nevertheless, you can't just discount someone as a potential murderer because they're a woman or because they're older."

"I guess you're right, but I wasn't discounting him because of his age. It was more because of his profession."

I hadn't expected that. "What's his profession?"

He smiled. "Martin Hurston is a minister. He's the pastor of New Bison Unitarian Church and a confirmed pacifist."

# CHAPTER 10

If there were any doubts about the success of Baby Cakes' roadside bakery, they were alleviated early. When I left the house at six forty-five, there was already a line of cars. I stopped to take a picture. **#TheEarlyBirdGetsTheCroissants #BestWayToStartYourDay #BabyCakes #Yum**

Hannah and Leroy were already there by the time I was showered, dressed, and Baby and I had finished our breakfast. We opened the doors at seven. By seven thirty, we had sold out of pastries. By eight, we were out of croissants and thumbprint cookies, and before noon, the only thing we had left were a few slices of cake.

"We might as well close up. Maybe you can post something on your phone so folks will stop coming," Hannah said as she swept a few crumbs off the display counter. I took a picture of the empty display cases. **#SoldOut #BabyCakesBakery #Thanks-ForTheSupport #PostACommentAndGetADiscount**

Leroy groaned. "You're giving another discount? I'm going to be up all night baking croissants."

"Maybe you should just stay here. I've got plenty of room. I'll even be your sous-chef and help out."

"Really? That would be great. Sometimes when Miss Octavia knew we'd have a lot of baking to do, I'd stay over at the bakery."

"The bakery. I almost forgot. Mr. Russell called earlier, but we were so busy, I didn't bother to respond." I swiped through the messages on my phone until I found the one from my lawyer. It simply said, *Call me.*

I called and waited until he picked up. "Mr. Russell, I'm sorry I missed your call. We were rather busy today."

He'd called to tell me that I needed to meet the claims adjuster at two. I checked my watch and realized I had only fifteen minutes if I wanted to keep that appointment.

Leroy and Hannah promised to clean up and get started on the baking for tomorrow, while Baby and I went to meet with the adjuster.

"Actually, I was hoping I could leave Baby here." I glanced over in time to see Baby sliding a piece of cake off the counter. "Never mind. Our inventory will stand a better chance if I take him with me."

I arrived at Baby Cakes just as the clock struck two, but, seeing that there was a white Ford truck with a sign for New Bison Casualty and Life in the parking spot next to mine, I knew the adjuster was already there. There was still a lot of broken glass from the fire, so I left Baby in the car.

When he realized he wasn't going inside with me, he wasn't happy.

"I'm sorry, but it's just not safe. You could cut your paw or something. It's best if you just wait here."

He yowled, but without hands, there wasn't much he could do.

I got out and headed to the back of the bakery when Jackson Abernathy came around the side of the building.

Baby barked, lunged, and made every effort to attack the breeder through the car.

"Mr. Abernathy, I wasn't aware that my aunt Octavia had

insurance with your company or that you were an insurance adjuster in addition to being a dog breeder."

He grunted. "My dad owned the company, and Octavia had a policy with him. He died about six months ago. I was sure she'd cancel her policy, but I guess she died before she got the chance."

Baby's barking grew louder and more intense, and Abernathy's face screamed condemnation.

I hurried to unlock the door to the building, and we entered.

Jackson Abernathy walked around the building, and I followed him. After a whirlwind tour that took less than five minutes, he started firing questions at the speed of light. *When was the last time the plumbing had been updated? When was the wiring last inspected? Did we have receipts for the kitchen items that were destroyed?* On and on the questions continued. My response was the same. *I don't know.* Finally, I stopped him.

"Look, I don't know the answer to any of these questions. My aunt Octavia owned the bakery. She took care of the plumbing, the wiring, and everything. I've only been here five days." *Wow! Has it only been five days? It feels like years.*

He suggested that I might want to look through my aunt's things and find receipts for the equipment.

"Will I be able to rebuild?"

"Octavia insured the bakery for five hundred thousand dollars. However, there are definite signs that the fire was deliberate."

"Whoever killed Mayor Rivers must have set the fire to hide the murder or to destroy evidence," I said.

"We won't be able to pay out until the police wrap up their investigation and determine that *you* didn't set the fire yourself."

"Why would I do that? I mean, I just got here. I certainly had no reason to burn down the bakery or to kill Mayor Rivers."

He snorted and spat on the floor, which would have been bad enough outside, but we weren't outside. I tried to focus and not look at the spit wad he'd left *inside* my bakery, but my eyes were drawn to it, and I couldn't hear anything else he said.

He waved a hand in front of my face. "Hey, are you listening? Earth to Madison."

"I'm sorry. What were you saying?"

He mumbled something that sounded like *space cadet*. Whatever he said had the power to pull my attention from the spit.

"Will New Bison Casualty and Life honor their policy?" I said. "I can't believe you can legally withhold money. I'll have to ask my attorney." I pulled my phone out of my purse.

He frowned and clenched his jaw until I saw a vein pulsing on the side of his head. He stared at me, but I didn't flinch. After a while, I won the game of chicken, and he conceded. "As long as you didn't set the fire, then New Bison Casualty and Life will honor the policy. It'll take a while to get the money."

"How much?"

"The building was insured for five hundred thousand, plus another hundred thousand for equipment and supplies."

I hid my excitement at the idea of over half of a million dollars. I could turn Baby Cakes into a high-end bakery. I could expand the floor space of the bakery and enlarge the kitchen and the area for classes. I'd need to talk to Hannah and Leroy, of course. They would know exactly what equipment we'd need, but I could envision the space that would put Baby Cakes on the map.

"How much can you give me now? We're continuing the bakery, and we have expenses. Plus, I've got to pay my staff." I wasn't sure what Leroy got paid or even if Hannah got paid at all. Regardless, they deserved to be paid. They were putting in a lot of time and effort, and Hannah was even using her own ingredients. I needed to be able to pay them. I'm sure there were records somewhere. I made a mental note to take a look when I got home.

From the expression on Abernathy's face, it was clear that he wasn't interested in paying me anything. After a few minutes, he forced a smile. "Well, I'm not sure that you fully understand all of the technical details of your aunt's policy. There are lots of forms that need to be filled out. Plus, the police are involved, and that always makes things take twice as long." He shook his head. "Seeing as you're new to town, and I suspect new to running a business and filling out all of the paperwork, I can work as your agent of record and take care of completing all the forms and filling out all the paperwork. Why, you probably haven't even been in town long enough to set up a bank account."

My heart constricted. I didn't have a bank account. In fact, I didn't even know what bank Aunt Octavia used for her business. Was there money in the account? How did I pay Leroy and Hannah? How did I pay for ingredients? I didn't even know what to do with the money we made this morning. Leroy had put it in a lockbox, but where would I even take it? For a split second, I considered letting Jackson Abernathy take care of everything. That's what I'd done my entire life. My dad filed my taxes and completed any legal forms I needed. After all, I wasn't good at making decisions. I wasn't good at business or paperwork. I opened my mouth, but just as I was about to speak, I heard Baby barking, and it snapped me out of the hypnotic state that I'd lulled myself into.

"I appreciate the offer, but I will complete the papers myself. If I'm going to run a business, then I need to learn as much about the business as I can. Just email me whatever papers you need completed, and I'll get them back to you. In the meantime, given the fact that the policy is for over a half million dollars, I think ten percent seems fair for an advance to help keep the business afloat. So, why don't you write a check for fifty thousand, or are you able to electronically transfer the money?"

Jackson Abernathy was stunned. "Don't you think you're being a bit hasty. Maybe you should talk to your attorney. Something like this might just provide the out you need."

"Out? I don't understand."

"This fire may be your ticket out of that crazy will Octavia created. You can take your six hundred thousand dollars and go back to California," he said.

I hadn't thought about the fire as a way out of the bakery. In fact, I wasn't sure I wanted a way out. Regardless, I wasn't about to take advice from Jackson Abernathy. "Aunt Octavia was an intelligent, hardworking, talented woman. And, I neither want nor need a way out of her will. Now, about that check?"

I ignored the steam coming from his ears and waited. After a few seconds, he mumbled that he'd have the money electronically deposited in three to five business days and then stomped out of the building.

When I was sure he was gone, I indulged in a happy dance. I did it. I made a decision, and I knew in my heart that I'd made the right decision. I didn't like Jackson Abernathy, but that didn't mean he wasn't a good insurance agent. However, I don't believe Aunt Octavia trusted him, and she was a pretty good judge of character. Baby sure didn't like him. I may not be a business mogul, but since coming to New Bison, I'd discovered that I had skills. If I couldn't figure out what I was doing, I'd ask Tyler. If all else failed, I'd ask Chris Russell.

I went back to the car and found Baby propped up behind the wheel. Long strings of drool hung from practically every surface, and the steering wheel was soaked.

"Ugh." I went back inside and rummaged through the cabinets until I found a bottle of cleaner and a roll of paper towels that were only slightly singed, along with a pair of rubber gloves.

It took longer than I thought to clean, and I had the feeling that Baby was insulted. He sat in the passenger seat and barely made eye contact with me the entire time.

"Look, there's no point in getting mad at me. I'm not judging. I know you can't help it . . . well, I'm fairly sure you can't. But humans aren't fond of sitting in doggy drool."

"Who are you talking to?"

My heart skipped a beat, and I nearly jumped ten feet. I turned around so quickly that I hit my head on the door frame. I rubbed the spot and scowled at Michael Portman. "Ouch, you shouldn't sneak up on people like that."

"Who's sneaking? I merely walked up to the car. Maybe if you weren't talking to . . . who are you talking to, by the way?"

"Baby."

"I see."

I rubbed my head and forced myself not to wince.

"Let me take a look." He moved close to get a closer look at my head.

I swatted his hands away. "Ouch. That hurt."

"I'm sorry. Will you let me take a look? I am a doctor."

"You're a veterinarian."

"I'm still able to take care of a little bump. Now, suck it up, sailor."

I glared for a few more moments, but then I lowered my hand and let him examine the bump.

He leaned closer, reached up, and probed the area with his fingers. I could smell his aftershave, which had a light aroma that I recognized as Dolce & Gabbana's Light Blue for Men, one of my favorites. I inhaled the light, breezy scent. We were so close I could feel his breath on my forehead. I started to feel light-headed, but I couldn't tell if it was because of the bump on my head or Michael Portman's proximity.

After what felt like forever, he looked in my eyes. Our gazes locked, and for a few moments, I felt like I was drowning.

My skin burned where his hands touched me. My heart raced, and I could feel the blood rushing in my ears.

His touch lightened from a probe to a caress.

We leaned closer. When we were only a breath apart—

"Maddy, is that you?"

Michael swore and then stepped back and turned away.

Bradley Ellison ran toward us. "I thought I recognized your

car. Are we still on for dinner tonight?" He was winded from the effort of trotting down the alley and bent over and panted to catch his breath.

"Dinner?" I stared.

"Yeah, don't tell me you forgot?"

"Of course, I didn't forget." I checked the time. "I just had to meet the insurance adjuster. How about you pick me up at seven?"

"That'll be great." He glanced at Michael. "What's going on?"

"Nothing. I bumped my head, and he was just looking it over to make sure I didn't need medical attention."

Brad chuckled. "Medical attention from a vet?"

Michael stood up straighter, and the air crackled with tension. He turned toward Brad.

Baby must have felt the tension, too, because he wound up like a spring and tried to lunge over me and through the car door.

Brad bolted backward, and Michael blocked the open door with his body and then quickly pushed the mastiff back and slammed the door.

"That dog needs to be muzzled," Brad said. "He's a menace."

"Baby isn't a menace, and he most certainly does *not* need to be muzzled. He's a well-trained dog, and you're in his space." I wasn't sure if any of that was true or not, but Baby was my dog now, and I wasn't going to let anyone cast disparaging remarks at him.

A growl rumbled inside him, but I'd had enough. "Baby, down."

Asking more than two hundred pounds of muscle to lie down on the front seat of a car was asking a lot. To my complete surprise, with his front legs across my thighs, he scooted his rear back and lay down. His focus never wavered from his target, and I could feel the tension inside him.

My stomach tightened at the thought of what would happen

when that knot uncoiled. Baby *was* a well-trained dog, but I wasn't willing to test him too far. I put the car in reverse and hightailed it home.

It wasn't easy driving or turning the steering wheel with Baby on my lap. After we were well away from the bakery, he relaxed, and I had him move to the passenger seat.

"What was that all about? What do you have against Bradley Ellison?"

I could tell by the way his ears rose that he had heard me, but Baby must have decided to keep his thoughts to himself.

We drove in silence for a few blocks, and then I remembered that I wanted to check on Garrett Kelley. I did a U-turn and headed for New Bison Hospital, which was a few blocks from downtown and one of the tallest buildings in the area.

When I pulled into the parking lot, I looked at Baby. "There's no way they're going to let you go inside, so you'll have to wait here."

Again, he didn't look like he liked being left, but he endured it without the same nervous energy he'd shown at the bakery.

"Oh, wait. I almost forgot." I reached into my purse and pulled out a dog bone that I'd shoved in earlier and handed it to him. I sat and watched him gnaw on his bone for a few moments. "If anyone had told me just a week ago that I'd be hauling a two-hundred-fifty-pound dog around a town with no designer stores, cleaning up drool, and lugging dog bones in my Louis Vuitton purse, I would have told them they were crazy." I shook my head and got out, leaving the windows cracked and Baby neck deep in drool with his bone.

Inside, I asked the receptionist for directions to the gift shop and for Garrett Kelley's room.

By the time I'd picked up a nice card and an overpriced bouquet of flowers and made my way down a multitude of corridors and taken an elevator, I had worked through my approach to questioning him. I needed to understand why he was in the bakery in the first place. When I found his room and entered, I was surprised to discover that he wasn't alone.

"April, I'm sorry. I didn't mean to interrupt."

"You're not interrupting anything. I just wanted to stop in and check on Mr. Kelley."

I was relieved to see that there were no visible burns that disfigured Garrett Kelley's face, but he did have what looked like a severe sunburn on one side of his face. His arms were bandaged, and another bandage crossed his forehead.

I placed the flowers on a dresser and sat down in one of the two chairs. The speech I'd rehearsed in the gift shop and while traversing miles of hospital halls vanished, and I sat staring at Garrett Kelley for several moments. Eventually, the silence became too much, and I blurted out, "I'm so sorry for your injuries, but what on earth were you doing in the bakery?"

Garrett Kelley stared at me for several seconds and then said, "Who are you?"

"Madison Montgomery. Octavia Baker was my great-aunt. I know we only met once, the other day when you were helping out at the bakery."

He gave me a blank stare. "I don't know you."

"Well, no. I just moved here a few days ago. Aunt Octavia left me her bakery and house."

"What do you want?"

I wasn't expecting such a blunt response, but then I didn't really know him. Maybe this was how he was all the time. "I just wanted to check on you to make sure that you were okay."

He raised his bandaged arms. "I've got burns on my arms, and my lungs feel like they're on fire. And I can't remember how I got this way."

"I don't understand." I stared from Garrett to April.

April leaned forward. "Garrett has what the doctors feel is short-term memory loss due to the trauma. He doesn't remember anything related to the fire."

"But surely you remember something. I mean, you don't recall what brought you there in the first place?"

Garrett Kelley merely stared for several moments and then shook his head.

We sat in awkward silence for several moments. Eventually, April broke the silence. "There's a really good chance that Garrett will regain his memory in time, so I'm sure we'll get to the bottom of this mystery soon and discover what happened."

"But . . . surely, you remember what led you and Mayor Rivers to be in the bakery after hours. I mean, it's not like either of you would have a reason to be in Baby Cakes."

Garrett Kelley shook his head. "April tells me that Paul is dead, but I'm afraid I don't remember going to the bakery at all. The last thing I remember is locking up my bookstore and walking down the street." He paused. "The next thing I remember is waking up in here. I'm sorry, but I just don't remember anything that will be of use to you."

I didn't stay long. I never was great with hospitals. I'd only known Garrett Kelley for a few days, and those days were now lost. Apart from that, we didn't have much to talk about. Besides, Baby was probably finished with his bone and may have started eating the steering wheel.

April followed me out of the room. In the hall, I turned to her. "Do you think he will regain his memory?" Behind her eyes, I saw a flash that led me to ask, "You don't believe him?"

"I think he may have some gaps, but I think he remembers more than he's letting on," she whispered.

"Why? You don't think he actually killed Mayor Rivers, do you?"

"Frankly, I don't know what to believe. Why was he in the bakery anyway? There's something fishy here, and I intend to get to the bottom of it."

I thought about Garrett Kelley the entire ride home. Baby finished off his bone.

Leroy's car was still parked in the driveway, and when I pulled into the garage, I could smell that he'd been busy.

"This smells wonderful."

He didn't respond immediately. Instead, he removed a tray of croissants from the oven and replaced it with another one. "Thanks, how did it go with the claims adjuster."

"Did you know that Jackson Abernathy was Aunt Octavia's insurance agent?"

He leaned against the counter and stared. "She never mentioned it. Seems odd, though. She really didn't like Abernathy."

I explained what happened at the bakery. "I need to find any receipts for equipment that Octavia had. Any ideas where she would have kept things like that?"

"I'd check her computer. She was meticulous about invoices and receipts."

"She had a computer? I didn't see one when I toured the house."

"Of course." He gave the croissants in the oven one last look, wiped his hands on a dish towel, and then headed down the hall.

I followed him upstairs to the study. He opened the closet. Aunt Octavia had converted a large walk-in closet to an office. There was a built-in desk, a laptop computer, and a large monitor along with two filing cabinets fitted with shelves full of binders.

"Wow. It's efficient, but there's so much space in this house, why didn't she just convert one of the bedrooms to an office?"

"Miss Octavia didn't like clutter. She said having a small space made her work faster so she could get out of here and spend time doing what she loved to do: cook or read mysteries."

I looked at the laptop. "I don't suppose you know her password?"

He grinned. "Actually, I do." He tapped something into the laptop and was rewarded when the splash screen was replaced by a picture of Baby as the background image: BabyCakes123.

I checked my watch. "I'll tackle finding the receipts after I help with the baking."

"I can handle it. You work on this."

"Are you sure?"

"It'll take a little longer, but I've got all night. This is important." He went back downstairs.

Aunt Octavia used a popular bookkeeping software program, and it didn't take long for me to see that she had been thorough about entering income and expenses. She was also detailed in the notes she provided. In a folder labeled INSURANCE, I found a detailed list of equipment with models and serial numbers of the big-ticket items along with the prices and digital copies of her receipts. I also made a note of all the banking information. Aunt Octavia used New Bison Federal Credit Union. There were notes about Leroy's and Hannah's salaries, and I breathed a sigh of relief when I realized that there was plenty of money to pay them. I printed the lists for Mr. Abernathy and was about to shut down when I noticed a box labeled 11-02. That stopped me in my tracks. November 2 was my birthday. I got the box from the shelf. Inside were the letters my dad had sent her and pictures of me as a small baby. I opened some of the letters. She was right, they were reports.

*March 15th. Madison age 12, 80 lbs, 5 ft 2 inches. She is smart and likes to read. She spends hours reading romance novels and mysteries. She likes clothes, especially shoes, and has a knack for solving puzzles. We are heading to the Middle East next month. Will consider sending her to visit when we return.*

*Jefferson*

All of the letters started the same, with the date, my age, weight, and height. Each one ended the same way, too, with a date in the future when I might be sent for a visit and his name. I would have liked to have seen Aunt Octavia's letters. I couldn't help smiling. I can't imagine anyone being bold enough to put Admiral Jefferson Augustus Montgomery in his place; however, from what I'd seen, it would have been Aunt Octavia. She wouldn't have cared about his medals or how many men he commanded. She would have ordered him around like a drill sergeant, and he would have sucked it up and taken it. My dad was tough, but he was also polite and very respectful, especially to women.

I rummaged through the box, read through my dad's letters, and relived memories as I looked at my life in pictures. Like most young girls, I went through phases. Pictures from my tomboy phase, girly-girl phase, goth phase—when I refused to wear anything other than black—and a really unfortunate phase that I can only call my abstract expressionist phase. Thankfully, my hair and one of my eyebrows grew back, and this picture was the only record of what I'd done to myself. I resisted the urge to shred the photo, but I buried it deep in the bottom of the box.

I was about to return the box when I spotted another one on the shelf. It was narrow and fit behind the one labeled with my birthday. When I picked it up, I saw it was a plastic case like the one I'd seen at Chris Russell's office.

In the master bedroom, there was a television with a box attached to it that looked like the one Mr. Russell had checked out from the library. I took my box and the video to the bedroom. It took a few tries before I managed to get the box to stop spitting the tape back at me. Eventually, I figured it out and turned on the television to watch. Just as in Mr. Russell's office, Aunt Octavia's face popped on the screen. She fumbled with what I assume was the camera and eventually backed up and sat down.

"*I hope this thing is recording,*" she mumbled. "*Madison, I hope you're the one watching this tape.*"

I gasped at her mentioning my name and leaned forward to hear more.

*"I didn't want to tell everything in front of that lawyer. I hope you're settling into the house and the bakery. Your father said you can't cook."* She snorted. *"Well, I figure that's because you never had to. Your grandmother was a great cook. She taught me, your aunt, and your mom to cook. I'm sure with a little help, you'll do just fine. It's in your DNA. Leroy will help. He's a talented baker. Hannah's a good cook, too. When her mind is clear, she'll be a big help. I left you my recipes. They're in a box labeled 'taxes.'"* She laughed. *"No one likes doing taxes, and I figured if anyone came looking for my secrets, they'd avoid taxes like the plague."*

She chuckled but then got serious. *"There's something strange going on in New Bison. That real estate developer is pressuring folks to sell their property so he can build condominiums. The mayor's in on it. I can't prove it, but I know it. I can feel it in my bones. That crook Rivers doesn't have the sense God gave a turnip. And that young whippersnapper, Ellison, is too wet behind the ears to have cooked up this scheme. No, there's got to be someone else involved . . . someone who's pulling the strings, a Moriarty. Your dad said you liked to read Sherlock Holmes, so you'll understand what I mean by that."* She looked over her shoulder as though she were afraid someone was listening to her. I couldn't help but wonder if Aunt Octavia was paranoid.

*"Be careful who you trust. I'd trust Leroy, Hannah, Garrett, and April with my life. I think Tyler is okay, too."* She paused. *"It breaks my heart to say it, but one of them may be a Judas. Someone is leaking information, and I think I know who. You be careful. Don't tell anyone about this video. It could put you in danger."* She shook her head. *"I hate to think that someone might hurt you, but there's lots of money at stake, and like the Good Book says, 'The love of money is the root of all evil.' Take care of Baby. He's a good judge of character. Baby won't steer you wrong. If all else fails, trust him to take care of you."* She

glanced around like a scared rabbit. "*I better go. I'll try to leave you some clues to help you. But keep it to yourself. Until I can find the spy in my camp, it's not safe.*"

She smiled and her eyes softened. "*I wish I could be there with you. You look so much like your mother. She would be so proud of the woman you've grown up to be.*" She sniffed and wiped at her eyes. "*Now, don't waste too much money on Jimmy Shoes . . . oh, if you ever need some quick cash, check in the deep freezer, in a container with Baby's name on it. That's where I keep my mad money.*" She paused again and listened. "*I better go before someone finds me. Take care, honey.*"

I sat for a few minutes, staring at the black screen. After a few minutes, I pressed rewind and replayed the video. I watched it twice but still couldn't figure out if my great-aunt was serious. Did she truly believe that there was something sinister about the mayor and Bradley Ellison? Or was she merely a crazy old woman? Either way, she'd left me with a lot to think about.

# CHAPTER 11

Baby sat next to me, and each time Octavia's face popped up on the screen, he sat up taller and stared. I wondered if he knew and understood that she was gone. When I turned off the tape, he lay down on the bed and placed his head in my lap and whined.

I comforted him the best that I could, but I was a poor substitute. "You miss her, don't you?"

He whined.

"I don't know if Aunt Octavia was batty or not. I mean, I find it hard to believe that any of her friends would harm her, but then . . . what do I really know about any of these people?"

Baby gave a soft bark.

"She trusted you, and I know you'd never reveal any secrets, would you?"

He rolled on his back, legs in the air, and exposed his belly, and I took the hint and scratched his stomach.

"I don't know what to do. I mean, part of me thinks she must have just been a bit paranoid. The type of conspiracy she's talking about, spies in the camp, and a Judas . . . well, that's just stuff from books. Maybe Alma Hurston was right. Maybe she did read too many mysteries. That stuff doesn't happen in real life, does it?"

Baby's response was to use his paw to move my hand to a spot that, when scratched, made his entire body wiggle.

I laughed. "It's all about you, isn't it?"

Baby opened his mouth and smiled.

With the hand that wasn't busy, I eased my cell phone out of my pocket and snapped a quick picture. Years ago, I mastered the art of one-handed cell phone operation. I could text and send pictures without looking at my phone. Within seconds, I had uploaded the photo. **#MastiffLife #EnjoyingTheGoodLife #LoveThatMastiffSmile #BellyScratchesMakeMeSmile**

"We may not be able to confirm if she was crazy or not, but we can check the two things she mentioned in her recording." I got off the bed and hurried back to the office. I found the box labeled TAXES and in the bottom were handwritten recipes.

"One down, one to go." I headed to the kitchen.

Leroy had made a lot of progress. There were trays and trays of croissants, thumbprint cookies, and turnovers. I grabbed one of the apple turnovers as I passed by on my way to the freezer, which I'd seen in the garage. In a corner, I found a tub with Baby's name written on it with a permanent marker. I removed the lid and gasped. Inside the container was a ziplock bag stuffed with money in rolls.

Back in the kitchen, Leroy did a double take when he saw the bag that I'd placed on the counter.

He whistled. "That gives a new take to the term cold, hard cash. What made you look in the freezer?"

Was Leroy the Judas she was worried about? I didn't believe he would betray me or Aunt Octavia, but I had made up my mind to trust no one, except Baby. "I found some instructions when I was going through her records." Which was partly true. I had found instructions.

"Do you want me to deposit that in the bank along with the money from today?"

"Aunt Octavia called it her *mad money*. I'm going to count it."

I sat down and took the cash out of the bag. It was stiff but warmed up quickly from the heat from the kitchen and the warmth from my hands. The bag contained mostly twenty-dollar bills, so it took quite a while.

Leroy prepared Baby's food and continued to bake.

When I finished the last roll, I stared in surprised. "Ten thousand dollars. I can't believe she kept ten thousand dollars in an ice cream tub in her freezer."

Leroy shook his head. "I'm pretty surprised at that amount, too. Miss Octavia wasn't exceptionally frugal, but I just never imagined she had squirreled away that much money."

"She called it her"—I used air quotes—" 'mad money.' "

"What's that? I've heard of rainy-day savings, but—"

"When I first started dating, my dad used to give me *mad money*." I smiled. "He said it was for emergencies. If my date got *fresh* and I got *mad* and needed to take a taxi or an Uber."

"Do Ubers accept cash?"

"Not everywhere, it depends on where you are. We've lived in places where you needed to carry around bribe money, so cash can come in handy."

"Wow. Did you ever need to use it?"

I shook my head. "Before college, I dated a lot of sailors. They were too afraid of The Admiral to get fresh. He literally took out his service revolver and threatened to have my dates court-martialed and executed if he heard they hadn't behaved in a manner befitting a member of the armed forces."

He chuckled. "That had to make you real popular."

"He wasn't around much, so I learned to take care of myself. I took a few basic self-defense classes. Still, it didn't hurt to have the threat that I'd tell The Admiral. They weren't really afraid that he'd shoot them, but he could certainly make their lives miserable." I laughed. "I think they were more afraid of ending up on permanent latrine duty or finding themselves on a sub in the middle of the Arctic."

"I didn't know we have subs in the Arctic."

"I never said we did." I put my fingers to my lips.

"Got it. Apart from the money, did you find anything else useful?"

I debated whether to tell Leroy about the video and Aunt Octavia's fears but decided against it. I could tell by his face that he knew I'd found something. It would seem suspicious to deny it. I searched my brain for something to say. "I found her secret recipes."

That got his attention. There was a sparkle in his eyes. "Really?"

I chuckled. "Yeah, I'm now the keeper of the family secrets." I pulled out one of the recipes that I snagged from the box. "This is a recipe for something called Chocolate Soul Cake. I thought maybe we could try it together. We could give out samples and take special orders. What do you think?"

Leroy stared at the recipe. I wasn't sure he heard me until he glanced up. "Coffee . . . I never thought of adding coffee to the batter, but she's right. It would enhance the chocolate and keep the mixture moist. She was a genius. You know, she had a degree in chemistry. She used to work for the Environmental Protection Agency before she opened Baby Cakes. She said cooking was just chemistry you could eat. She loved to try different ingredients and watch how they interacted." He waved the recipe. "This is gold. It's worth far more than that pile of money. Miss Octavia's chocolate cakes were amazing. Did you know she won the New Bison Fall Festival's Baking Contest every year for the past fourteen years?"

"No, I didn't know that."

"She called it Chocolate Soul Cake because it was so good, people would sell their soul for a slice." He chuckled. "She's a legend around here. Two years ago, she entered this chocolate cake recipe and won. The next year, when she made it again,

three bakers withdrew their entries from the competition before the judging even started."

"Wow. Now I really want to give it a try."

Leroy reviewed the ingredient list and made sure we had
everything on the list on hand. He worked with a nervous excitement that I found endearing. He could care less about ten
thousand dollars in cash, but a recipe for chocolate cake made
him giddy.

While he prepared the ingredients, I packed the cash away
and returned it to the freezer. By the time I was washed up and
ready to assist, Leroy had sobered up. "What's the matter?" I
asked.

He stepped back. "You should be the one to make this. I
mean, it's your family's secret recipe. I think Miss Octavia
would want you to make it."

"But I can't cook."

"You can follow directions." He slipped an apron over my
head, wrapped the ties around my waist several times, and then
knotted them. "I'll be your sous-chef."

For several moments, we debated who would take the lead,
but he was adamant that it should be me. So, I took a deep
breath and looked over the recipe card. I called off the ingredients, and Leroy assisted, stepping in only to prevent catastrophe on my part or to explain terms I wasn't familiar with.

He demonstrated the proper way to chop a block of dark
chocolate without losing any of my digits. He brewed a cup of
coffee and prepared the pans. By the time the pans were ready
to go into the oven, I was covered in flour, and my hands were
dark from the chocolate.

Leroy took a few pictures while I worked.

When the cakes were done, the house was warm and smelled
chocolatey and sweet. While the cakes cooled, we mixed the
frosting. The layers weren't completely even, but Leroy showed
me how to use frosting to camouflage any flaws. When it was

done, we snapped pictures and posted them online. **#Octavias-AwardWinningChocolateCake #FreeSamples #BabyCakes**

I stared at the finished cake with awe. "I can't believe I did that."

Leroy smiled. "Believe it. I knew you could do it."

"Can we taste it?"

"We should probably taste a small slice, just to make sure that we did everything right."

We pulled out plates, and Leroy cut us both a very narrow sliver of the chocolatey goodness.

I watched Leroy take a bite and didn't realize I'd been holding my breath until he sighed, and then I knew it was a success. I took a bite. It was heavenly. I must have moaned because Leroy started laughing.

"It's delicious," he said.

"Is it really as good as Aunt Octavia's?"

"Absolutely. You did a great job."

"I couldn't have done it without your help." I took another bite. "You know, this would be great with a bit of orange."

He smiled. "Already making modifications?"

"No, it's delicious. I just . . . thought."

"You're right. Once, Miss Octavia made this for a dinner party. She made a white chocolate raspberry vanilla ice cream to go with it and drizzled the entire thing with a warm milk chocolate sauce. It was the best thing I've ever tasted."

"She made ice cream?"

"Usually she only made ice cream in the summer. She saw a woman on QVC selling stand mixers. They demonstrated the various attachments, and one of them was an ice cream bowl." He laughed. "She loved that stand mixer."

I looked over at the huge contraption that seemed to take up so much space, but it certainly made mixing a snap.

Baby had been lounging on the floor, but he suddenly perked up. He growled, ran to the front door, and barked.

I followed him to the door and took a peek outside. It was Brad Ellison. "Darn it. We're supposed to go to dinner." I yelled back at Leroy, "Can you take Baby out to the garage?"

He grabbed Baby by the collar and escorted him out of the room, mumbling, "I guess it would be pretty bad if your dog ate your date."

"Not funny."

When I was sure Baby was safely locked away, I opened the door. Bradley Ellison stood on the porch with flowers, candy, and a large teddy bear with a sign that read, I'M SORRY.

"Wow. Is all that for me?"

"Will you forgive me? I didn't mean any disrespect toward Baby. I'm sure once we get to know each other, we'll become great friends. In the meantime, I do appreciate you for not allowing him to eat me."

I took the flowers, candy, and bear. "He's really a sweet dog. I have no idea why he doesn't like you. He likes most people, except . . . Mr. Abernathy. He didn't like him, either."

He followed me into the kitchen. "Ah, Leroy. Still baking?"

"Actually, Maddy made that, and it's delicious. Would you like to try a slice?"

"You made this?"

"I did."

He hesitated. "There aren't any nuts or peanut butter, are there? I'm allergic." He pulled out his EpiPen and held it up.

I shook my head. "No nuts."

"Then, of course, I'd love to try a piece."

Leroy cut another sliver and put it on a plate in front of him. He took a bite, and his eyes got large. "This is delicious."

My chest nearly burst with pride. "Thank you."

I left Brad eating in the kitchen while I went to get dressed. One quick look in the mirror showed that I was covered in flour and smelled like chocolate. I quickly hopped in the shower. Normally, I could spend hours in the shower, especially washing my hair. However, I didn't have that kind of time tonight. Instead, I made quick work of making myself presentable.

No time to dry my hair tonight. I used gel to get my curls under control and pulled it back into a bun. I wrapped a scarf over it while I put on makeup and dressed. It would be stiff tomorrow when the gel dried, but I decided I would deal with that problem tomorrow.

I put on a skirt with a turtleneck sweater and boots. I was ready in record time . . . well, record time for me. When I returned to the kitchen, Brad and Leroy were making awkward conversation about sports, and both looked anxious for rescue.

"Sorry for the delay, but I'm ready."

Brad whistled. "Well worth the wait."

He helped me on with my coat and then hesitated. He turned to Leroy. "Can I drop you somewhere?"

Leroy blushed. "No . . . thank you."

"He's staying here." I noted the shocked look on Brad's face but chose to ignore it. I walked to the door and waited for Brad to catch up and open it.

I wasn't surprised to see that Brad drove an expensive luxury sedan. He started the motor, but before he put the car in gear, he turned. "Are you sure it's safe to leave him there alone? I mean, you haven't been here long, and you hardly know him."

I smiled. "He's not alone. Baby's there."

"I mean—"

"I know what you meant, but I trust Leroy." The words were barely out of my mouth when I realized that I meant them. I did trust Leroy. I may have known him only for a week, but deep down I knew he wasn't a Judas. If anyone betrayed Aunt Octavia, and I wasn't sure they had, it wasn't Leroy. Besides, she told me to trust Baby, and he liked Leroy.

Brad Ellison frowned but didn't say anything more. We drove in an uncomfortable silence for several minutes. When the silence went on too long, I decided to cut him some slack and explain, even though he didn't deserve an explanation.

"We've got a lot of baking to do, and with the bakery out of commission, it makes sense for Leroy to bake here. Besides, it's a big house, and there's plenty of room."

I struggled to make decisions, but I decided to trust Leroy. Only time would tell if I'd made the wrong choice. What I didn't know was whether I could trust Bradley Ellison.

Brad drove me around New Bison, pointing out the new condominiums he'd been instrumental in creating on the shores of Lake Michigan. His voice rang with pride as he talked about the previously wasted waterfront, which would be teeming with tourists in the summer.

"Why wasn't the waterfront developed?" I asked.

"No one had the vision, the expertise, or the financial backers to make it happen."

*Until now.* He left it unsaid, but I knew it was what he was thinking. Bradley Ellison wasn't indecisive when he was talking about himself. He had a monumentally high opinion of himself, but I couldn't fault him for it. In fact, I found it hard to believe that no one else thought tourists might like beachfront property. I stared at the white boxes, which blocked the shore from the road, and was reminded of beachfront property in big cities across the country. I'd never really thought about beachfront property beyond wanting to make sure that I had a great view and access to the beach and any amenities the property offered. Today, I thought about people like my aunt Octavia. In order to build those boxes, it would mean tearing down homes like mine. Perhaps I was being selfish. After all, condos would mean that a lot more people could enjoy the lake. But I'd miss not seeing the sunset as it sank into Lake Michigan each evening.

"Earth to Maddy."

I shook myself out of my daydreams. "I'm sorry. The condos are very . . . tall."

He smiled. "I wanted to make them taller, but New Bison

zoning regulations wouldn't allow buildings over six stories on the waterfront. Can you believe that?"

Something about his demeanor told me there was more to the story than what he was sharing. "I'm sure an intelligent man like you wouldn't allow silly zoning regulations to stop you." I leaned closer. "You have a plan up your sleeve, don't you?"

At first, he tried to look innocent and deny that he had any other plans, but I batted my eyelashes and stroked his ego by throwing out compliments that would have required waist-high wading boots to navigate. Eventually, he caved in.

"I would never do anything illegal, but I did make sure that the architects allowed for additional stories to be added later if the zoning regulations were to change in the future."

*Or if anyone putting up resistance were to die.*

# CHAPTER 12

We dined at a French restaurant located near the dock. Inside, the décor was nice but predictable. Over the years, I'd eaten at hundreds of similar restaurants and enjoyed myself. However, tonight, I found myself mentally picking apart everything, from the dimmed lighting to the white-shirted, black-trousered scrver.

Brad ordered a white wine, one of his favorites, for the table. It was a gesture that I normally would have appreciated. I wasn't a wine connoisseur, so I was all in favor of one less decision to make. Tonight, it rubbed me the wrong way.

"This is *the* nicest restaurant in New Bison. They know me and they know about my allergy. They always make sure that I'm safe. Plus, the chef was recruited from France and has several Michelin stars," he said with a pride that made me wonder if he'd been the one who'd recruited him. "He insisted on bringing his entire waitstaff with him. He wanted to make sure everything was authentic."

"That's nice."

"Nice?" He chuckled. "That's more than nice. I mean, most

chefs would give their front teeth for a Michelin star. I can tell you, no one else in New Bison has one. But it's things like that that will help attract just the right people to the town." He swirled his wine in his glass, held it up to the light, and then sniffed it.

"Who would that be?"

"What?" He tore his focus away from his glass to glance in my direction. He smiled and then took a sip. "You should try it. This is my favorite wine."

"Let me guess. It's an award-winning wine."

"What can I say? I like the best. Which is probably what attracted me to you." He grinned.

I was starting to understand why Aunt Octavia hadn't liked Brad Ellison. He was a snob. Sadly, there was a part of my brain that realized I was a lot like him. I liked the best, too. For a moment, I wondered if Aunt Octavia would have liked me any better than Bradley Ellison if she'd met me in person.

"Is something wrong?" He reached across the table and covered my hand with his.

His hand felt clammy, and I had to force myself not to move my hand away and wipe it on my napkin. "I have a bit of a headache. It's been a long day."

"Maybe you should eat something. Have you eaten today?"

Other than a few croissants and the chocolate cake, I hadn't eaten since breakfast. "Actually, I don't think I did."

He snapped his fingers to get our waiter's attention. "Can you please bring the lady some fresh bread, and if you'll permit me, I can order for both of us." He didn't wait for my response. In rough French, he ordered oysters, grilled salmon, and rum-soaked yeast cakes.

One advantage of traveling the world with the military was that I was fluent in a number of languages, especially the romance languages. Before the waiter left, I stopped him. "Excusez-moi. Je voudrais le coq au vin."

The waiter's eyes lit up when he heard my accent. I had excellent language coaches who prided themselves on making sure no foreign accents were detected. He'd trained a number of military personnel, and in special cases, lives depended on ensuring there were no accents.

The waiter and I chatted in French for a few moments before he headed off to the kitchen to place our orders.

"You're full of surprises," Brad said. "You didn't tell me you spoke French."

"You didn't ask."

In fact, I was fluent in several languages. Years of practice taught me how to skillfully avoid questions. Instead of answering, I directed the conversation back to a topic Brad would enjoy. "Tell me about yourself."

Brad talked about his upbringing on the South Side of Chicago, public schools, and how he dropped out of college and got started in real estate.

"By the time many of my friends were graduating from college, and up to their eyeballs in school loan debt, I'd closed on my first million-dollar listing and paid cash for my first BMW."

Dining with Brad was much like dining with Elliott. Little interaction was needed on my part. The occasional, *Oh, my, aren't you clever* or *Isn't that fascinating* was pretty much all that I had to contribute. It was comfortable, and I was good at it. However, it wasn't satisfying. He didn't ask if I'd attended college or what I'd majored in. My mind was free to wander, and for the life of me, I couldn't figure out why it wandered to Michael Portman. I was piqued out of my reverie when Brad mentioned Mayor Paul Rivers.

"Were you well acquainted with the mayor?"

"When I first came to town, I made a point of introducing myself to all the influential people in New Bison."

"Who do you think murdered him?"

"I have no idea. I just know it wasn't me."

"Really, do you have an alibi?"

His eyes narrowed, and he stared at me. After a few seconds, he chuckled. "You had me going for a few moments. I know there's no way anyone would believe me capable of murder. Although, that dingbat of a sheriff probably couldn't find a killer if she caught him standing over the body with the knife still in his hand." He laughed. "It was probably a robbery gone bad, and they started the fire to cover up their mistake."

I wondered.

The food was delicious, which was frustrating, since I didn't want to like the restaurant. However, I took comfort in the fact that Aunt Octavia's chocolate cake was better than the Savarin au Rhum. Aunt Octavia may not have had a Michelin star, but I'll bet this French chef hadn't won a baking contest fourteen years in a row, either. I took a picture of the food anyway. **#BestFrenchCuisineInNewBison #LoveCoqAuVin #Michelin-StarChef**

After dinner, Brad wanted to take me to a new bar that had opened near the New Bison Yacht Club, but I needed a break. "Actually, I'm really exhausted. Would you mind very much if we saved the bar for another time?"

His initial disappointment vanished. "Another time . . . so, a second date?"

I gave him a coy smile but didn't respond. It worked.

"Sure, I know you've been working hard getting things going after the fire. I'll take you home. Friday nights are always much better anyway."

"I'm surprised the yacht club is open in the winter."

"Of course, it's too cold to go on the water, but the club is open year-round." He spent the remainder of the drive telling me about the yacht he had been researching and hoped to buy before the year was up.

"You must love boats."

"Not really, but if you want to make big deals, you need to be where the dealmakers are. I plan to make a lot of *big deals*."

He pulled up to the garage, and I leaped from the car before he had come to a full stop. "No need to get out. Thank you for a lovely evening. . . . Brrr, it's cold. I'm going to run. Drive carefully." I ran to the door, pushed the code, and turned to wave goodbye.

Baby stood on his back two legs and hugged me when I got inside. I was so glad to be home that I gave him a big hug. "You missed me, didn't you? Well, I missed you, too."

Leroy took a tray of croissants out of the oven and placed them on the counter to cool. "You're home early. I planned to be downstairs and out of the way in case you and Brad wanted to be alone."

"*Ha!* I've had enough alone time with Bradley Ellison, thank you very much."

He smiled. "Bad date?"

I hesitated. "No . . . not really. I mean, Brad was pleasant. He took me to—"

"Let me guess. La Petite Maison."

"How'd you know?" I kicked off my boots and perched on a barstool at the island.

"Easy. It's the most expensive restaurant in New Bison. If I wanted to impress a girl . . . and I had a ton of money, I'd take her there. The food is supposed to be excellent . . . plus"—he held up his cell phone—"you posted about French cuisine, and it's the *only* French restaurant in New Bison."

"The food is excellent, but I think that chocolate cake was better." I pointed to the cake on the counter.

He grinned. "You're just saying that because you made it."

I shook my head. "I'm saying it because it's true—and because *we* made it."

Practically every surface was full of baked goods. "You've

been busy. Is there anything I can help you with? I just need to go and change—" I hopped down from my stool.

"I'm all done. I actually got a start on a few things for Thursday, so we're ahead of the game."

"Are you tired?"

"Not really. I love baking, so it was fun."

"Good." I put my boots back on.

"Why? What do you have in mind?"

"I want you to take me to the casino."

He stared at me as though I had been speaking a foreign language that he needed to translate. After a few moments, he said, "Why me? I wouldn't have taken you for a gambler."

"I'll admit that I'm not much of a gambler, but I was hoping we might run into Candy Hurston. I want to confirm her alibi for when her husband was murdered."

"Confirm her alibi? Are you crazy? You can't just walk up to her and say, *Where were you when your husband was murdered? And can anyone confirm that?*" He paced the kitchen, waving his hands as he talked. "That might work in those detective novels that Miss Octavia read, but that isn't going to work in real life."

"Why not?"

He stopped pacing. "What?"

"Why not?"

"First, because in real life, people don't just go around asking potential murder suspects, *Where were you at the time of the crime?* Second, they don't do it because *real* people would never answer them. Unless you're the police, you have no right to ask those questions, and thirdly because people know they don't have to answer you." He ticked each item off on his fingers.

"Give me some credit. First, I'm not going to just walk up to her and ask her where she was at the time of the crime. I'll be subtle. I'll just talk to her. When the conversation naturally lends itself to her murdered husband, then I'll discreetly ask her where she was."

"Discreetly? How do you discreetly ask someone if they murdered their husband?"

"I don't know."

He paused, but if I had thought he was done objecting, then I would have been wrong. "Fourthly, real people don't interrogate murder suspects because it's freakin' dangerous. They are *murder suspects!*"

We were so engrossed in our conversation, we didn't notice that Baby had moved to the back door until he started barking.

I got up to answer the door, but Leroy stopped me. "It's late. Maybe I should go."

"That's very kind, but I can tell it's a friend." I pointed at Baby. "He doesn't get that excited for just any serial-killing ax murderer."

I opened the door and was pleasantly surprised to see April. After she greeted Baby, she greeted me.

"I hope you aren't here on official police business," I said.

"Good grief, no. I came to let you know that we have finished with our investigation, and you're free to go back into the building." She flashed a smile at Leroy. "Hey there. I thought I recognized your truck outside."

"Yeah, I'm getting a jump start on the baking for tomorrow," he said.

"Well, that's great. I was—oh, my word, is that Miss Octavia's award-winning chocolate cake?" April walked over to the counter where the cake sat on the glass cake stand. She leaned over the cover and took a large whiff. "Mmm, it is. I'd know that chocolate decadence anywhere."

Leroy opened a drawer and pulled out the cake slicer and a small dessert plate. "It is, and Maddy made it all by herself."

April tore her gaze from the cake to stare at me.

"I found Aunt Octavia's secret recipe"—I pointed to Leroy—"and *we* made it."

He sliced the cake and put it on the plate. "We're giving away free samples tomorrow."

April took a bite of the cake and closed her eyes and savored it for several seconds before chewing. She moaned and then quickly ate the remainder. "This is the best chocolate cake I've ever had. I was afraid the secret had died with Miss Octavia. This is wonderful."

I tried to keep from smiling, but my lips had a mind of their own. By the time April finished eating, my cheeks hurt and my chest was puffed out with pride.

"I can't believe you're giving away free samples," April said.

"You know what they say," I said, "the first one's free, the rest you pay for."

April all but licked the plate. When she was done, she sighed. "I feel like I need a cigarette, but I don't smoke."

Leroy made the mistake of taking a sip of water and nearly spit it out. He broke into a coughing fit, which I wasn't sure was due to choking on the water or surprise at April's comment.

"Well, now that I've shocked everyone. I'd better be on my way." April put her plate in the dishwasher and turned to leave.

Leroy's eyes reminded me of Baby's when I'd left him in the car. For a split second, he looked as though he were going to say something, but the second passed.

"Where are you going?" I asked.

"Home. I just came from checking out a rental."

From the look on her face, I knew she wasn't thrilled. "That bad?"

"It's a rat trap. There's mold in the bathroom, and the ceiling leaks. Sadly, it's the only thing I can afford. So, tomorrow I'll swallow my pride and shell out the money for first and last month's rent."

Lightning struck. "Why don't you move in here?"

"What?"

"There's plenty of room. In fact, I was thinking about renting the lower level out. You'd have your own private entrance and—"

"You don't need to sell me on the idea. I love this place, but I can't afford to stay here. It's fully furnished and on the lake. Do you know how much you could get if you rented that basement out?"

"I don't care. I wouldn't want to rent to just anyone. I know you. You're the sheriff. Baby loves you, and it would get my dad off my back. He can't say that it's not safe if the sheriff is my tenant. Who would break in?" I was so excited, I felt giddy.

April looked shocked. "Are you sure? I don't want to take advantage of you. I would have been happy renting the apartment over the garage, but . . . this?" Her eyes were as big as silver dollars. "Are you sure?"

"Yes. I'm sure."

She slumped down onto a stool. "I can't believe this. Living here would be a dream. I can provide letters of reference from my last landlord."

"Baby is the only one you need to convince."

Baby had been sitting at her feet, staring at her with love and adoration while drool dripped from his jowls.

She took his huge head in her hands, leaned down, and looked him in the eyes. "What do you say, Baby? Are you okay with me moving in?"

Baby gave one bark and wrapped his paws around her waist.

I smiled. "I'd say that's a definite yes."

We walked downstairs, and I showed her the space, although she was already very familiar with it. April was determined that everything be fair and above board, and I promised to find a lease online for her to sign. We agreed on an amount for the monthly rent, although April kept saying it was well below the market. However, I told her that she could make up for the difference by helping teach me to cook and by helping me paint, remove wallpaper, and update some of the interiors. Finally, she agreed and said she would start bringing things by tomorrow, along with her deposit.

When that was settled, we went back upstairs.

April flopped down into the chair. "This is a dream. I'm going to need some time to process this." She glanced around. "What are you two doing?"

"I was just trying to convince Leroy to take me to the casino." I shot a glance at Leroy and mentally willed him to keep quiet.

April caught the look. "Which one of you is going to tell me what's really going on?"

"What do you mean? I just told you."

She raised an eyebrow and then turned to look at Leroy. "She's a terrible liar. Okay, you tell me."

I knew Leroy wouldn't be able to hold out against a full-on assault from April. He squirmed and avoided eye contact, but she was a cool customer and fixed him with a silent stare.

Unable to withstand the pressure of denying a request to the love of his life, he caved in like a sinkhole in the desert. Like a raging torrent, the words tumbled out. "She wants me to take her to the casino so she can question Candace Hurston about whether or not she murdered Rivers, but I told her we couldn't do that and this is real life and not a book. We aren't the police, and there's no reason anyone would answer our questions. Plus, she might be a murderer, although I don't believe Candy murdered anyone, but—"

April held up her hand, and he finally stopped talking. "Take a breath."

He inhaled and released it.

"Good." She turned to me. "He's right. You can't just walk up to people and ask questions. It's dangerous. Besides, that's my job. I'm the police."

Leroy smiled, and his face screamed, *I told you so*, even though he never opened his mouth.

I took a deep breath and tried to decide if I wanted to try the *It's a free country* defense or if I'd just lie and pretend that I was giving up and then venture out on my own, since Leroy had proved that he was not going to make a good sidekick. That's when she gave me the same stop sign.

"I can see your wheels turning, but let me finish."

I reluctantly yielded.

"Now, Leroy's right. It's dangerous. This isn't a book. There's a real killer out there, and chances are good he or she won't answer questions you don't have the authority to ask."

"But I'm not a threat. I'm just a person. People don't like talking to the police, but they'll tell people things that they won't say to the police and—"

"And that's why I need to be with you."

"What?" I asked.

She smiled. "Why not? I'm off duty. There's no rule that says I can't go to the casino. If we happen to run into Candy Hurston, and if we just happened to start talking, then maybe she will tell us what happened. That way, if she gets her panties in a wad, I can pull out my shield and tell her she can talk with me there or we can go to the precinct."

I stared at her and then reached over and pulled her into a hug, while Leroy stared at us with his mouth open.

When I released her, I looked down at her uniform. "You can't go like that."

"I can go home and change."

"I think we're close in size. Come with me." I grabbed her by the hand and pulled her upstairs.

April was taller and curvier than me, but I found a skirt and a silk blouse that looked fabulous and brought out the color of her eyes. Her feet were larger than mine, so shoes were a challenge until I found a pair of Aunt Octavia's shoes that were a perfect fit.

"I can't believe Aunt Octavia had these. I didn't know her, but I imagined she would wear sensible old-lady shoes."

April chuckled. "Miss Octavia wore sensible old-lady shoes six days per week. On Sundays, she got gussied up for church. That's when she pulled out all the stops. She wore what she called 'first-lady clothes.'"

"Really? What kind of church did she attend, and what are first-lady clothes?"

"Miss Octavia was Methodist. Most Sundays she went to the New Bison AME Church. Sometimes she wanted something livelier and she would go to the Baptist church with Miss Hannah. The pastor's wife is referred to as the 'first lady,' and they often wore very stylish clothes with matching hats and shoes."

The Admiral didn't often attend church services, so, my religious education was limited. However, I do remember going to something called Vacation Bible School during the summers when we were in the States, which wasn't often.

Aunt Octavia had several outfits that were fancy and a number of nice pairs of shoes.

"Well, I suppose I can pack these up and take them to the Goodwill."

April gasped. "Are you serious? Can I . . . I mean, I'd be willing to pay you for them, but these are some nice things."

"Take whatever you want."

"Okay, now I know I'm dreaming, but if anyone pinches me, I'll take out my revolver and shoot them."

I laughed.

By the time we made our way back downstairs, Leroy had combed his hair and changed his clothes. Before I could ask, he held up his duffel bag. "Good thing I packed a bag so I could stay late and bake."

He looked at April, and I thought his eyes would fall out of his head.

"Okay, let's go," April said. "I haven't gone out on the town as a regular person in so long, I'm not sure I remember how to have a good time."

Baby's tail wagged expectantly.

I gave his ear a scratch. "You need to stay home this time, but I don't trust you in the kitchen with all of the treats, so you can just go to the bedroom and get in bed."

He wagged his tail more and wouldn't move until I got a treat and led the way back up to the bedroom. Once he was settled on the bed with his treat, I turned on the television to keep him company.

"I'm not sure what you like to watch, but let's try something calm and soothing." I flipped the channels until I ran across one that made him look up and pay attention. "Oh, you like that? To each his own." I put down the remote and walked out, leaving him watching reruns of the Britcom *Absolutely Fabulous.*

Downstairs, I asked, "Did Aunt Octavia watch a lot of British comedies?"

April smiled. "Lord, yes. Miss Octavia loved all those old British television shows. She and Baby would watch them all, and God knows they've seen them a thousand times."

"She used to say they didn't make them like that anymore," Leroy said.

"There's a reason for that." I grabbed my purse and donned my red beret and scarf. "Why don't we take my car? I cleaned up most of Baby's drool, so it should be okay, but I don't know where I'm going, so, Leroy . . ." I held up the key fob.

He took it. "Now *I* might be dreaming. I'm out on the town with two of the hottest women in New Bison and driving a Land Rover."

I was standing behind April, so I was able to see the flush that went up the back of her neck. That was the first sign I had that she might share Leroy's feelings. "Would you mind if I ride in the backseat? I'm thinking about buying the car, and I want to check out the leg room in the back."

April agreed, although a flash in her eyes told me that she knew what I was doing.

New Bison Casino wasn't far. It took only about ten minutes to get there. We took that opportunity to share with April what we'd learned from Alma Hurston. I told them what I'd learned from Brad Ellison, which wasn't much.

April listened quietly. "I'm not sure Brad Ellison had a motive. Mayor Rivers was in favor of the development. He was Ellison's inside track to get zoning and other regulations changed."

"Good point." I tried to hide my disappointment. I wasn't sure why the idea that Brad Ellison wasn't a cold-blooded killer was disappointing, but it was. I'd have to analyze my feelings later.

The New Bison Casino was a surprise. I'd been to Vegas, Atlantic City, and Monte Carlo. My expectations for a casino in New Bison was a community hall with a few folding tables and a bingo wheel. Boy, was I wrong. New Bison Casino was much grander. First off, it was huge. The building was stone with a massive entrance. Leroy pulled up to the front, and a valet came out and exchanged the key fob for a ticket, then wished us luck.

It was cold, but the casino had overhead heaters, and we didn't have far to go. April and Leroy suggested leaving our coats in the car to limit the smoke on our clothing. Fortunately, we didn't have far to walk, and we hurried inside.

The entrance was equally grand, with a massive marble-floored lobby and two large stone fireplaces on either side. The casino had slot machines, table games, and multiple bars and restaurants. It would have fit quite nicely on the strip in Vegas.

The décor was earthy, with references to buffalo in the mosaic tile inlays, the chandeliers, and the carpets. I snapped several pictures. **#NewBisonCasino #TimeForSomeFun #Feeling-Lucky**

"Where do we go?" I asked.

We did a lap around the entire casino, which wasn't a small feat. I was wondering if we'd ever find anyone in a building this size when Leroy tapped my arm and nodded to a small girl delivering drinks nearby.

April caught the movement, put on a big smile, and walked over to her. "Candy? Candy Hurston? It's been ages. How are you?"

Candy looked up, slightly surprised. "April, how are you? Or should I call you Sheriff Johnson?"

"April's fine. I'm off duty and just hanging out with my friends." She turned to us. "You know Leroy, but I don't think you've met your mom's neighbor. This is Miss Octavia's great-niece, Madison Montgomery."

I plastered on a big smile and reached out a hand. "Please call me Maddy."

Candy balanced her tray to enable her to shake. "Nice to meet you. I've been meaning to come over and introduce myself, but . . . I've been really busy."

"No worries. Although I'd love to meet some young people. When's your break? Maybe we can sit down and talk?"

"I get my dinner in thirty minutes."

April smiled. "Great. Why don't we meet you in Timbers, and we can all get better acquainted."

If Candy thought we had an ulterior motive, she hid it well. "Okay."

Timbers was one of the casino's restaurants, which served expensive burgers and sandwiches. We sat down at some of the penny slots nearest to the restaurant and played for a bit. I made sure to give Leroy and April plenty of space by choosing a machine that was still within eyeshot of the restaurant but not close to them. I played twenty dollars in a penny slot machine. I had three dollars left and decided that rather than cashing out I'd just hit the max bet and risk it all. I pushed the button and stood up to leave when I went into the bonus round. A video of Michael Jackson popped onto the screen singing "Bad" as he danced. Before long, he was covering all of the reels and the machine was flashing.

"Are you breaking the bank?"

I turned around to see Michael Portman standing behind me.

"I have no idea what just happened, but it looks good."

He smiled. "You just got a big win."

I was curious to know where he came from, but with lights flashing and videos playing, I was excited to see how much I'd won. When the music died down and the flashing stopped, I was amazed to see that I'd won over a thousand dollars. I turned to Michael. "What happens now?"

He smiled. "What do you want to happen?"

"I want to take my money and run like the wind."

He laughed, reached down, and pressed the button to cash out.

My machine spit out my ticket, which I stared at in disbelief. "That was my last spin. I just hit the max bet because I was done playing. I can't believe I won."

"Congratulations." Michael smiled. "You must be lucky."

I held up my ticket. "Where do I cash this in?"

He guided me to a machine that doubled as an ATM, where I inserted my ticket and waited for my cash. I grabbed the money and shoved it in my purse.

He glanced around. "Where's Ellison? Didn't you two have a date?"

"Beats me. After dinner, I had him drop me at home."

He raised an eyebrow. "Let me guess, La Petite Maison?"

"The food was delicious."

"It's great if you like that fancy stuff. I prefer simple food."

"Like what?" We walked away from the money machine in the direction of the restaurant.

"There's a place not very far from your house that makes the best hamburgers on the planet."

"Best on the planet is saying a lot. I'll have to give them a try."

"So, you ditched Ellison and came to the casino alone?" He placed his hand on my back as we walked.

"No, April and Leroy are here, but . . ." I glanced around in the direction where I'd last seen them. "I wanted to give them a little room in case . . . well, you know."

He smiled. "In case Leroy ever got up the nerve to tell April that he's madly in love with her?"

I stopped and stared. "You know?"

"You'd have to be deaf, dumb, and completely blind not to see that he's crazy about her."

"Do you think she knows?"

"April is a lot of things, but she is not deaf, dumb, or blind."

I sighed. "I think she knows, too, and I think she might like him, too. Anyway, I'll find out, and hopefully as they spend more time together, things might heat up." I crossed my fingers and my arms.

He shook his head. "I didn't take you for a matchmaker in addition to a sleuth, social influencer, aspiring baker, entrepreneur, dog wrangler, and—"

"I'm a woman of many talents."

"You are indeed."

I stole a glance at him but I didn't detect cynicism. I was going to ask what brought him to the casino when he tapped my arm and pointed. "I think you're being flagged down."

April and Leroy were seated at the restaurant, which was tucked away at the back of the casino but was completely open to the machines.

I waved.

"I'd better leave you to enjoy your friends." He turned to leave.

"You're welcome to join us. We're actually here on business more than pleasure."

That stopped him. "What type of business?"

I leaned close and whispered, "We're going to question Candace Hurston about Paul Rivers's murder."

His eyes grew larger. "You can't just question someone here . . . in the middle of the casino."

"Shush." I waved my hands for him to lower his voice. "Well, I'm not questioning her, April is. And it's not really questioning. It's just some friendly conversation."

His frown got deeper. "I don't like this. What if she's the one who murdered him?"

"Then April will arrest her. Now, do you want to come with us or not?"

He scowled, but curiosity must have gotten the better of him because he followed me to the table.

Leroy and April looked pleased to see him—too pleased.

"Michael, what a surprise," April said. "Are you here alone?" She flashed a big smile his way, which, for a brief moment, made me wonder if she might have a crush on him. I felt a flutter in my stomach that I refused to analyze.

"I delivered a colt for the general manager over the weekend. Part of my payment included dinner and some casino bucks." He held up the casino's red rewards card that I'd seen others sliding into the machines before they played.

"So, you're alone?" April asked with a singsong voice.

"Yep."

April smiled broadly and then stood up from her seat across from Leroy and slid in next to him. "Great. Why don't you sit down and join us?" She looked up just as Candace Hurston spotted us and headed toward the table.

I slid into the booth and gave April a stare that said, *What are you doing?* She ignored it.

Michael stood until Candace arrived and then pulled out a chair.

Candace flopped down on the chair. "Thank you, Dr. Portman."

"Please call me Michael." He smiled and slid in next to me.

The booths were small. I could feel his leg, and every time he turned, I got a whiff of his cologne.

The restaurant waitresses weren't required to wear the scanty squaw costumes and were allowed to maintain their dignity in brown slacks and a T-shirt bearing the name of the casino on the front. "What can I get you?"

We all asked for coffee, except for Candy, who ordered a burger and a large Coke without ice.

When we were alone, the tension at the table was awkward, so I took the plunge. "I was talking to your mother earlier, and I gave her my condolences. I was sorry to hear about your husband's death."

"Thanks, but Paul Rivers wasn't much of a husband. We were separated, and in just a few weeks, I planned to divorce him." She sipped her Coke.

Obviously, she wasn't the grieving widow.

April leaned closer and reached out a hand to Candy. "I'm sorry to hear about your marriage. I hope you will be able to at least come out of this okay."

Candy smiled. "You're right. Now that he's dead, I get everything. At least, that's what Chris Russell says." She took another large sip of her Coke. "He was Paul's attorney. He said, I get his insurance money, the hardware store, the house—everything, which is good, because if I'd divorced him, I wouldn't have gotten anything."

"What do you mean? Don't tell me that lowlife made you sign a prenup?"

"He sure did. He said it was just a formality, since we were soul mates and would be married until death do us part. Well, that was a joke. You know, I don't think he loved me at all."

"What would make you think that?"

The waitress returned with Candy's burger and four coffees.

"As soon as we got married, he started trying to get me to use my influence to help him convince my mom and Miss Octavia to sell their houses. When I refused, he wanted me to spy on them and tell him what they were saying about the developments."

Maybe Aunt Octavia wasn't crazy, after all. She might really have had a spy in her camp. "Did you?"

"Absolutely not! I would never do that. I liked Miss Octavia. She was my unofficial godmother and was always nice to me. She used to make her special Lemon Zucchini Bread for me because she knew I loved it."

"When's the last time you talked to your husband?" April asked.

Candy swallowed and took a quick sip. Then she chewed on her straw as she thought. "Well, he kept trying to get back together. So, he came here the night he was murdered and tried to sweet-talk me into coming home—"

"Wait, are you saying Paul Rivers was here with you the night he was murdered?"

"Yep. In fact, we were right here . . . well, not at this table." She pointed to a two-person table in a corner. "We sat there. Paul used to say it was our special table. It's where he proposed to me."

"He proposed to you right here at the casino?" Leroy asked.

"Yep. He got down on one knee and everything." She gazed into the distance as though remembering, but then she shook it off and took a bite of her burger.

"What happened that night?" April asked.

"When he proposed?"

"No, when he died."

"Well, he wanted me to come home. He said he had a plan, and everything was going to be okay. He said things were going to be just fine. We were going to have all the things he'd promised. I almost gave in. He had a way with words . . . but then his phone rang, and he took the call." She gave us a wide-eyed stare as though we should know why that was a problem.

The importance was lost on us because we just exchanged glances. However, April was great. She tsked and shook her head. Apparently, that was an appropriate response.

"Can you believe that?" Candy said. "I got spitting mad. Here we were sitting in the same spot where he proposed, and instead of sweet-talking me, he was taking a phone call. Well, that just burned my butt, and I was fuming."

By now, we had all figured out we needed to agree, so we provided appropriate responses until she continued.

"You can bet I planned to give him a piece of my mind just as soon as he hung up."

She was engrossed in her story and didn't hear Michael mumble, "I'm not sure she can spare any pieces."

"Did you say something?" Candy asked.

April and I both kicked him under the table.

"Ouch!"

"I'm sorry, was that your leg?" I said, smiling sweetly. "I thought it was the table leg."

He rubbed his knee. "Apparently both of you did."

I ignored him and turned to Candy. "Did you give him a piece of your mind?"

She poked out her lower lip and pouted. "No, I didn't get a chance to. His call got really heated, and he started yelling. People were staring at us."

April leaned closer and asked, "I don't suppose you can remember anything that was said or who he was talking to?"

"Oh, he was yelling so much, I couldn't help but overhear. He said he would meet them at the hardware store, and they'd talk things over and get everything settled once and for all. Then he slammed his phone down." She crammed the last bite of her burger in her mouth and slurped the last of her Coke.

"I'm surprised he didn't crack the glass on his phone, but he didn't. At least, I don't think he did. Anyway, he got up and said he had to go but he'd call me later. But I was angry. So, I told him he didn't need to bother calling me because I wouldn't be taking calls from him.

"Well, my break is over, and I have to get back to work." She sucked the last drops of Coke from the glass and stood to leave.

"Do you by any chance know who he was talking to?" April asked.

Candy smoothed her short skirt. "It was Garrett Kelley."

# CHAPTER 13

It took a few seconds for the shock to pass. When it did, I reached out. "Are you absolutely positive that he was planning to meet Garrett Kelley? I mean, is there any chance that's not who he was talking to?"

Candy was shaking her head before the words left my mouth. "Nope. It was Garrett. Before I marched off, I heard him say, 'Garrett was a pain in the'—well, Paul didn't always use the best language. My dad doesn't like it when I use words like that. I gotta go, but it was nice hanging out with all of you."

She hurried off, and for several moments we sat in stunned silence.

I got a text message on my cell phone. I glanced at it and then sent a reply.

"I'm going to need to question Garrett Kelley again," April said.

"How?" I said. "He doesn't remember anything."

"I just can't believe Garrett Kelley would have anything to do with Paul Rivers," Leroy said. "He was so crazy about Miss Octavia. If she'd known he was in league with Rivers and the real estate scheme, she would have carved him up like a Thanksgiving turkey."

"I need to get back," April said. "I need to figure out if I can talk to Garrett Kelley or if I need a doctor's authorization first. This is a hot mess." She grabbed her purse and stood up. "Would you mind too much if we left?"

Leroy slid out of the booth, prepared to chauffeur April wherever she wanted to go.

"Actually, I was thinking about staying a bit. I had a winning streak on that Michael Jackson machine, and I want to play a bit longer." I turned to Michael. "Would you mind bringing me home?"

He hesitated a split second but quickly agreed out of good breeding, if not a desire to spend more time with me. "Of course not. I'll be happy to drive you home."

I gave him a big smile and then turned to April. When I was sure Michael wasn't looking, I gave her a wink, which I knew she would mistake for me wanting to be alone with Michael.

"But it's your car," Leroy said. "Maybe we should get a ride back with Michael, and you can—"

I kicked him, and he nearly toppled over.

April took his arm to steady him. "Maddy's right. I think that's a great idea. Leroy and I will head back, and you two can take your time." April smiled and practically dragged Leroy out of the casino.

When we were alone, Michael turned and faced me. "Now, what do you have up your sleeve?"

"I have no idea what you mean." I sipped my now cold coffee.

"I'll admit my ego would like to believe that every beautiful woman I meet wants to be alone with me, but I'm smart enough to know that isn't true. Spill it."

The fact that he thought I was beautiful tossed around in my head a few times before I circled in on the rest of his statement.

"First, I think April and Leroy could use a little additional alone time together."

"Okay, continue."

"Secondly, while we were talking to Candy, I got a text message." I pulled out my phone and showed it to him.

*Couldn't talk in front of the sheriff. Meet me at Baby Cakes. I'll tell you everything*

*When?*

*Midnight. I have one loose end to tie up first*

*Okay*

Michael read the texts and then gave me a look that I'd seen many times whenever The Admiral was dead set against something. "You must be out of your mind."

"Nope. I'm pretty sure that I'm not."

"You must be if you think this is a good idea."

"I didn't say it was a good idea, but how else are we going to get to the truth? He reached out to me. Besides, I'm not convinced Garrett Kelley is dangerous."

"Why not? You just heard what Candy said."

"That's only one side of the story, and she only heard Paul Rivers's side of it at that. I mean, she isn't exactly the brightest bulb in the pack. What if she got it wrong?"

"What if she got it right? Even a broken clock is right twice each day."

"Miss Hannah give you that one?"

"That doesn't make it wrong."

"Well, I'm going to meet with him."

He was angry, but he took a deep breath. "I'm not going to stand by and let you meet with a possible murder suspect in the middle of the night. It's crazy, and it's dangerous."

I smiled. "I thought you'd say that."

"What?"

"Miss Hannah obviously raised you to be a gentleman. Plus, you were a part of the military, and most of the military men I know are gentlemen, even the GIs." I flashed him a smile. "So, I figured you wouldn't want me to go alone, and since you could see that I'm determined to go, then I knew—"

"You knew I'd insist on going with you." He narrowed his eyes and stared at me, and then he shook his head. "I just got played. So, all that stuff about Leroy and April was—"

"True. I do think they need more time alone, but I figured Garrett wouldn't talk with April there. So . . ."

"Well played, Sherlock."

"Elementary."

# CHAPTER 14

Michael wasn't really angry. At least, I didn't think he was. He fumed for a few moments but he got over it quickly. We sat and talked for thirty minutes. Then he glanced at his watch and motioned for the waitress to come over with our bill.

I reached for the bill, but he slid it away. "I know I'm old-fashioned, but I just can't have a woman pay for my meal." He pulled out a twenty and handed it along with the check to the server. "Keep the change."

"You are old-fashioned. Technically, it would have been on the casino because I was going to use my winnings." I slid out of the booth.

"You can pay me back in thumbprint cookies. Or save me a slice of that chocolate cake you made."

"How'd you know about that?"

He held up his phone. "Gotta love social media."

I turned away so he couldn't see my smile. *He was following me!*

We walked to the front. I waited while he gave his ticket to the valet. We walked over to the coat check. He handed over his ticket and held out a hand for mine.

"I didn't check my coat."

He stared. "It's freezing outside. You didn't come out in this weather without a coat?"

"Of course not. I had one when I left home, but I left it in the car so it wouldn't get all smoky."

"In the car that you let Leroy and April take home?"

"I'll be fine." I crossed my arms across my chest. "It's not like we're going to walk home, are we? You do have heat, right?"

"Of course I have heat."

The coat check person returned with a wool tweed coat.

Michael gave the guy a tip that made his eyes bug a bit, and then took the coat and wrapped it around my shoulders and buttoned the front.

I glanced up at him. "Thank you."

He stared into my eyes for several moments, and I felt heat that had nothing to do with the wool coat.

"Are you warm enough?" he asked.

I nodded.

We went outside, and he led me to a sleek black Tesla Model 3. He opened the passenger door, and I slid onto the luxurious leather seats.

He hurried around to the driver's side.

The valet held a huge smile. "Man, that is one sweet ride."

They fist-bumped, and Michael gave him a tip and then got inside. He turned up the heat to full blast and adjusted the seat warmer. "How's that?"

"Perfect."

He drove off, but he kept glancing in my direction as he drove down the dark country roads. "What?"

"Nothing. I just didn't expect this." I waved my hands across the dashboard. "I expected a veterinarian would drive a pickup truck."

He chuckled. "I have a pickup truck. It comes in handy, especially when I need to transport a two-hundred-fifty-pound

English mastiff around. Or hitch a horse trailer on the back. But can you imagine my grandmother climbing in and out of a pickup truck?"

"No, I can't imagine that."

"Plus, it's practical. All-wheel drive and electric."

"Doesn't hurt that it's super sexy, either."

"Glad you think my car's sexy."

If our relationship were different, I might have said something more. Instead, I just smiled.

It didn't take long to drive downtown. Before I realized it, we were pulling in behind Baby Cakes. There was a dark blue Subaru parked behind the building, and the door to the bakery was slightly open.

Michael parked. "Maddy, I don't think this is a good idea. In fact, I know this isn't a good idea. What's really going on?"

"What do you mean?"

"You're too smart not to see that this is a bad idea. Every slasher horror movie on the planet has a scene where the beautiful but naive heroine does something really dumb, like going into a dark building to meet a killer. You're too smart for that. Give me one good reason why I shouldn't back up, turn around, and take you home."

"Because you're smart, and you know that if you take me home, I'll just get in my car and come back by myself."

He pushed out a deep breath and rubbed the back of his neck. "Why? I don't get it. Why is this so important to you?" He sighed and turned to face me full on. "One thing four years in the military taught me is to trust my gut. My gut tells me this is a bad idea."

I sifted through my thoughts to figure out how to answer.

He waited, but I should have known he wasn't done. He'd merely regrouped and was going back to finish the battle. I was well accustomed to that battle strategy. The Admiral was a master.

"You don't know Garrett Kelley. You only met Paul Rivers

a couple of times, and you didn't even like him. Two weeks ago, you didn't know any of them. April doesn't believe you killed him. There's nothing tying you to any of this. Two weeks ago, you barely knew you had a great-aunt Octavia. Why are you now willing to risk your life to do this?"

I gasped. His last words hurt, and I felt as if I'd been punched in the gut even though he hadn't laid a hand on me. I took several deep breaths and blinked back the tears that were stinging the back of my eyes. Whoever said *Sticks and stones may break your bones, but words will never hurt you* was an idiot. Nothing hurt more than words. Broken bones heal, but words left scars that cut deep and sometimes never healed. I wanted to lash out, but instead I swallowed the pain.

"You're right. I didn't know Paul Rivers and I don't know Garrett Kelley. And I didn't know much about Aunt Octavia. But she's my family. She loved my mom, and I know she loved me, too. She trusted me with everything that was precious to her: her house, business, secret recipes, and Baby." I smiled but made a decision that sobered me. "Two weeks ago, I didn't know you, either, but I trust you."

"Then trust me when I tell you this is a bad idea. We need to call April and—"

I held up a hand. "I trust you, so I'm going to tell you what I learned today."

I told him everything. I told him about the box with the pictures and the letters from my dad. I told him about the video and everything Aunt Octavia said.

He listened patiently.

"I didn't know her, but she knew something was wrong. I feel like she deserves to have someone believe her. I just want to find out what he knew. Michael, she was scared, and I think something happened to her. I just want to find out what, if anything, Garrett Kelley knew that might help." I sat quietly waiting for him to back up and take me home.

After a few moments, he sighed. "I don't suppose you'll stay in the car and let me go in and check things out."

"Absolutely not. Classic slasher horror movie mistake. Never split up and investigate alone. That's when the beautiful but naive girl gets killed."

He shook his head, opened his door, and got out.

I wasn't sure he'd open the door for me, so I hopped out.

He closed my door but wasn't finished giving orders. He moved so his face was mere inches away. He looked me in the eyes. "Stay behind me."

He walked silently with the stealth of a cat. I stayed within inches. Inside, he paused and listened. The hairs stood up on my arm, and I knew something was wrong. When we were near the kitchen, he turned, placed his finger to his lips, and indicated that I should stay.

It took everything in me to obey, but my legs had turned to stone, and I wouldn't have been able to lift them if I tried.

He slipped into the kitchen and came back with the samurai sword I'd discarded in favor of a smaller weapon when I'd come here with Baby the first night. He started down the hall, and I tugged his sleeve to get his attention. When he turned, I whispered, "I'll be right back."

I didn't wait for him to object. Instead, I slipped into the kitchen. Within seconds, I was back with a cast-iron skillet.

If he had a comment about the skillet, he kept it to himself, but his lips twitched briefly.

We crept down the hall and into the store. If I thought it was dark before, I was wrong. Last time, the windows weren't boarded up, and moonlight and streetlights pierced the darkness. Tonight, the room was pitch-black.

He stopped suddenly, and I bumped into his back. We waited and listened. There was a squeaking noise. Michael looked back, and with his eyes asked what the noise was. I couldn't place anything that would make that noise and shook my head.

We walked into the bakery. Michael stopped and turned. "Let's go."

"What happened?" I glanced around him, and that's when I saw the source of the squeaking.

A chain was hanging from the ceiling. Swinging from the bottom of the chain was Garrett Kelley.

# CHAPTER 15

A scream rose within me. Michael covered my mouth with his hand to prevent it from escaping.

He propelled me backward. "Let's go. We need to get out of here."

My legs went from concrete to jelly. My heart raced. The blood rushed and pounded inside my head. I felt dizzy. There was a loud crash, and everything went black.

When I woke up, I was back in Michael's car.

Within seconds, he put the pedal to the metal, and the car sped through the alley. Michael drove like a NASCAR driver for several blocks.

"What happened?" I asked.

"You fainted."

"Impossible. I don't faint."

"Well, you sure gave a good rendition of a faint."

My stomach roiled. "Was that Garrett Kelley?"

"Yep." He glanced at me. "You look kind of green."

I put my hand to my mouth.

He reached across and pushed my head down between my legs. "No puking."

"I'm not going to puke." I swiped his hand away and sat up.

He sucked in a large amount of air. I turned and looked at him for the first time. "I might be green, but you're looking pale. Are you okay? What happened?"

He put his head back on the seat rest and flinched.

That's when I noticed the blood on his shirt.

"Oh, my God. You've been shot."

"Ironic, isn't it. Four years in the military, and I get shot in a bakery in New Bison, Michigan."

"You shouldn't be driving. Stop. Pull over. Why are you driving?"

"Considering you passed out, and someone was shooting at us, I figured one of us needed to get *us* out of there." He pulled into a parking lot.

I opened the door and hurried around to the driver's side. His left arm was drenched in blood. For a split second, the dizziness returned.

"Hey, squid. No passing out on me again. I don't know if I can carry you with only one good arm."

"How'd you carry me the first time?"

"Adrenaline."

For a few moments, I panicked. What was I supposed to do? My mind went blank. Then I looked into Michael's eyes. This man risked his life for me. Impulse took over, and I leaned in and kissed him. He hadn't expected it, but his response sent warmth through my body. After a few seconds, I pulled away.

He gazed at me. "Not that I'm complaining, but what brought that on?"

"Isn't that what you're supposed to do to prevent shock?"

"That's not what they taught in vet school, but I'm not objecting to your methods. Maybe you can do that again when I have use of both arms and am not about to pass out."

"Don't you dare pass out on me, soldier," I said, channeling The Admiral and spitting out orders. "Now, tell me what to do."

"I need a tourniquet to stop the bleeding."

A tourniquet . . . geez, it's not like there are plenty of those lying around. That's when it hit me, and I reached up and took off the scarf that was holding my hair up.

"Now tie it around my arm near the shoulder."

I tied it, and he took his right hand and pulled it tighter. When it was done, he put his head back on the seat rest.

"I'm so sorry, Michael, I didn't mean to put you in a situation where you'd get shot, but I'm going to need you to come out of this okay."

He grimaced. "I'll be fine. Now, get in, and I'll drive—"

"Oh, no, you won't drive. Not with only one good arm. You're going to sit there and I'm going to call nine-one-one."

"I'm perfectly capable of driving myself. It's just a puncture wound. I . . ."

He droned on, but I stopped listening. I grabbed my phone and dialed. Within moments, the ambulance arrived. The EMTs went to work and got him onto a stretcher. Before they loaded the stretcher into the back of the ambulance, he reached out his hand to me.

I grabbed his hand and felt his key fob. "Be gentle with her."

They loaded him into the back of the ambulance and drove away.

I pulled out my cell phone and placed another call.

"April, it's Maddy. Garrett Kelley's dead."

# CHAPTER 16

I drove Michael's Tesla back to Baby Cakes. April pulled up to the alley. She got out and walked over to the car.

"Wow!" She smiled. "Things between you and Michael must have progressed nicely if he let you drive his fancy new car."

I got out of the car.

She gasped. "You're bleeding. Are you hurt? Where's Michael? What happened?"

I held up a hand to fend off the barrage of questions.

She paused for a second and then stretched out her arms and pulled me into a hug.

I don't know when the tears started, but once the waterworks were going, I couldn't stop them. I cried until I was weak and my knees buckled.

She opened the car door. "Sit down."

I sat. For the second time in one night, I felt someone pushing my head down through my knees. The irony of the situation made me laugh.

"You're in shock. Do you want me to slap you?"

That helped to sober me up. I shivered. "I'm just cold."

"You're in shock. You need to go to the hospital."

I shook my head. "No, that's where they took Michael. I can't face him, not after what I did."

She glanced at me and then moved over to the passenger seat and got in. "Madison, I like you, and it would break my heart to have to arrest you. Plus, it'll mean I won't get to move into the basement of Miss Octavia's . . . your house. But I do need to warn you that I swore an oath to uphold justice. Anything you say can be used against you in a court of law. Now, do you want to call your attorney?"

"No. I don't need an attorney. I need a shrink, but not an attorney."

"Good. Maybe you should tell me what happened. Why is Garrett Kelley hanging from a beam in your bakery? Why're you driving Michael Portman's Tesla? Why're you wearing Michael's coat? And why are you covered in blood?"

I sat in Michael's car with the heat blasting and told April everything. I have no idea how long I talked. When I was out of words and energy, I leaned my head back on the seat rest, exhausted.

April stared ahead. "You have no idea what Garrett wanted to tell you?"

I shook my head.

She stared at me. "You can't drive. You're in shock, and you're exhausted."

I didn't have the strength to object. I sat staring out the window, wishing I could go back in time and relive this night from the moment I got the text message from Garrett Kelley asking me to meet him. "If I'd only said no when Garrett Kelley sent that message, then none of this would have happened. Maybe he'd be alive today. Definitely, Michael wouldn't be in the hospital with a bullet in his arm."

"It is a capital mistake to theorize before one has data," April said, quoting a famous passage. "Insensibly one begins to twist facts to suit theories, instead of theories to suit facts."

"Sherlock Holmes, 'A Scandal in Bohemia.' He isn't real. I

can't believe I thought I could solve a murder based on books with fictional detectives."

"Just because he wasn't a real person doesn't mean he was wrong."

I turned to stare at April. "You must be in shock, too. That doesn't make sense."

"You're tired, and your brain isn't functioning on full capacity. If it were, you would have noted that Garrett Kelley was probably dead long before you and Michael arrived."

"What do you mean?"

"Those beams are at least twenty feet if they're a foot. Garrett Kelley was about five six. His feet were so far off the ground, you bumped into them. How'd he get up there by himself? Unless you and Michael tossed the ladder away that he must have used to get up there, then someone else must have killed him and then hoisted him up."

I sat up. "Are you sure?"

"We won't know for sure what killed him until the medical examiner gets done." She gestured toward the building. "Plus, there's the biggest question of all."

I looked at her and waited.

"If Garrett Kelley was hanging from the rafters, who shot Michael?"

# CHAPTER 17

April tried to convince me to go to the hospital, but I refused. I just wanted to go home.

"I need to take care of Baby. Plus, we're supposed to be open for business in"—I glanced at my watch—"two hours. At some point, I have to work up the courage to tell Mrs. Portman that I'm the reason her grandson is in the hospital with a bullet in his arm."

"You might want my Kevlar vest."

"Thanks, but given how I feel right now, I'm just going to lay down and let her club me to death." I reached on the backseat and picked up the cast-iron skillet I'd taken from the kitchen.

One of the uniformed deputies drove me home in the Tesla, while Doughboy followed in a police car.

I wasn't surprised to find that Leroy and Baby were both up waiting in the kitchen for me. Leroy was baking something that smelled like cinnamon and apples.

When I walked in, Baby got up on his hind legs and put his paws around me.

I stood there and hugged my dog. At that moment, I knew that Baby was mine. He might have started as a part of Aunt Octavia's life, but now he was totally and completely mine.

When Baby and I separated, Leroy walked over and stretched his arms open. "Is it okay for me to hug my boss?"

I walked into his arms, placed my head on his chest, and absorbed his warmth, comfort, and energy. "Whatever you're baking, I'm going to need all of them. I'm starving."

We separated, and he pulled out a chair and helped me sit. Then he went to the oven and peeked in. "I bake when I'm nervous, so I've been baking like my life depended on it. I hope you don't mind."

"Of course not."

He got a plate and piled on three apple turnovers, and then brought me a cup of coffee to wash it down.

To both of our surprise, I ate all three turnovers while I told Leroy everything that happened. He deserved that much.

"Wow. Who's going to tell Miss Hannah?"

"Tell me what?"

We were so engrossed, neither of us had heard Hannah enter the kitchen.

My heart sank into the pit of my stomach, and I immediately regretted all the turnovers I ate, but I needed to get this over with. "I'm afraid I have some bad news. Maybe you'd better sit down."

"I don't think I can take any more bad news today. First, I get a call that Michael's been shot and is in the hospital and Garrett Kelley's dead. I'm old, and my heart can't take too many more shocks." Hannah frowned and flopped down.

"You know Michael's been shot? Who told you?"

"He did. He called from the emergency room." She glanced around. "You got any more of that coffee?"

Leroy made her a cup and placed it on the counter.

"But . . . aren't you upset?" I asked. "I mean, I'm glad you're not angry at me, but . . . why aren't you angry? I figured you'd beat me to death with this skillet for getting your grandson in a situation where he got shot."

"Lord, what would I do that for? Michael's a grown man. When he joined the Army, I was a basket case. Octavia saw how worried I was, and she reminded me that worrying wouldn't change anything. I needed to turn it over to the Lord and stop worrying myself about things that I had no control over. And she was right. I prayed and gave it to the Lord, and He's kept Michael safe." She waved her hand to the heavens in a praise.

"But he was shot."

"He said it was in his arm. God knows it could have been worse. Michael's strong and stubborn. He was arguing with the doctor at the hospital, trying to convince him to let him remove his own bullet." She shook her head. "He's not even going to need surgery. They're going to dig the bullet out, put a bandage on it, and send him home. He's probably already there."

I was staring at her with my mouth open. "Are you sure? They don't need to operate?"

She shook her head. "Nope. I don't even think they plan to admit him. He said you helped stop the bleeding, which is probably where you got all that blood on his coat. I'll need to soak that in cold water, or the stain'll never come out."

I looked down, not realizing I was still wearing his coat. I took it off.

"He told me you were trying to get to the truth about what happened to Octavia. He couldn't let you go alone. Now, the way he tells it, he saved your life, but men like to exaggerate. Why don't you tell me what really happened?"

I was stunned silent for a few moments, but for what felt like the hundredth time, I replayed what happened.

Hannah sipped her coffee and ate a turnover while I talked. When I finished, she said, "That's about what he told me. I'm proud of him. He's always been the type who helped others. I suppose that's why he became a vet, so he could help animals. He's a good catch. He'll make someone a great husband." She winked at me.

I shook my head. I must be dreaming. I'd just told this woman that I was responsible for her grandson getting shot, and she was worried about getting the bloodstains out of his coat and trying to hook us up. This couldn't really be happening. Maybe she was having one of her dementia episodes. "Mrs. Portman, do you want to lie down?"

"For what? I just got up. We need to get out there and start selling these baked goods before folks start knocking down the door." She hoisted herself out of the chair. "Well, maybe Leroy and I should go. Frankly, you look like one of those zombies from that *Walking Dead*. Maybe you should go upstairs and lie down. Leroy and I got this." She picked up a platter of pastries and headed outside.

I looked at her back until she was gone and then turned to Leroy. "Is she crazy, or am I?"

"She's not crazy. In fact, she's right. You do look like you could do with a nap." He grabbed two trays and headed out.

I was halfway upstairs before I realized he had only verified that Hannah wasn't crazy without commenting on my mental state.

# CHAPTER 18

It took all my strength to climb the stairs, and all I wanted to do when I got to the top was crawl between the sheets and crash. But an overwhelming desire to wash away the memories and filth of the past twenty-four hours compelled me to take a long shower. When I got out, I closed the curtains and climbed in beside Baby, who had already claimed two-thirds of the bed.

I was tired, but my brain wouldn't stop working. Thoughts of Michael Portman drifted in among thoughts of Aunt Octavia, Mayor Paul Rivers, Garrett Kelley, Brad Ellison, and Jackson Abernathy. I forced thoughts of Michael to the side, as those were too distracting on a lot of different levels, and focused on the others.

Was Aunt Octavia paranoid? As much as I hated to admit it, Michael was right. I didn't know her. Maybe she was just a kooky woman like the aunts from *Arsenic and Old Lace*. Although I doubted that Aunt Octavia was a murderer, maybe she was one of those people who saw conspiracies everywhere. I was risking my life and the lives of people who I cared about. For what? I couldn't answer that question. I rolled over and found Baby's muzzle just inches from my face.

"You knew Aunt Octavia. Was she nuts?"

Baby yawned, and I nearly passed out. "We're going to need to work on your oral hygiene."

He must not have thought much of that idea because he merely stretched and closed his eyes.

"This isn't getting me anywhere. I'm talking to a dog. No offense." I glanced at Baby, but he'd started snoring.

April's quote from earlier this morning raced through my mind. *It is a capital mistake to theorize before one has data. Insensibly one begins to twist facts to suit theories, instead of theories to suit facts.* "I need data. I need to stick to the facts. What are the facts?" Mayor Paul Rivers was a con man who was trying to cheat Aunt Octavia and Alma Hurston out of their lakefront property. That was confirmed by Alma Hurston and Candy Hurston-Rivers. "Plus, he tried to buy Baby Cakes as soon as I arrived. I'd call that a fact." I needed to write that down.

I sat up and got a notepad and pen from the nightstand. I leaned back and scribbled down what I knew about Paul Rivers. Then I added Jackson Abernathy's name. What did I know about him? He bred English mastiffs. He owned an insurance company that held the policy on the bakery and house. If Aunt Octavia didn't trust him, would she do business with him? Maybe she just never got around to moving her policy after his father died. Or maybe she just didn't like him because he wanted to buy Baby. That didn't make him a murderer. Baby didn't like him. I glanced at my sleeping dog. "Baby's a good judge of character, but again, just because Baby doesn't like him doesn't mean he's a killer.

"Bradley Ellison . . ." I hesitated. Something deep down didn't want to look at Brad. That was when thoughts of Michael flitted back through my mind, and I took a deep breath and forced myself to face the reality. "What do I know about him?" Bradley Ellison was young, ambitious, a social climber, someone who liked the best things in life. He was cocky, shallow, and self-centered. The reality hit me. "He's just like me." I wasn't prepared for a self-assessment, but I couldn't move on until I dealt with the facts about Brad and about myself. "Aunt Octavia said I was spoiled, and she was right." The Admiral had showered me with money, clothes, shoes, and pretty much anything else I wanted . . . everything except his time. "He's a busy man who makes life-and-death decisions with world-changing implications. He doesn't have time to teach me to understand the value of money. Or how to be self-sufficient. Or how to cook." Could he even cook? I had no idea. I couldn't remember him cooking. We'd never baked cookies together. The idea consumed me. I needed to know if my dad could cook.

I picked up my cell phone and was just about to swipe The Admiral's name in my favorites when his picture popped on my phone. Maybe we were closer than I realized with some type of father-daughter telepathic bond that caused us to need to talk at the same time.

"Dad, I was just about to call—"

That's as far as I got before he launched into a ten-minute tirade that included a lot of questions. *What were you thinking? How did you get mixed up in a murder . . . two murders? When were you planning to tell me? You nearly got yourself killed.* There were a lot more questions, but I zoned out after the first five minutes. When I sensed that he was winding down, I asked, "Dad, can you cook?"

"What? What does that have to do with anything? Madison, this is why you shouldn't be on your own. You're asking questions that couldn't possibly matter."

"It does matter. It matters to me." I was tired. "I really need to know the answer to this. Can you cook?"

He paused so long I didn't think he was going to answer. I glanced at the phone and saw that the call hadn't dropped. He was still there. He let out a long breath. "Yes. I can cook. The military teaches self-sufficiency, dedication, and hard work. Now, what does that have to do with two dead bodies and a lunatic shooting at you? According to the *New Bison Times*, you were nearly killed last night. What were you doing at that bakery at midnight? And what time will you be arriving?"

"Arriving where?"

"Home. Surely, this latest incident is enough to prove to you that New Bison is dangerous. There's a killer on the loose, and he or she apparently has you in their crosshairs. You're not equipped for this. You need to give up this foolish venture and come home. Now, if you tell me what flight you're on, I'll make sure that someone is there to pick you up."

"I'm not coming—"

"What?"

I had to move the phone away from my ear to protect my eardrums from his shouts. He launched into another barrage, but I'd had enough. "Dad, I know you don't understand, and I'm not sure I can explain it to you, but New Bison is a beautiful town, and I'm staying. I own beachfront property on Lake Michigan. I own my own bakery, and people from all over the area are coming to eat things that I helped bake. Yesterday, I made a chocolate cake."

Baby must have sensed that I needed comfort because he placed his head on my lap and looked at me with love and adoration.

I smiled. "And I have a dog. His name is Baby, and he's an English mastiff." I stroked his ears. "I have friends here. Tyler owns a knit shop and makes the most amazing sweaters and afghans. Leroy is an amazing baker, and April is the sheriff. Then there's Michael. Michael is the grandson of Hannah, who was Aunt Octavia's best friend. He served in the Army, but you shouldn't hold that against him. He's nice and thoughtful and he saved my life. There's something strange here, and I'm going to figure it out." In the past, my need to overshare when I was nervous or scared hadn't included The Admiral. Oversharing to a parent usually resorted in having my driving privileges revoked, so I'd learned early to curtail it where he was concerned. However, once the words started, I couldn't stop them. "I'm not going home . . . actually, I *am* home. So, try not to worry about me, but I need to see this through. I'll call you in a few days, but I need to go." I hung up without waiting for a response.

"I've never talked to The Admiral like that before," I said to Baby. "Either he'll respect my decision or he'll send the Navy to invade New Bison and have me forcibly removed for insubordination. Either way, we better get busy and figure out who killed Mayor Rivers and Garrett Kelley. I'm pretty sure New Bison's defenses won't hold against a full-blown assault, and I don't look good in stripes. Plus, I don't care what anyone says. Orange is *not* the new black."

# CHAPTER 19

Sleep eluded me, and after my altercation with The Admiral, I needed to move so I wouldn't be forced to think. I dressed, and with a little prodding I convinced Baby that we should check on how things were going at our makeshift bakery. I might have tempted him with the T-word, but he'd earned it.

I made it as far as the kitchen when I heard Leroy and Hannah. "I was just coming out to help."

"Sold out," Hannah said.

I glanced at the clock. "It's only ten. We've only been open three hours."

"It was amazing," Leroy said. "There were cars all the way down the street, around the corner, and onto Red Arrow Highway. I've never seen anything like it. They bought everything, even the extras that I baked."

"Like buzzards, they stripped us dry," Hannah said. "There ain't a crumb left big enough to feed a bird."

"Why?" I asked. "I mean, I know we have terrific baked goods, but this is . . . odd. Isn't it?"

"I've never seen anything like it," Hannah said. "I mean,

that chocolate cake was a *huge* hit, and I have a list of folks who want to order cakes." She pulled a list from her pocket that she'd written on the back of register tape. The list looked to be a mile long.

"Do we do custom orders?" I asked Leroy.

"It's your bakery. You can do whatever you want."

"Octavia took orders for special occasions and holidays like Easter, Thanksgiving, or Christmas," Hannah said. "She had a few special friends that she'd bake for, but she did what she wanted, when she wanted." She handed me the list. "Leroy's right. It's your bakery. You can do special orders or not. I didn't promise anything. I said I'd ask. So, if you don't want to do it, no worries."

I looked over the list of names. "It would bring in more money, but it's hard when we don't have the extra kitchen in the building." I glanced from Hannah to Leroy. "Maybe if we divided the list up and all made cakes, it wouldn't be overwhelming."

There was a long pause. "That's Octavia's family recipe," Hannah said. "I don't know if she would want anyone who wasn't family to have it."

That's when I made a decision. I ripped the list into three sections. I handed one list to Leroy and another to Hannah. Then I went to the drawer where I'd stored the card with the recipe. "You and Leroy are family, but I only have this one card. We'll need to make two copies." I hurried to the office and tried to use the printer, but it was out of ink. Before leaving, I grabbed the documents that Jackson Abernathy needed. I could drop them off on my way to the library to use their printer.

"I'm going to run down to New Bison Casualty and Life to drop off the receipts he needed, and then I'll swing by the library to make copies. I should also pick up a new ink cartridge. Anything else I need to do while I'm out?"

202 / *Valerie Burns*

"I ordered groceries," Leroy said. "You're running low on just about everything. I was going to pick them up, but if you can do that, I can get started on more croissants." He lifted the last bag of flour from the pantry. "I ordered curbside pickup. If you know what ink cartridge you need, I can add it to the order and update the pickup information, so they'll be expecting you, and I'll forward the confirmation email." He wiped his hands on his apron and pulled out his cell phone.

"I could use a ride home," Hannah said. "Michael told me to call him and he'd pick me up, but I think he should rest." She stood and grabbed her purse.

"I'd like to check on him, too, if you don't mind."

"Of course I don't mind."

"Mrs. Portman, how did you get here? Doesn't Michael usually drive you?"

"He called someone named Uber, and he picked me up and brought me here."

Unfortunately, Leroy chose that exact moment to take a sip of water. He choked and spewed water all over himself.

I patted him on his back and swallowed the laughter that tried to escape.

We left Baby with Leroy. With two adults, I knew we would be pushing our luck to throw in a two-hundred-fifty-pound dog and a rear compartment filled with food.

I was surprised to learn that New Bison Casualty's office was in the same building where Chris Russell had his office, which explained why Abernathy was there my first day in town.

Hannah opted to wait in the car while I ran inside. I checked the directory board. Abernathy's office was on the third floor. When I came before, the antique elevator had a sign declaring it OUT OF ORDER. The sign was still there, so I opted to take the stairs. There were only two offices on this floor. The one I wanted was slightly open. So, I stuck my head in. "Hello, is anyone here?"

The lights were on, but the reception area was empty. I slipped inside and looked around. Unlike Chris Russell's office, which was neat and orderly, with classic charm, Abernathy's was shabby, messy, and chaotic. Folders, papers, used coffee cups, and fast-food wrappers were strewn across every horizontal surface. I was just about to turn and leave when I heard raised voices coming from the private office behind the reception area.

The voices were heated, but it was hard to make out the words. Obviously, Abernathy wasn't pleased with someone—maybe his cleaning staff.

Noting the mess, I decided against laying my receipts down, to be swallowed up by the chaos. I grabbed the handle and was almost out when I heard my name. My blood froze, and I stopped in my tracks.

I turned and strained my ears to make out who was talking about me and what was being said, but it was no use. I could only make out about every fifth word, and sometimes those words were muffled. So I tiptoed closer to the door. There were three distinct voices, but I didn't recognize all of them.

"She's just as stubborn as that crazy aunt of hers."

I couldn't stake my life on it, but that sounded like Abernathy.

"You're supposed to convince her to sell."

No matter how hard I tried, the voice was too soft for me to figure out whom it belonged to, although something about it was familiar.

"I'm working on it, but, holy guacamole, she's a hard nut to crack, and now that she knows she has a half million dollars coming, it's going to be even harder."

I'd bet all my mad money that whiny voice belonged to Bradley Ellison. The idea that he was supposed to *convince* me made my blood boil.

"Work harder. There's too much at stake to let a flighty airhead stand in our way."

*Airhead*? I was so mad, my curls started straightening out from the steam coming from my ears. *This airhead was going to give him a piece of her mind.* I stood up straighter, pushed my shoulders back, held my head high, and marched the few feet to the door. I grabbed the knob and was just about to fling the door open and spew fire when my blood, which was boiling just moments before, chilled.

"If she gets in my way again, I won't miss next time."

There was frost in his tone, and I knew from the depths of my soul that Abernathy's soft-voiced companion meant business. I heard a chair sliding across the floor, and I nearly wet my pants. *They're coming.* I ran like a jackrabbit to the door. When I was safely outside, I took the steps two at a time and jumped the last three. I didn't breathe until I was in the car.

My hands shook as I started the engine, but I wasn't about to stop to steady them. When the motor started, I burned rubber and sped down the street.

Two blocks later, I stopped at a red light.

Hannah reached over and touched my hand. "What in heaven's name happened up in that office? You look like you've just seen the devil."

"No, but I think I heard him."

# CHAPTER 20

Hannah ordered me to pull over. So, I did. Once we were parked, she turned to face me. "Now, what happened?"

I took several deep breaths and told her everything I'd heard. Even to my ears, it sounded bizarre. In retrospect, I realized that I hadn't heard anything super damning. I hadn't seen anyone. I *thought* I recognized Bradley Ellison's and Jackson Abernathy's voices. The fact that they were in Abernathy's office made it highly probable that he was one of the three men. When I dissected it, what really happened?

"You need to report them to the police," Hannah said.

"For what, calling me an airhead? Insulting someone isn't a crime."

"For threatening you."

"Technically, all he said was if I got in his way again, he wouldn't miss next time. He didn't say it to my face. Maybe he meant, he wouldn't miss sending me flowers or eating the last piece of chocolate cake. He didn't say he wouldn't miss shooting at me."

"Well, you knew what he meant. I saw your face when you

ran outta that building like the very hounds of hell were on your trail. You were shaking like a leaf."

"It wasn't so much *what* he said but *how* he said it. That's what scared me. He was so calm." I shivered.

Hannah pursed her lips. "Well, I still think you need to tell April."

"I will. I'll tell her later." I took a couple of deep breaths and restarted the car. "Let's go see how Michael's doing."

We drove to the hospital. I pulled up to the curb and let Hannah out and then parked. Inside, I met Hannah at the reception desk for the emergency room.

They'd removed the bullet, and Michael went home.

"How?"

"What?" the nurse asked.

"How'd he go home? I have his car."

"No idea."

I sent him a text.

*Where r u?*

*Home. Where r u?*

*At the hospital looking 4 u.*

*I'm home.*

*How'd u get home? I have ur car.*

*Uber*

I relayed the message to Hannah.

"I should have known his friend would take him home, too," Hannah said.

I was tempted to explain that Uber wasn't a person but decided to let it go. "Shall we go to your house?"

We turned, but I stopped and pointed to the gift shop. "Since we're here, I'm going to get him a card and maybe a flower."

We headed for the gift shop. For the first time since we set out, I felt awkward. Hannah was Michael's grandmother. Grandmothers could bring flowers and balloons, and there wasn't anything you could do. They were family. I didn't have a title for my relationship to Michael. I wasn't family. I wasn't his girlfriend. Heck, I didn't even know if he had a girlfriend. I was just the girl who kissed him when he was shot and bleeding. What kind of card do you buy for that? *Sorry you got shot trying to protect me. Cordially yours, The woman you've known for less than two weeks but who kissed you when you were vulnerable.*

"Maddy, what's taking you so long to pick a card?" Hannah asked.

I grabbed a card and a peace lily and headed for the register. Hannah stared. "You can't give him that."

I looked down at the plant. "Why not? What's wrong with it?"

"They take those to funerals. Besides, he isn't going to take care of a plant, and I'm going to have to be the one to try to keep it alive."

I felt myself getting flushed. "I don't really know him well enough to know what he would like and what he won't like."

Hannah took the lily from my hand. "He likes animals. He likes exercising, and he likes food. Now go pick something else."

Like a child sent back to the board to redo a math problem, I headed back into the small gift shop to find something that would meet Hannah's exacting standards. I circled the store and stopped when I got to a stand with paperback books. Most were older, well-known best sellers. There were a few thrillers, and I finally found my inspiration. This time, when I went to the cash register, my purchases passed Hannah's scrutiny and I was allowed to pay.

I brought the car up to the door and picked up Hannah and then followed her directions.

From the road, I turned at a sign for the New Bison Animal

Clinic. There was a small brick building with a gravel parking lot. Behind the building was a farmhouse. That's where Hannah told me to go.

The farmhouse was white with dark green shutters. It was old but nice. And nothing like what I would have envisioned.

We entered the back door at the kitchen. Inside, Hannah dropped her purse on the counter. "Michael."

"In the den."

We followed the voice around a formal living room to a wood-paneled room that looked out onto what was probably a garden during the summer. I followed Hannah through the house. Once we were just outside of the room, I felt shy and hesitant, but Hannah barged in, dragging me with her.

Fortunately, Michael was sitting up on a well-worn sofa watching television. He smiled when he saw us. "Two of my favorite women."

Hannah gave him a kiss and tight hug. "How's your arm?"

He held it up. "Still attached. I tried to get the doctor to let me dig it out myself, but he wouldn't let me."

"Why did you want to dig it out yourself?" I asked.

"So I could keep it for a souvenir." He grinned. "Actually, all gunshots have to be reported to the police, so I knew if he took the bullet out, then I wouldn't be able to keep it."

"Evidence?"

"Yeah, but I doubt that April will be able to match the bullet. If the shooter is smart, he'll have pitched that gun into Lake Michigan by now."

"Smart? If the shooter were smart, they wouldn't have been shooting at us in the first place. If they'd just let us find Garrett Kelley strung from the ceiling, we might have thought he killed himself."

"Maybe. I wonder why he didn't."

"Either we surprised him or . . ."

"Or what?"

Hannah looked vacant. "Mrs. Portman, are you okay?"

Michael rose to get up, but I stopped him. "I'll help her if you tell me where to go."

He pointed. "Down the hall and the first room on the left."

"Mrs. Portman, I think you should lie down." I helped her up from the sofa.

"Who are you?" she asked as we walked down the hall.

"My name is Madison. I'm Octavia's great-niece." I led her to a room that was decorated with pink. The walls were pink. The bedspread, curtains, carpet, and all the accessories were pink.

I removed her shoes and helped her lie down, and before I left the room, I could hear her snoring lightly. I turned off the light and closed the door.

Back in the den, I sat on a chair near the sofa.

"Thanks," Michael said.

"You're welcome. She was amazing today. It was the least I could do."

"Can I get you something to drink?" He started to rise again.

Again I waved him back. "Absolutely not. You shouldn't be waiting on me. You're the one who's been shot. Can I get you something?"

He held up a mug. "I'm good, thanks, but you know you don't have to do this."

"What?"

"Wait on me. I'm fine, really. The bullet hit me in the muscle. It was clean. No bone fractures. It didn't hit anything important like a blood vessel. It's basically just a puncture wound. They dug it out and patched me up. I didn't even need stitches. I'm fine." He grinned. "Although I kind of like the idea of you waiting on me, but . . . it really isn't necessary."

"Wait, they didn't even put in stitches?"

He shook his head. "Nope. It'll be a little sore for a few days, but I'm good. Now, what's in the bag?"

I handed him the bag. "I thought you'd appreciate these." I watched while he pulled out the books. "It's Tom Clancy's *The Hunt for Red October* and Stephen Coonts's *Flight of the Intruder.* Both are great books."

He grinned. "The fact that they're both published by the Naval Institute Press didn't have anything to do with your selections, I'm sure."

"Really? Were they? I had no idea." I feigned surprise. "Have you read them?"

"No. I've seen the movie with Sean Connery, but I haven't read either of them, yet. Thank you." He opened the card.

I decided to go simple. The card said *Get Well Soon* on the front. The inside was blank, but I'd written a note.

*IOU one chocolate cake, plus a dozen thumbprint cookies*

He rubbed his hands together. "Now, that's a gift I can use. Thank you."

"Your grandmother said you liked food, so . . ."

"I do like food. I like books, too."

I glanced around.

"What are you looking for?"

"Nothing. It's just that you're a vet. I kind of expected that you'd have a dog or a cat or something."

He smiled and stood up. "Come with me."

I followed him out a side passage that led to an old garage. He stopped at the back door and pointed through the window.

The garage had been converted into an office. Inside, there was a three-legged Saint Bernard curled up on an old sofa. Two cats were sprawled on the desk, and a birdcage was near the window.

"Wow!"

"Those are just the ones I keep inside. I have two horses and a goat in the stable."

"That's a lot of animals."

"Comes with the territory, I guess. I can't just euthanize an animal because their owners can't care for them anymore. So, the ones I can't find homes for end up here."

"That's really . . ."

"Dumb?"

"I was going to say sweet."

We stared in awkward silence. A shiver went up my spine.

"You're cold," he said. "We better go back into the house." He turned and led the way back inside the main house, and I felt colder.

"I can't stay long. I've got to pick up groceries, and I left Leroy baking. I just wanted to come and see how you were doing, and . . . I wanted to say thank you. You saved my life, and I owe you."

"I'll add it to your tab."

Our eyes fixed, and I could feel the heat coming from my body. He leaned forward to kiss me, but at the last minute I took a step back.

"Well, it's getting late, and I still have to pick up groceries. Tons of baking to do before tomorrow morning."

His eyes held a question, but I couldn't or wouldn't answer. I wanted to say a hundred things. I wanted to tell him about my encounter at Abernathy's. Instead, I said goodbye, turned, and walked out.

In the car, I put my head on the steering wheel. Michael Portman was a nice man. He saved animals, and he'd saved me. If I told him what I heard, he would keep helping me. He wouldn't stop. He'd keep trying to help. THIS WE'LL DEFEND had been ingrained in him from his days in the Army. He'd defend with his life what he cared about. He'd proved that the other night at the bakery while someone was shooting at me.

He'd taken a bullet and still gotten me out alive. Next time, the killer wouldn't miss. I couldn't risk that happening. This wasn't even Michael's fight. It had something to do with Jackson Abernathy, Brad Ellison, Paul Rivers, Garrett Kelley, and Aunt Octavia. And now me. Another shiver went up my spine when I realized that half of those people were now dead. I needed to figure out what was going on. Who murdered Paul Rivers and Garrett Kelley? And I needed to stop them. Or I knew in my heart that I'd be next.

# CHAPTER 21

I was so intent on trying to figure out who the murderer was that I nearly forgot the groceries. I was almost home when I remembered. So I turned around and headed back. New Bison was so small that everything was still within easy distance, so it wasn't a major time waster.

The grocery store was located on a road that ran parallel to the lake, so I was able to watch the waves crashing across the rocks while I waited for a young, pimply-faced teen to load the cartons into the back of the SUV. When he finished, I drove home.

Leroy and Baby came out to help unload the boxes.

"How's Michael? I'll bet he's a horrible patient. They say doctors are."

"He's fine. They didn't even admit him, just dug the bullet out and slapped a bandage on."

"Wow. I knew he was tough, but that sounds painful."

I sighed. "Yeah, I guess."

Baby heard the car pull up before either of us and was at the back door with his rear wagging before the doorbell rang.

"Come in," I yelled.

April came through the door, dragging a suitcase and two garbage bags. Leroy hurried to help, but she declined. "I've got it, but thanks."

He headed for the door. "I can help bring in the rest of your things."

"No need. This is it."

"You're joking, right?" I asked.

"Nope. I did a major purge and realized that most of the stuff I owned was crap. The halfway decent crap I hauled to the Goodwill. Everything else went into a dumpster." She flopped down into a chair. "It was eye-opening. My schedule is so sporadic that I barely keep food in the house. It was a studio, and hardly big enough to swing a cat around in."

"How much space do you need to swing a cat?"

"Not much." April had to fend off Baby, who was standing on his hind legs with his paws on her shoulders.

Leroy took out a large bone, which got his attention. Baby took his treat and curled up in a dog bed in the corner.

"Thanks," April said. "God knows I love that dog, but he is definitely a handful."

I sat down across from April. "So, you're done? This is everything?"

"Yep. It was actually quite freeing. I mean, I feel like I'm starting a new life." She gazed at me. "You haven't changed your mind, have you?"

"Of course not, but I haven't had time to get a rental contract, but I can go get something off the Internet." I rose, but April waved me back down.

"I knew you'd be knocked out after last night. So I found a standard rental contract, and I figured we could add or subtract whatever we needed." She pulled a document from her purse.

I looked it over. "This amount for the monthly rent is more

than we agreed to last night." *Was it only last night*? It felt as if a lifetime had passed.

"I figured I should pay more for utilities."

I crossed out the amount and wrote in the figure we'd previously agreed on. "No changing things. I'd have to pay the utilities whether you lived here or not."

"But they'll be higher with two people staying here."

She reached for the pen, but I slapped away her hand. "You can pay utilities by helping Leroy teach me to cook or by parking your patrol car outside. I've heard that helps deter criminals. Plus, you can help Leroy with some of the baking. It would be faster if we used the kitchen downstairs and the kitchen up here. And you can help with Baby."

She stared. "Are you serious?"

"Is that too much?"

"No, but I'd watch Baby and help Leroy bake for free. Plus, if I'm living here, then my patrol car will *have to* be parked outside."

"Oh, good. I've signed and initialed all of the changes. I think if you do the same, then we're in business." I slid the contract across.

She stared for a few seconds, but then picked up the pen and signed. "You drive a hard deal, but you're driving in the wrong direction."

I pulled a key off the keyring and handed it over. "Great. Now, let's get your stuff downstairs and moved in."

Leroy had already taken her things downstairs while we were negotiating.

April hung her things in the closet, put her toiletries in the bathroom, and was completely moved in within less than an hour. She smiled and looked around. "I feel like I need to pinch myself. I can't believe I get to live here." She stared out at Lake Michigan. "And wake up to that every day."

I sniffed. "Is something burning?"

"The croissants," Leroy said, and rushed upstairs.

April and I sat on the sofa and looked out at the waves. After a few moments, April turned to me. "Okay, what's bothering you?"

"How'd you know anything was bothering me?"

"You keep sighing."

I told her about what I'd heard in Jackson Abernathy's office, although after a few hours, it all seemed very vague and ridiculous. "It was probably nothing. I don't even know who the man was."

"No, but you thought you recognized something about his voice, and you don't know many people around here." She stared harder at me. "What else is bothering you?"

I told her that I felt I needed to put some distance between Michael and myself.

"Why?"

"He got shot because of me. I don't want anything to happen to him."

She put her hand on mine. "Michael's a big boy. He's also tough and well able to take care of himself. If I were in trouble, there's no one else I'd rather have guarding my back."

"I was thinking maybe we could figure out who the killer is and then you could arrest them."

"That's the plan, but . . . Miss Octavia had the brains. She was the one who helped solve things. The Baker Street Irregulars did the legwork."

"Actually, I think you're underestimating yourself. You figured out that Garrett Kelley didn't commit suicide."

"That was easy. Anyone would have figured out he couldn't have gotten up there by himself and then started taking potshots at you."

I pulled out a piece of paper from my back pocket. "I started working on this while I was at the grocery store. I think we need to find out who else Garrett Kelley called last night. Maybe that can help us determine who knew he was going to Baby Cakes."

"I'm working on a subpoena to get his cell phone records, but that could take some time."

"Why? Don't tell me there's a huge crime ring in New Bison that's clogging up the court system."

"Hardly. Two murders is more than we get in a year. Winter is generally pretty slow, crime wise. So the one judge takes his annual fishing trip to Florida. I have to go to Berrien County, and that could take time. But . . ."

"What?"

"Luke Carter works at the phone company. I'll bet he'd let you get a glance at the records if you were to cozy up to him."

"What! You can't be suggesting that I flirt with someone to get information? That's sexist and underhanded . . . and . . ."

"I didn't say anything about flirting. Heck, you've never met Luke Carter. He's about six feet eight and a hundred and fifty pounds dripping wet and dumb as a bag of hammers. Personally, I think he must have a tapeworm because he eats all the time and never gains an ounce. All you've got to do is to take him some of that chocolate cake."

"Really?"

"I'd do it, but that would be breaking the law. But if you were to ask him real nice, smile, and wave that cake under his nose . . . Miss Octavia said he'd sell his soul for a doughnut."

"Good thing I bought extra chocolate."

"I think we need to be cautious, though. You're sure it was a man's voice you heard?"

"Yes."

"Then I think we need to work on this alone. I don't think we should tell any of the guys, Tyler, Leroy, or Michael."

I started to protest but April held up a hand to stop me. "Look, I know what you're going to say. You trust them. So do I. So did Miss Octavia. She trusted them, but she knew some-one had betrayed her. I'm not saying it's one of them, and I pray to God it's not. But until we know for sure, I think we need to play it safe. Until we can completely rule them out, we don't lay out all of our cards."

# CHAPTER 22

I pondered April's comments. "It can't be Leroy. He was with you last night."

She shook her head. "He drove me back here, and then I went home. He had plenty of time to go to Baby Cakes, kill Garrett, and make it back here."

"But—" The tortured look in her eyes made me stop.

She made sure we were still alone. "Look, I like Leroy, too. He's cute and nice, and I love the schoolboy crush he has on me."

"You know?"

She gave me a look that said, *You must be joking.*

"He'll be devastated. He thinks you don't know."

"I like him, too, but . . . let's just say it's complicated." She took a deep breath and moved on. "But we have to be certain."

"I don't know Tyler very well, but . . . he seems so nice. I just can't believe he'd be involved in something shady like this."

"Tyler *is* nice. They're all nice. But he wasn't joking when he said he was in favor of the development. He was on board with all that Brad Ellison and Mayor Rivers wanted to do. He said it would be good for business. I'm not saying he would kill anyone, but . . . we can't just rule him out because he's nice and we like him. We have to be sure."

"And Michael?" My voice cracked. "He was with me the entire night. He couldn't have killed Garrett Kelley."

"What about before you ran into him?"

I stared at her as though she'd suddenly lost her mind. "I didn't get the text message until after we were together."

"He could have killed Garrett earlier and then somehow arranged to have the messages sent later. Maybe he even kept his cell phone after he killed him, so it would look like the messages arrived later."

"But he was shot. He couldn't shoot himself."

"Why not? You fainted. Did you see him get shot?"

My silence answered her question.

"You only have his word that's what happened."

My head knew she was right, but my heart couldn't accept it. "I don't believe it, but . . . I can't prove he didn't do it. I just *know* that he didn't." I stared at her. "What do we do?"

"We work together and figure out who did it."

# CHAPTER 23

"How are we going to figure out who murdered Paul Rivers and Garrett Kelley?" I asked.

"Hey, that's your job. You're the brains in this operation."

"I don't know where you got that crazy idea. I'm indecisive, irrational, and immature. Just ask my dad."

"I got that idea from Miss Octavia. She said you were smart."

"She obviously didn't know me very well."

"Did you attend a fancy college?"

I shrugged. "Yeah."

"Graduate with honors? Speak multiple languages?"

"It sounds more impressive than it is, trust me. I was a military brat, and my dad dragged me all over the world. I had tons of help with languages and classes."

She placed her hand on her hip. "I can barely speak English. Stop putting yourself down. You are smart. Miss Octavia may not have spent a ton of time with you, but she did her research. She wasn't someone who tossed out compliments lightly." She smiled. "Now, she didn't have anything good to say about your extravagant shoes, but she said you had a good head on your shoulders. All you needed was to be around 'real people.' "

"Real people as opposed to . . . fake people?"

"Real people who were normal, hardworking folks—not celebrities. She didn't have anything good to say about them. Except for Frank Sinatra. She loved him."

"Well, there's no accounting for taste." I chuckled but then got serious. "Honestly, I don't know the first thing about catching a murderer."

"Me, either, and I'm the sheriff and it's my job. But Miss Octavia used to say the best detective would be a combination of Sherlock Holmes and Miss Marple. She said Sherlock was a genius, but he didn't know people. Miss Marple knew people, but she needed more technical expertise."

"You realize both of those people are fictional characters, right?"

"Doesn't matter. Let's just talk this through."

"First, we need Garrett Kelley's cell phone records. I'll try the chocolate cake, but I can't believe this Luke Carter person is just going to turn over someone else's records in exchange for cake."

"You haven't met Luke. He'd sell his grandmother's soul to the devil for cake."

"What about the bullet that was removed from Michael's arm? Any chance you can trace it to a gun owned by Jackson Abernathy or Bradley Ellison?"

She shook her head. "No such luck. We ran it through the ballistics database, but we didn't get a match."

"Michael said if the shooter were smart, he'd have tossed the gun into Lake Michigan."

"That's what I'd do. It's a great way to get rid of it."

One question had been flitting around in my brain. "Who's the mayor now that Paul Rivers is dead?"

April stopped pacing. "That would be the mayor pro tem, Jackson Abernathy."

"Interesting. I wonder what Mayor Abernathy will do now that he's in control."

# CHAPTER 24

"We need to know as much about our suspects as possible. Can you find out about them?" I hated thinking of my new friends as suspects, but the only way to prove they were innocent was to find out who was guilty.

"I'm on it," April said. "I'll run Leroy, Tyler, and Michael's names and see what I can find out."

"Don't run just them. We need to run Bradley Ellison, Jackson Abernathy, and Garrett Kelley, too."

"Why Garrett? He's dead."

"True, but maybe there's something in his past that can explain why he was murdered or that could link him to one of the others."

She clapped her hands. "Good point. I'm on it. What are you going to do?"

"I'm going to see if Aunt Octavia left me any more messages. She was on to something. Maybe if I can figure out what, I can figure out why someone considered her a threat." I got a text message. I looked at my phone and then put it down. After a few minutes, I picked it up and replied.

"What is it? Something's got you frowning."

"Nothing . . . Brad Ellison wants to go on another date."

"I hope you told him to jump in Lake Michigan." At my silence, she paused. "No. Please tell me you did not agree to go out with that sleazeball, again."

"Okay, I won't tell you."

"Maddy, are you crazy? He could be a murderer, not to mention he called you an airhead. Even if he's not a murderer, he hangs out with scary people. He's the enemy. You *cannot* go out on a date with that guy. It's too dangerous."

"That's why I have to go. I need to try and find out what he knows."

We argued for quite some time, but eventually she must have realized that she couldn't stop me. That's when she went into protection mode. "Okay, fine. I can't stop you, but at least you have to be safe. Do you have a gun?"

"No, and I don't want one. My dad tried to get me to learn to shoot, but I just don't like guns."

She rummaged through her purse. "Then you need to at least take this with you." She handed me something that looked like a cell phone.

"What is it?"

"It's a taser."

I started to protest, but she dug in her heels.

"Fine. I'll put it in my purse, but I won't need it. Brad isn't the violent type. He might get his hands dirty."

"There's a first time for everything. And there's one more thing. You need to download this app." She held up her cell phone.

"What is it?"

"It's a GPS tracker. I'll be able to track your location in real time as long as your cell is turned on. So you need to make sure your cell phone is turned on."

"My phone is always on." I downloaded the app.

"I don't like it. I don't like it at all. You make sure you stay in a public area where you're surrounded by people."

I laughed. "Trust me. I'm not trying to be *alone* with Bradley Ellison." I glanced at my phone. "He wants to take me to some winery."

She smacked her head and groaned. "No. That'll be the New Bison Winery, and it's out in the middle of nowhere. Nothing but country roads and farms as far as the eye can see."

My confidence failed for an instant. "Okay, I've got it." I picked up my phone and typed. After a few moments, I breathed a sigh of relief.

"What?"

"I asked if he would mind if we went to back to La Petite Maison. I raved about the food, and he agreed. I suggested we could try the winery next time." I got up.

"Where are you going?"

"I'm going to bake a chocolate cake to bribe Luke Carter into letting me see Garrett Kelley's cell phone records. Then I'm going to search the house for anything Aunt Octavia might have left me. Lastly, I'm going to get dressed to go out on the town with Bradley Ellison."

# CHAPTER 25

Leroy had the fan on full blast, and Baby had flakes on his nose that looked a lot like burnt croissants. However, I wasn't one to judge. I washed up and made two chocolate cakes, with only a small amount of assistance.

While they baked, I snapped a picture of Baby with the croissant flakes on his nose.

**#BabyCakesClosedThursday #CroissantMishap #BabyIsnt-Talking #BackOnFriday**

I told Leroy we were closing tomorrow, and he breathed a sigh of relief. That would give him time to build up some inventory. He flopped down in the chair, and for the first time, I realized how exhausted he was.

"I'm sorry that I've not been much help. You're used to Aunt Octavia doing the bulk of the baking."

He shook his head. "It isn't that. It's just that I'm used to an industrial stand mixer and much larger bowls and racks and, well . . . it's just harder. It's a commercial-grade kitchen, but . . ."

"But it's not the same as Baby Cakes?"

"Yeah. Did Abernathy give you the check? We'll be able to go back soon, right?"

That's the first time I thought about the papers I was supposed to take to Abernathy. In all the confusion, I'd forgotten about them. I grabbed my purse and rummaged, but the copies of the receipts weren't there. I must have dropped them at Abernathy's office when I fled. My heart tightened. If he found them, then he would know I was there. He might guess that I'd overheard their conversation. If he did, then I could be in danger.

"What's wrong?" Leroy asked.

"Nothing. I just lost the receipts. They must have fallen out of my pocket . . . or my purse. Or maybe I dropped them somewhere." I was babbling, but I couldn't stop myself.

"You could just print another copy." He held up the ink cartridge.

"Good idea." I grabbed the ink and headed upstairs to the printer.

Baby followed me and when he was inside the room, I closed the door and flopped down at the desk. "I need to stop panicking." I forced myself to take several deep breaths. "I mean, so what if he finds the receipts. It doesn't mean I was there at the same time they were having their clandestine meeting where they may or may not have been talking about me, right?"

Baby shook his head, flinging drool around the room.

"Don't look at me like that. It's possible." I stood up and paced. "It's also possible that he may never find the receipts. The way that office looked, you could lose a small child in all that chaos."

He sat on his haunches and gave me a look that I interpreted as, *You must be kidding.*

"Well, there's nothing I can do about it now. I have my taser, and I just need to stay away from Jackson Abernathy." I sat down and reprinted the information. This time, I found an envelope and put the documents inside. "I'll drop this in the mail and that's it."

Baby yawned.

I checked the clock and decided that I had enough time to tempt Luke Carter and still get dressed for dinner with Brad Ellison.

Leroy made the frosting while I was upstairs, so there wasn't much left for me to do except to pack up the cake.

I drove to the phone company. Inside, there were only two people, and, going by April's description, it didn't take me long to figure out which one was Luke Carter.

"Hello. I'm—"

"Madison Montgomery. You're Octavia Baker's niece and the new owner of Baby Cakes." He sniffed the air. "And that smells like chocolate. . . . Oh, my word, please tell me that's Miss Octavia's chocolate cake."

"It is."

He bounced up and down and clapped. "I seriously have dreams about that cake. It's the most amazing thing I've ever eaten."

"I was hoping you might be able to help me. I was wondering if you could get me a copy of Garrett Kelley's cell phone records for the past few days." During the ride over, I tried to think up a good reason why I needed it, but nothing came to mind. Instead, I lifted the lid of the box so Luke could see the cake in all its glory.

His eyes enlarged, and I thought he might pass out from excitement. "All I have to do to get that cake is give you a list of Garrett Kelley's phone bill?"

"Yes."

"Done." He tapped on the computer and reached down and tore something from the printer. He barely looked at it and then handed it over.

"Thank you." I took the paper and slid the box across the counter.

Feeling like I'd just robbed a bank, I headed for the door.

Before I left, I took one glance back. Luke Carter's window now displayed a sign that read CLOSED, and he was nowhere to be seen.

"I can't believe it was that easy," I mumbled.

Baby had moved to the driver's seat during my absence, so I ordered him to move back into his spot. Then I took a couple of minutes to dry off the drool that he'd left in his wake. Once I was in the car, I read the printout, which consisted of a list of telephone numbers along with the time and duration of each call. Sadly, that's when it dawned on me that I didn't recognize any of the numbers except my own. There were two numbers called around the same time that Garrett Kelley had texted me.

I entered the first one. I got a recording for Russell, Russell, and Stevenson. "Well, that makes sense. If you're about to confess to murder, then you would probably want your attorney close by." I hung up and dialed the second number, which looked vaguely familiar.

"Hey, Maddy," Leroy said. "Did you forget something?"

"Umm, No. I'm . . . good . . . I just wondered if you . . . um . . . needed anything while I was out?"

"No, I've got plenty to keep me busy."

I hung up and sat staring from the list to my phone. I hadn't made a mistake. The number I entered was the number on the printout. And that number belonged to Leroy Danielson. Leroy, my head baker and friend. "Why had Garrett Kelley called Leroy less than one hour before he died?"

I stared at Baby, and he stared back.

"Was he correcting an earlier mistake? Did Leroy save Garrett Kelley from dying in the fire at Baby Cakes? Or had he been thwarted in his attempt to murder both Paul Rivers and Garrett Kelley the first time?"

# CHAPTER 26

My head spun, and I felt dizzy. I leaned my head against the steering wheel. "How could I have been so wrong about Leroy? So much for trusting my gut."

Baby leaned down and licked my neck, dripping drool down my shirt.

I wiped away the drool and sat up.

"Leroy seemed loyal and trustworthy, but he might have been spying on Aunt Octavia—and me." I gave Baby's ear a scratch. "He fooled you, too."

Baby shook, flinging drool across the dashboard.

I wiped it off. "There's no need to get in a mood. I mean, he fooled a lot of people."

*Woof.*

I ignored him. "What am I going to do? I can't run Baby Cakes by myself, but I can't have someone I don't trust working for me." I snapped back and gazed out the window. "What am I saying? This isn't just about trust. This is bigger than me and you and Baby Cakes. He might be in league with the enemy, but Leroy could also be a murderer."

*Woof, woof.*

"You're right. He would be a double murderer."

I put the car in drive and pulled away from the curb. I drove until I saw the sign for Interstate 94. I didn't care which direction, east or west. I just needed to think. I knew Chicago was west, so I chose east and headed toward Detroit. Driving always relaxed me. In LA, I spent a lot of time on the freeway—usually stopped in bumper-to-bumper traffic—but when The Admiral was stationed in Italy, I loved to drive the autostrada. I could think, and if you scream in your car, no one can hear you.

I set the cruise control for ten miles over the speed limit. Based on the way cars were passing me as if I were standing still, I could have easily increased my speed. But I wasn't familiar with the local speed traps, so I decided to err on the side of caution. There wasn't much to distract me, so I was able to let my mind drift while I drove.

"Why would Garrett Kelley call Leroy at eleven at night?"

Baby gazed out the passenger window.

"Maybe it was something completely innocent. Maybe he called Leroy to get my number."

That suggestion didn't even merit a glance in my direction. Baby looked out the window with his jowls dripping drool.

"If it was totally innocent, then why didn't Leroy mention it? Why not come forward and say, *Garrett Kelley's dead? That's strange. He just called me last night to thank me for saving his life. Or to get Maddy's telephone number. Or . . . to borrow my bowling shoes.* Right? He should have spoken up if there wasn't anything sinister going on."

Baby yawned.

"You're right. I shouldn't be asking you. I need to be asking Leroy these questions."

*Woof.*

I got off at the next exit. After two short turns, I was back on

Interstate 94. This time headed west and home. "I'll ask him. I'll just confront him with the evidence and see what he has to say."

By the time I got home, Leroy was nowhere to be found. Had my earlier call alerted him to the fact that I was on to him? A note on the refrigerator said he had gone to dinner with his mom.

"Leroy has a mom?"

Baby turned his back and walked away.

"All right. Stupid question. Everybody has a mom, but you knew what I meant."

I didn't have a lot of time to search to see if Aunt Octavia had left me any more clues, but I did a quick search in the closet near where I'd found the other tape. Whoever said lightning never struck in the same place twice didn't know my aunt Octavia. Behind a box labeled BABY'S STUFF was another recording.

"Eureka!" I waved the tape in the air as though I had just found the Holy Grail. I might have done a happy dance before I raced to the bedroom to play the tape and prayed it wasn't a video of Baby playing.

Aunt Octavia's face appeared on the screen. She looked as though she'd aged considerably since the previous tape, and I wondered how much time had passed.

*"Maddy, I hope this is you. Of course it's you. You're a smart girl. I knew you'd find this."* She smiled and her eyes reflected how proud she was of me. I teared up at the idea that this great-aunt whom I've never met believed in me, while my own father didn't. I'd never seen The Admiral look at me like this, anyway.

*"I don't know which tapes you've found, but I know I don't have a lot of time."* She looked around like a frightened rabbit.

*"Something's not right in New Bison. The mayor and Abernathy are up to their eyeballs in it, along with that developer. But . . . there's got to be someone else behind this. I don't know who, but Jackson Abernathy and that fool Rivers don't have the*

*intelligence to pull off something like this."* She paused but shook her head and continued.

*"I have my suspicions, but . . . I need to check on it. I don't want to accuse the wrong person. I think Ellison is working for some dangerous people. He's got the mayor and Abernathy under his thumb. They've changed zoning regulations to get those high-rise condominimums built."*

I smiled at "condo-minimums."

*"There's no way that land is stable enough for all those buildings. That used to be a landfill. Plus, I'm positive there was toxic waste dumped there, but all the records seemed to have conveniently disappeared. I know that fool Rivers must have been involved, but he's just not bright enough to come up with a scheme like this. No, there's someone else behind this. I've been asking questions and digging through the records and . . . well, I think they might be on to me."* She glanced over her shoulder.

*"I'm not worried for myself. I'm an old woman. I've had a good life, but I do worry about you. I probably shouldn't have told you any of this. I don't want them coming after you. I've made sure that the important papers will get into the right hands . . . if anything happens to me. But I want you to stay safe. You're young and you have your entire life ahead of you. Plus, you need to take care of Baby."* She smiled.

I looked over at Baby, who was sitting up and staring at the television.

*"Now, you promise me that you'll just keep out of this. I need you to stay safe."* She sniffed. *"Your mama would never forgive me if I let anything happen to you. She loved you so much. You and your daddy were her sunshine. Now, I hope you are liking life in New Bison. It'll be a shock from what you're accustomed to, but if you give it a chance, I think you'll like the people. There's even some nice-looking young men around. Hannah's grandson, Michael, is a nice, well-mannered young man. I tell*

*you if I were forty years younger . . .*" She laughed. She had a deep laugh, and her eyes crinkled at the corners. "*Ha. You might laugh, but when I was younger, I could turn a head or two. Just like you do. It runs in the family, just like baking.*" She took a deep breath. "*Well, I can't stay here jawing all day. I got work to do. You do like I said. You take care of yourself and Baby. Don't worry about me. I'm going to get to the bottom of this.*"

There was a click, and Aunt Octavia looked around. Then she stopped the recording.

I sat staring at the black screen until I heard a howl.

Baby stared at the screen as though he were trying to command his old mistress to come back.

"I'm sorry, Aunt Octavia. I know you told me to stay out of it, but I can't. However, I will be careful, and I will take care of Baby." I turned off the television and gave Baby a hug.

After a few moments, he settled down. I'm not sure how long we sat that way, but eventually, I glanced at the time. It was later than I thought. "I know you miss her, and even though I don't remember her, I miss her, too. She must have been a very special lady."

I hurried downstairs and got Baby's dinner, then I rushed to take a shower and get dressed.

I took extra care on my hair and makeup and put on an expensive designer dress that I'd picked up in Paris. It seemed like overkill for New Bison, but I really loved it. It was an Oscar de la Renta, and it reminded me of Grace Kelly. It floated over my hips and made me want to swirl around so I could feel the feathery light fabric caress my skin.

"What do you think?" I asked Baby.

He was lying across the bed. He lifted one ear and then jumped off the bed and headed downstairs. Two seconds later, the doorbell rang.

I assumed it was Brad and took Baby to the garage. If I'd been paying attention, I would have noted that Baby wasn't barking and trying to beat down the door.

I opened the door and was surprised to see Michael Portman. "Oh . . . I wasn't expecting . . . I'm sorry, please come in." I stepped aside.

"You look amazing." He glanced around. "Obviously, you're going out. I didn't mean to interrupt." He turned to leave.

"Wait. You're not interrupting."

"Clearly, I should have called before coming over. I thought maybe you wanted to talk about . . . things."

"I do want to talk, but I promised Brad—"

"Ellison. I understand."

I started to explain, but he held up a hand. "No need to explain. You don't owe me an explanation. I should have called. Have a nice evening." He turned and walked out.

"Michael."

He climbed into his pickup truck and pulled away.

I stared after him until he was out of sight. I considered texting him, but I wasn't sure he'd respond. I still had his Tesla. I closed the door.

I let Baby back inside, and we went back upstairs so I could finish dressing. Funny, but this time when I looked at myself in the mirror, I didn't have the same feeling. I didn't have time to analyze my feelings, but I knew I couldn't wear my beautiful dress on a date with Bradley Ellison. I took it off.

I looked through the clothes I'd brought and stopped at a white Alaïa gown. It was white knit with long sleeves. The sleeves and the skirt had laser cutouts, while the waist had a black leather belt design that resembled a corset. Where the de la Renta dress was old-fashioned, feminine, and flirtatious, the Alaïa was edgy and futuristic. When the dress was featured in *Vogue*, the model wore combat boots. I didn't think La Petite Maison and New Bison were quite ready for that type of fashion statement. Instead, I put on a pair of thigh-high Jimmy Choo boots, which had cost a fortune but were as soft as butter. The boots also hid my legs, so the modesty police would be pleased.

I grabbed my purse, turned on the television for Baby, closed the door, and went downstairs. This time, when the doorbell rang, I was ready.

"Wow. You look . . . lovely," Brad said. "Is that Alaïa?"

"I didn't know you were into fashion?"

He helped me on with my coat. "I read *Vogue* and try to stay up on the latest fashion trends. Just because I'm here in this backwater doesn't mean I have to dress like the local yokels." He chuckled.

I gritted my teeth and forced a smile. *And he called me an airhead.*

He drove to the restaurant and escorted me to our table, like a peacock. His face held an arrogant smile like that of a sovereign looking down on his subjects.

He grinned. "I knew you'd like this place as much as I do."

"The food is delicious," I said grudgingly. "What's not to like?"

He made a production of the wine presentation. He examined the cork. Swirled the wine in the glass. He held the glass up to the light, sniffed, sipped, and swished it around in his mouth. I'd spent a lot of time around wine connoisseurs and I recognized their reasons for doing it, but in Brad Ellison, the gesture seemed contrived. I was sure if someone slapped a ribbon and an expensive price tag on a five-dollar bottle of salad dressing, he wouldn't have been able to tell the difference.

"Why don't you order for both of us?" he said.

He'd apparently learned something since our last date.

We had a different waiter, and I ordered Brad's favorite, and this time I ordered Sole meunière.

"Sole meunière sounds exotic." Brad grinned.

"Not really, it's just fish in a butter sauce."

"No nuts, right?" Brad reminded me of his nut allergy.

"No nuts," I reassured him.

He droned on for several minutes about some local idiot who'd refused his excessively generous offer to buy his fishing cabin. "He has a strip of land on some of the best property in the county and what does he do? He builds a fishing shack."

When he stopped for a breath, I asked, "Are you sure New Bison is the best place to consider expanding your real estate business?"

"Absolutely, it's right on the pristine shores of Lake Michigan. It's underdeveloped and a gold mine. Why? Don't tell me you're fed up with small-town life already?"

"I'm just wondering if it's safe. I've only been here two weeks, and already both the mayor and a local business owner have been murdered." I shivered. "It's scary. My dad thinks I should get on the first flight back to California and, well . . . I'm not sure."

He leaned forward. "If you decide to leave, I can make you a great offer on your house. You'll be able to go back to California with a substantial increase in your bank account and forget that New Bison even exists." He reached across and took my hand. "Although, I hope you won't forget *everything* about New Bison."

I took a sip of my wine and choked down the response that came to my lips. "I don't know. New Bison has some really nice people, and I was hoping things might . . . develop."

Brad smiled, and his teeth reminded me of the wolf's in "Little Red Riding Hood"—*All the better to eat you with*. "I'm glad to hear you say that. I was starting to think you weren't attracted to me. You've been resistant to my charm."

"How could any woman resist your charm?" I wondered what Father Calloway would say about lying for a good cause. I definitely would have a lot to confess the next time we met.

"But, seriously, what do you think about all of these murders? Who could possibly be behind them?"

He looked slightly confused by my quick change of subject. "I think there must be some stranger passing through the town. I'm sure you don't have anything to worry about."

"But I do worry. I worry about you."

"Me?" He released my hand and leaned back. "Why would you worry about me?"

"Will your investors want to continue investing in a town where the business owners are dropping like flies? I mean, who will want to buy a lakefront condo if they have to worry about getting killed by a maniac?"

"I'm sure it's just a fluke. In fact, I'm confident the murderer has already been stopped."

"What do you mean?"

"Garrett Kelley. He killed Mayor Rivers and then committed suicide."

"But I don't think—"

"Trust me. The sheriff is going to find that Kelley left a note confessing to everything. It was probably just some personal dispute between the two of them. And now that they're both dead, that'll be the end of it."

The waiter arrived with our food. I took a picture and posted it online. **#BestFrenchCuisineInNewBison #LaPetite-Maison #Yum**

Brad changed the subject, and there wasn't a good opportunity to get him back into talking about the murders.

We finished our meal and left the restaurant. It was too cold to walk on the beach, so we got in the car and he drove to a point where we could look out at the waves. It should have been a romantic scene, but whenever Brad got too cozy, I managed to get him talking about something I knew he valued a lot more than making out with me—money. I even implied that I would sell him my house.

Now, that got his juices going. His eyes flashed, and he started talking ninety miles an hour. "Excellent. That's a great move. I knew you weren't just a pretty face. You've got brains, too. You won't regret it. Holy guacamole, when you combine your half million from the insurance with the millions you'll get for selling the house, you should be set for life. You'll be able to travel the world and live just about anywhere you want."

A chill ran up my spine. I'd heard, "holy guacamole" before and in an instant I remembered where. My mind drifted back to the conversation I had overheard in Abernathy's office. Abernathy's the one who could have told him about my insurance money and he was the only one I'd heard use that phrase. Brad Ellison was supposed to convince me to sell. I forced myself not to shudder. It was Brad Ellison. He'd been in the room with Abernathy. My heart raced. I forced a smile and prayed it didn't look as phony as it felt.

Brad rambled on for several moments, but my silence alerted him that something wasn't right. He stopped and stared at me. Then he smacked his forehead. "I can't believe you tricked me."

"I don't know what you're talking about." I pretended that I had no clue what he was talking about.

"Don't play dumb."

"Brad, honestly I have no idea what you're talking about." I slowly reached a hand into my pocket and made sure my phone was in silent mode. Then, I tapped the side button five times. I immediately started tapping my fingernail on the glass using the tap code my dad had taught me as a child and prayed the emergency operator would recognize it.

"I've said too much. Darn it."

For the first time since I had met Bradley Ellison, instead of the arrogant gaze that normally met me, his eyes held intelligence and something else . . . something dark and sinister.

"Here I thought you were just a dumb airhead, and all this time you were playing me for the fool."

"I don't know—"

He beat his hand on the steering wheel. "Don't lie to me."

My blood chilled.

He frowned. "What was it? What gave me away?"

"Nothing. I honestly don't know what you're talking about." I reached for the door, but he reached across and pried my hand off the handle. He forced me back against the seat. With his face just inches from mine, he stared into my eyes. "You're not going anywhere," he said through clenched teeth. He pulled a gun from his pocket and pointed it at my head. "One false move and you'll be as dead as that crazy aunt of yours."

# CHAPTER 27

My heart thudded in my chest. Blood was rushing in my ears, and I felt dizzy. "Brad, please. You don't have to do this."

"Oh, but I do. I promised my investors that they'd have those waterfront properties, and they don't like it when they don't get what they've paid for. And they've paid me a lot of money."

I was so scared I could barely hear. In spite of my fear, my only chance of getting out of this was to keep him talking. "What happened to the money? Maybe you could give it back."

"You can't be that dumb." He gave a snarky laugh. "Give it back? I can't give it back. I spent it. Where do you think I got the money for this car and my own beachfront condo, not to mention expensive dinners at French restaurants and six-hundred-dollar bottles of wine? Just because I'm among uncultured hicks who don't know the value of beachfront property doesn't mean I have to live like it."

"Brad, please. Just let me go. I promise I won't—"

"You won't what—tell anyone? You won't tell that idiot of a sheriff friend of yours that I killed Garrett Kelley? Or tell that overzealous boyfriend of yours that I shot him?" He snorted. "You really do take me for a fool."

"Did you kill Aunt Octavia?"

"I would love to take credit for knocking off that nosy busybody. Sadly, I only came up with the idea, but the execution of the plan was . . . left to someone else."

"What do you mean? Who?"

I stared into his eyes. As when Hannah disappeared, the person I knew wasn't there. However, the one that stared back at me was unhinged. "Are you saying someone killed Aunt Octavia?"

He was silent, but his smirk spoke volumes.

"Why? She was just an old lady."

"She was nosy. She kept asking questions—too many questions. She wouldn't stop. She kept looking for records about the landfill, even when it was too late. Even after construction was over, she just kept digging and digging, trying to get answers. We destroyed the records at city hall, but she sent away for that environmental report."

"Someone pushed her."

"I would have loved to have been the one to take her and Cujo out, but maybe when I'm done with you, I'll go and take out that dog of yours." He chuckled.

"Did you set the fire at the bakery, too?"

"No. That was Rivers, the idiot. I told him she wouldn't keep any important papers at the bakery."

"So you killed him?"

"Oh, no. I can't take credit for killing Rivers. That was all Garrett Kelley. Although, I might have played a minor role." He grinned. "I might have *implied* that Rivers was responsible for killing Octavia." He laughed. "Yeah, Garrett was head over heels in love with your aunt. All I had to do was drop a hint or two, and he took it and ran."

"Are you saying Paul Rivers killed Aunt Octavia?"

He snorted. "That wimp didn't have the guts to do what needed to be done. He was too much of a coward."

"Then who killed her?"

"You ask too many questions. She's gone. What difference does it make who did it?"

My brain hurt from the effort of trying to push down the fear and figure a way out of this nightmare. So far, the only thing that kept going through my mind was that I needed to keep him talking. The longer he talked, the longer I stayed alive. "Why kill Garrett?"

"I couldn't take the chance that he'd figure out that Rivers didn't kill Octavia. Besides, I needed a fall guy. Originally, I planned that Garrett Kelley would be so distraught over killing Rivers that he would commit suicide. I even had a nicely worded confession, but you showed up with Gomer Pyle, so I had to improvise. If I'd shot you both, then Garrett Kelley would have confessed to that, too. Before he hanged himself, of course." He glared. "Why did you show up?"

"He sent me a text message, asking me to meet him."

He hadn't expected that. "Why?"

I hesitated, and he pushed the gun into my temple.

"I don't know. He was going to tell me when I got there."

He eased up on the pressure. "What's that tapping?"

I froze. "I don't hear anything."

He paused and listened, then he put the gun back to my head. "This is taking too long. I need to finish you and get out of here."

"What?"

"It's time to say goodbye, Maddy."

# CHAPTER 28

"Don't. If you kill me . . . you'll leave DNA and blood evidence in your car." Helping Brad Ellison kill me without leaving evidence wasn't a smart move, but I was desperate. "You'll never get my blood out of this car. The police have chemicals they can use, and no matter how well you clean, there will be signs that I was here."

"You're right. No point in ruining my Italian leather seats. Get out."

"Wait. There were people who knew I was going out with you. Plus, the people at the restaurant. Besides . . . if you kill me, you'll never find the reports."

He narrowed his gaze. "What reports?"

"The ones Aunt Octavia sent away for. She hid them. She suspected someone was on to her, so she hid them."

"You're lying."

"No . . . she left me a tape."

He stared.

"The police will search the house, and they'll find the tapes and the reports."

He fumed and then beat his hand on the steering wheel. "I need to think."

I sat quietly and continued using the tap code on my phone. I tapped my name as softly as I could and prayed the 911 operator would figure out what was happening.

After an eternity, he started the engine. "You're going to give me the reports and tapes." He put the car in reverse and sped away.

I bought myself a little more time. Although the thought that I'd die in the comfort of my home rather than in the woods provided little comfort.

# CHAPTER 29

Brad drove the short distance to my house. I reached for the handle as soon as the car pulled to a stop, but he wrenched my hand away. He grabbed me by the hair and pulled me across the seat through the driver's door.

He propelled me toward the door. "Open it."

I fumbled in my purse for my keys and unlocked the door.

Inside, he kept the gun in my back and one arm around my neck. "Where are those reports?"

"Upstairs in my bedroom."

Together we walked up the steps.

I closed my eyes and pictured how I might apply the self-defense moves The Admiral had taught me. My elbow in the area just below the ribs and above the abdomen would be first. Then I'd jam my heel into his instep. My palm to his nose, and then I'd hit the groin area. I had to remember the acronym SING. I repeated it to myself over and over under my breath. "Solar plexus, instep, nose, groin."

"What are you muttering about?"

My brain flew into a scattered mess. Was it SING or SIGN or GINS? Did the order matter?

I walked to the bedroom door. "Brad, you don't have to kill me. You can go—"

"Stop. Just stop talking. It's too late for that. Let's just get this over with." He pushed me through the door.

As soon as the door opened, I made my move. I jammed my elbow into his solar plexus, lifted my foot and stomped the pointy heel of my Jimmy Choos onto his instep, leaned back and headbutted him in the nose, pulled the taser from my purse, and zapped him in the groin.

Brad dropped to the ground like a rock.

That's when I remembered Baby.

There was one growl, and with the grace of a tiger, he flew through the air.

I ducked and rolled to the side just as an explosion echoed through the room.

Baby landed on Brad's chest. His mouth missed his throat and landed on his shoulder.

Brad screamed.

Then the earth went silent.

# CHAPTER 30

Screams rang through the room and reverberated off the walls. I didn't realize I was the screamer until April pulled me to my feet and slapped me.

"Are you hurt? Maddy, are you hurt?"

When my teeth stopped rattling, I closed my mouth and the screams stopped.

April bear-hugged me. "Thank God."

My knees buckled, and she dragged me to the bed and pushed me down. After a few moments, she plopped down next to me.

"I thought I was going to have to use my revolver."

"Wait. If you didn't . . . oh, my God. Baby." I struggled to get up.

April tried to block my view, but I shoved her away.

Baby was on the floor next to Brad and there was a pool of blood.

*"Baby!"*

He lifted his head and tried to get up, but the effort was too much, and he yelped.

I dragged the bedspread off the bed and applied pressure.

April squatted next to me.

"Hold this." I grabbed her arm and pressed it down on the wound just as I'd done when Michael was shot. Then I pulled my cell phone out of my pocket and dialed Michael Portman.

"Baby's been shot. Come quick."

I could hear him moving as he asked a hundred questions. I couldn't think straight.

"Please. I don't know. I don't know. He's upstairs in the bedroom. There's so much blood. Michael, please. Don't let him die. I can't lose him."

# CHAPTER 31

It took less than fifteen minutes for Michael to arrive, but it felt as if I'd aged ten years.

He ran upstairs and quickly assessed the situation.

The room was crammed with practically every member of the New Bison police force, EMTs, Chris Russell, and all of the Baker Street Irregulars.

Brad Ellison was knocked unconscious, but he was fine. When he came to and looked up and saw Chris Russell, he demanded the lawyer help him.

Chris Russell looked as though he'd rather eat dirt than represent Bradley Ellison, but he handed him one of his business cards and said he'd meet him at the police station later.

Brad Ellison was okay, but Baby wasn't. Despite being shot, Baby harbored no ill feelings and even licked Brad multiple times before he was rolled away.

Michael enlisted everyone's assistance, including the EMTs. He'd brought as much equipment as he could carry but demanded the other things he needed.

"What do you need me to do?" I asked.

"Stay close by so he can smell you. It'll settle him down until this tranquilizer takes effect." He injected Baby with a needle that looked large enough to take down an elephant.

After a few moments, Baby drifted off to sleep, and that's when Michael and the EMTs went to work.

I moved out of the way, held my breath, and prayed.

# CHAPTER 32

After a lifetime, the activity settled down. Michael stood up. He removed his gloves and shook hands with the EMTs. He walked to the corner and squatted down to talk to me. "He's going to be fine. The bullet missed his heart. He's—"

I flung myself into his arms and wept.

He held me close and let me cry.

When I didn't have any more tears left, I pulled away. "Thank you."

He smiled. "Glad I could help. He's a good dog."

"He saved my life."

"He's going to be fine. Why don't you go downstairs and let the Irregulars know Baby's okay while I finish up?" He smiled. "As soon as my grandmother heard Baby was hurt, she was ready to go vigilante. It took everything in me to keep her from coming here with a rifle."

"How did all of those people find out?"

"She called Tyler and Leroy on the way over. I guess Chris Russell must have been listening to the police radio or maybe April called him." He glanced down at his patient. "I'd hate to see what those Irregulars would have done to Ellison if he'd taken Baby out."

"I'd better go down and let them know he's okay."

"Great. I'll be down soon. Then you can tell me what happened."

Chris, Hannah, Tyler, Leroy, and April were in the kitchen drinking coffee. They turned as I came down the stairs.

"He's going to be okay," I said.

Hannah threw her hands up in the air and praised God. "Thank the Lord."

April hugged Leroy, and Tyler gave a whoop.

Chris Russell heaved a sigh of relief. "That's great. It would be hard to defend him for killing three people and a dog."

"He's a liar and a murderer and he can't be trusted," Hannah said. "If I had my skillet, I'd save the cost of a trial."

I collapsed into a chair.

"Are you okay?" April asked. "Bring her a cup of coffee. She's shivering."

I held the cup in my hands and let the warmth seep into my body. I didn't realize I was shaking until my teeth chattered on the rim of the mug when I took a drink.

"Aunt Octavia was murdered," I said.

That sent a hush through the room.

"I told you all she was murdered, but no one believed me." Hannah crossed her arms across her chest and looked down her nose at us.

"I'm sorry." April patted my arm.

"I hardly knew her, but I feel this connection to her and now? Now she's gone and I feel . . . angry and sad and . . . hurt all at the same time." I shook my head to clear my thoughts. "I can only imagine how difficult this must be. You all knew her."

"Miss Octavia was a wonderful person, and I'll miss her, but I'm glad her murderer is going to finally get justice," Leroy said.

"He should get the electric chair, but some lawyer will probably get him off with just a slap on the wrist." Tyler glared at Chris Russell.

"Hey, don't look at me. I liked Octavia, too. Besides, I didn't write the constitution." Chris Russell held up his hands.

"Everyone is entitled to legal counsel." I smiled at the lawyer to try to ease his discomfort, although I did feel that he could have declined to represent Brad, considering he had been Aunt Octavia's lawyer and was now mine. Surely, that would be a conflict of interest.

"Thank you, Madison. I will, of course, decline to be his lawyer, but given his agitated state, I didn't want to make things worse. He really didn't look good."

"Really? I didn't notice," I mumbled. *I was too busy caring for my dog whom he'd just shot.*

"Leroy, why did Garrett Kelley call you the night he was murdered?" I asked.

Leroy shrugged. "No idea. He seemed kind of weird. He kept thanking me for saving his life. I told him it wasn't necessary, but he just kept at it. Then he started talking about Miss Octavia and how much he missed her." He shook his head and shuffled his feet around. Then he looked up. "He started crying and going on about how sorry he was and how much he missed her." He looked at me. "Honestly, it made me uncomfortable hearing him cry like that. So I lied and told him I had to go. I'm sorry, was it important?"

I shook my head. "No. I just wondered."

An army went through the house and I didn't have time to dwell on Garrett Kelley's motivation. When most of the commotion died down, I turned to April, who was just finishing a very stilted conversation. "You need a statement?"

"Eventually, but we got most of it already."

I stared. "How?"

"When you dialed nine-one-one, they recorded the call.

That's how we knew where you were." She wiped her brow. "I don't think I've ever prayed that hard in my life. Anyway, things probably worked out for the best."

Something in her tone made me suspicious. "What do you mean. Did something happen?" My heart raced. "Baby?"

She waved me down. "Baby's fine."

I closed my eyes and took several deep breaths. When my heartbeat went down from a mariachi band to a polka I looked closely at her face. "Brad?"

"Brad Ellison went into some type of shock. He's dead. I hate to say it, but it's probably for the best. He killed three people, tried to kill you, and shot Michael and Baby."

"He denied killing Aunt Octavia. Why would he lie?"

She shrugged. "Who knows what thoughts go through the minds of people like him. He's twisted and I don't think we can believe him. He's a killer and a liar."

Michael stuck his head around the corner. He looked tired and haggard. "Baby's sleeping. The EMTs are going to take him to my clinic, where I can monitor him and make sure he's quiet and stable. He's a tough boy."

I walked over and hugged him as hard as I could to infuse him with energy. When we pulled apart, I saw confusion in his eyes. "Can you excuse us for a moment," I announced as I took him by the hand and pulled him into the dining room.

When we were safely alone, I reached up and kissed him. I felt his body respond, and then his passion matched my own.

When he came up for air, I saw the question in his eyes. "If that's how you thank everyone who takes care of your dog, then I'm signing up to be Baby's only caregiver."

I gave his arm a playful punch. When he winced, I remembered that was the arm that had been shot. I apologized until he kissed me quiet.

"Hey, are you two—" April stopped and turned around to leave.

"We'll be right there, April," I said.

"I wonder how long I'd get for shooting the sheriff," Michael mumbled.

"I heard that," April said, backing out of the room.

I quickly explained that I went out with Brad only to get information. I could tell by the way he clinched his jaw that he didn't like the idea of my putting myself in danger, but he listened.

"When I think that both Baby and you were shot because of me, I feel sick."

"I think I can speak for Baby when I say, we'd do it all over again. You're worth protecting. But please don't make it necessary for us to prove that."

"I think it's safe to say my sleuthing days are over. What are the chances that we'll have another murder in New Bison, anyway? I plan to stick to learning to bake and promoting Baby Cakes."

"Speaking of Baby Cakes, was that chocolate cake I saw in the kitchen?"

"That's not just any chocolate cake. That was Aunt Octavia's award-winning chocolate cake, and I made it."

He raised an eyebrow. "You?"

"Keep it up, Army, and you'll never get a crumb."

He headed toward the kitchen, but I stopped him. I held up my cell phone. We leaned together, and I snapped a selfie.

#LoveVets #ItsAGoodLife #MyHero #LoveTheSweetLife #LovingMyBestLifeInNewBison

# Recipes from Baby Cakes Bakery

# Lemon Zucchini Bread

## *Ingredients*
1½ cups all-purpose flour
½ teaspoon baking soda
½ teaspoon baking powder
¼ teaspoon salt
¾ cup sugar
1 cup finely shredded unpeeled zucchini (don't squeeze or
   dry)
¼ cup cooking oil
1 egg
2 tablespoons freshly squeezed lemon juice
2 tablespoons lemon zest

## *For the glaze* (optional, but why wouldn't you?)
½ cup powdered sugar
1 tablespoon freshly squeezed lemon juice
1 teaspoon lemon zest

## *Directions*
1. Combine flour, baking soda, baking powder, and salt
   in a medium-sized mixing bowl and set aside.
2. Combine sugar, zucchini, cooking oil, egg, lemon
   juice, and lemon zest in a separate bowl and mix.
3. Add the dry ingredients to the zucchini mixture and
   stir until just combined.
4. Pour batter into a greased loaf pan.
5. Bake at 350 degrees F for 45–50 minutes or until
   golden brown.
6. Cool on a wire rack for 15 minutes, and then remove
   from the pan and cool completely.

## Optional

7. Combine ingredients for glaze and drizzle over bread. If the bread isn't cool, the glaze will soak into the bread and be even more lemony.

# Apple Turnovers

## Ingredients
1 lb. puff pastry (2 sheets) thawed according to package instructions
2 tablespoons butter
1 tablespoon all-purpose flour (for dusting)
1¼ pounds Granny Smith apples (3 medium) peeled, cored, and diced, ⅓ inch thick
¼ cup lightly packed brown sugar
½ teaspoon ground cinnamon
¼ teaspoon salt
1 egg and 1 tablespoon water for egg wash

## For the glaze
½ cup powdered sugar
1-2 tablespoons heavy whipping cream

## Directions
1. Preheat oven to 400 degrees F. Remove puff pastry from freezer and thaw.
2. Melt butter over medium heat in a medium pot. Add diced apples and cook, stirring occasionally until softened (5 minutes).
3. Reduce heat to low and stir in the brown sugar, cinnamon, and salt. Simmer until apples are soft and caramelized, and then remove from heat and cool.
4. Sprinkle the flour to prevent the dough from sticking and, using a rolling pin, roll the first sheet of thawed pastry to 11 inches square. Use a pizza cutter to cut into 4 equal squares.
5. Place cooled apple mixture in center of each square, leaving at least a ½-inch border.
6. Beat egg and water. Brush egg wash over edges of the

pastry. Bring the edges together and crimp tightly along the edges with a fork to seal and cut 3 slits into top to allow pastries to vent.

7. Transfer to a parchment-lined baking sheet, keeping the pastries at least 1 inch apart.
8. Place in the fridge for 20 minutes.
9. Remove the pastries from the fridge and brush the tops with the remaining egg wash and bake for 20 minutes or until golden brown and puffed.
10. Combine the powdered sugar and 1 tablespoon heavy whipping cream and stir. If the glaze is too thick, add more heavy whipping cream until you get the desired consistency and drizzle glaze over the turnovers.

# Thumbprint Cookies

## *Ingredients*
1 cup softened butter
½ cup powdered sugar
1 teaspoon pure vanilla extract (absolutely no imitation)
¼ teaspoon salt
2½ cups flour
⅔ cup finely chopped walnuts or pecans

## *Directions*
1. Preheat oven to 350 degrees F.
2. Cream the butter and sugar together. Add the vanilla and salt. Slowly add the flour and mix until the dough comes together. It will be dry (don't panic). Add the nuts and mix until combined.
3. Roll a small piece of the dough in your palms until it is about 1 inch in diameter.
4. Line a baking sheet with parchment paper and place the balls on the sheet, leaving an inch between each ball.

## *Variations—you can make three different types of cookies with this dough*
1. Option 1: Russian Tea Cookies—bake for 10–12 minutes. When they are done, roll the cookies in powdered sugar.

2. Option 2: Press your thumb in the middle of the balls before baking. Bake for 10–12 minutes. Cool and then fill with jam (e.g., raspberry, apricot, strawberry).

3. Option 3: Press your thumb in the middle of the balls and bake 10–12 minutes. While the cookies are cooling, make icing.

1 cup powdered sugar
1 tablespoon milk
1½ teaspoons almond extract
Food coloring (optional, if you're feeling really fancy)

1. Combine the powdered sugar, milk, and almond extract in a small bowl and mix well. If the mixture is too thick and dry, add a splash more milk. If using food coloring, separate the icing into separate bowls and place a drop of color into each.
2. Put a dollop of the icing in the centers of each cookie.